PRAISE FOR
IN THE PALACE OF REPOSE

hese are some accomplished, splendid, enticing—even masterful—stories. Holly Phillips steps out for her first time on stage, all unknown, and brings down the house with a restrained yet bold performance. We are present at the birth of something major." —*Asimov's*

"Phillips writes dark fantasy mostly with the aura of heroic fantasy, aiming to awe far more than to frighten—and succeeding, awesomely."—*Booklist,* starred review

"Phillips demonstrates a unique voice and an eclectic, often understated approach to the fantastic that often echoes mainstream short story construction more than genre tropes, in a book full of hauntings and the haunted, the real ghosts in Phillips's work are passion and identity, and she seems to understand a lot about both."—*Locus*

"This collection of nine fantasy and slipstream short stories from Canadian author Phillips, her first book, offers a neat package of quietly thoughtful, composed writing . . . readers will find themselves drawn in by elegant imagery and evocative settings, making this one stand out from the pack on the fantasy shelf."

—Publishers Weekly

CONTINUED

"The essential Holly Phillips story begins like this: In a world that felt too little, there lived a girl who saw too much."

—Sean Stewart

"*In the Palace of Repose*, a beautifully titled collection of original short fiction, has so much potential it makes your fingers ache to turn the pages. Phillips is a controlled and skillful writer with an uncanny knack for finding the quiet moment in a story, and dwelling in them with a tenderness that somehow resists sentiment. Though many of these tales have an element of the fantastic, the overall effect is never less than literary, and never less than entirely lovely, lovely and sad. A pervasive sorrow shadows this book, giving it a gravitas that many speculative collections do not possess. Combined with Phillips' searing eye, which illuminates the times and places of her tales with almost painful clarity, the result is that many of these narratives will not leave me for some time."—Catherynne M. Valente

"Holly Phillips recently came out with *In the Palace of Repose* . . . Dammit, the woman can write. In fact, as a fellow author once told me (he remains nameless because I haven't asked permission to quote him), 'She's a better writer than you or I will ever be.' I think he's right."—Peter Watts

AT THE EDGE
OF WAKING

OTHER BOOKS BY HOLLY PHILLIPS

In the Palace of Repose
The Burning Girl
The Engine's Child

AT THE EDGE
OF WAKING

HOLLY PHILLIPS

PRIME BOOKS

AT THE EDGE OF WAKING

Prime Books
www.prime-books.com

For more information, contact Prime Books:
prime@prime-books.com

ISBN: 978-1-60701-356-3

This one's for my dad, man of conscience, with love

CONTENTS

INTRODUCTION

Holly Phillips is spooky good.

Holly Phillips is possibly *too* good.

I don't think I've ever said that about another writer, and I'm not entirely certain of what I mean by it, but bear with me. I'd never read any of her work before—my loss, she's published a *lot*—and I only knew the name in a vague, glancing way. I'm having enough trouble keeping up with a new generation of brilliant young women writers suddenly showing up, seemingly all at once, like new spring butterflies. But even among those, Holly Phillips is quite simply Something Else.

I can't even be quite sure whether to call her a fantasy writer, though her web site makes a point of it. Yes, many of the stories in *At the Edge of Waking* flirt around the edges and elements of classic fantasy, but so have other writers done who aren't generally considered fantasists: E.M. Forster, Robert Nathan and, currently, Michael Gruber all come to mind. And as for vampires, zombies, sword-and-sorcery, apocalypses headed off at the last minute . . . well, she does suggest an apocalypse or two, but they occur almost incidentally, diffidently, without the usual drama and fanfare. Like Val Lewton, my favorite old film producer, creating quiet horror on a $1.98 budget, she knows what to do with shadows.

Her great gift, it seems to me, is for creating utterly believable worlds; indeed, in this respect I can't think of anyone to compare her to except Ursula K. LeGuin. World building is a good deal harder to pull off in a short story, as opposed to a novel or novella, where the writer has time to build up tension, character and atmosphere. But Ms. Phillips comes blasting out of the starting gate—rather like a guitar solo by Carlos Santana or the late Jerry Reed—habitually dropping you into what feels like the middle of the story, and leaving you to find your way in this strange but hauntingly real country and culture. Whether the tale is taking place in what *might* be an Antarctic scientific expedition (and, my God, can she do cold!), in a locale that *resembles* an 18th or 19th-century Spanish colonial possession, only not *quite;* or a city that could *almost* be modern-day London in an apparent England, held from magical chaos by the will of a—possibly—dead man . . . however you look at it, we are just not in Middle-earth, Oz or Camelot anymore. One way or another, Holly Phillips' worlds are all scary, even when nothing exactly scary is happening. Just like Val Lewton's movies.

Her other strength is the truly astonishing density and precision of her language. I'm not talking about the kind of Dreiserian clotted prose that simply beats you into surrender with its depth of detail, nor Thomas Mann's determination to leave absolutely nothing out of a scene or a setting, just in case. I have admired both of these writers since my youth; but I don't think either of them could have produced a passage like the following, from a story entitled "Cold Water Survival," describing the universe beneath an Antarctic iceberg from a videographer narrator's point of view.

INTRODUCTION

[Bubbles rise past the camera's lens. The mic catches the gurgle of the respirator, the groaning of the iceberg, the science-fiction sound effects of Weddell seals.]

The camera moves beneath a cathedral ceiling of ice. Great blue vaults and glassy pillars hang above the cold black deeps, sanctuary for the alien life forms of this bitter sea. Fringed jellies and jellies like winged cucumbers, huge red shrimp and tiny white ones, skates and spiders and boney fish with plated jaws. Algae paints the ice with living glyphs in murky green and brown, like lichen graffiti scrawled on a ruin's walls. Air, the alien element, puddles on the ceiling, trapped.

The water seems clear, filled with the haunting light that filters through the ice, but out in the farther reaches of the cathedral the light turns opaquely blue, the color of a winter dusk, and below there is no light at all. Bubbles spiral upward, beads of mercury that pool in the hollows of the cathedral ceiling, forming a fluid air-body that glides along the water-smoothed ice. It moves with all the determination of a living thing, seeking the highest point. [The camera follows; bubbles rise; the air-creature grows.] The ceiling vault soars upwards, smeared with algae [zoom in; does it shape pictures, words?] and full of strange swimming life [are there shadows coiling a the farthest edges of the frame?] and it narrows as it rises to a rough chimney. Water has smoothed this icy passage, sculpted it into a flute, a flower stem . . . a birth canal. The air-body takes on speed, rising unencumbered into brighter and brighter light. The upward passage branches into tunnels and more air-bodies appear, as shapeless and fluid as the first. Walls of clear ice are like windows into another frozen sea where other creatures hang suspended, clearer than jellyfish and more strange. And then the camera [lens streaked and running with droplets] rises from the water [how], ascending a rough crevice in the ice. The air-bodies, skimmed in water—or have they been water all along?—are still rising too, sliding with fluid grace through the ice-choked cracks in the widening passage. {The videographer sliding through too; how?} The host seeks out the highest places and at last comes up into the open air – ice still rising in towering walls, but with nothing but the sky above. Gray sky, blue-white ice, a splash of red. What is this? Fluid, many-limbed, curious, the water-beings flow weightlessly toward the splash of scarlet [blood]. They taste [blood], absorb [blood], until each glassy creature is tinted with the merest thread of red . . .

Dreamlike, but absolutely concrete at the same time; matching, as it happens, the descriptions of a friend of mine who spends part of every year doing exactly that sort of photography under Antarctic ice. All the stories in *At the Edge of Waking* are like that—deeply accurate, and yet more than accurate, as the word "surreal" was originally supposed to mean. Barry Lopez writes like that; so do Maxine Hong Kingston and the Indian writer Padma Hejmadi. Not too many others.

I don't always know at first glance what she's doing, but it doesn't matter. She does, and knows it so precisely that the reader comes quickly to trust her surefootedness, which is the big test any artist has to pass. And while I still can't say exactly what I mean by saying that Holly Phillips is "too good"—beyond, perhaps, the quiet inner rumbling that all writers feel when they encounter someone else's words and find themselves thinking *damn, I wish I'd done that*—what I can tell you is that she's an astonishing who-the-hell-is-this kind of discovery for anyone previously ignorant of her work. Until recently I was one such, which lamentable situation I am going to remedy by immediately reading every bit of her writing I can get my hands on. A new planet, to quote Keats, has definitely swum into my ken.

—Peter S. Beagle

THREE DAYS OF RAIN

They came down out of the buildings' shade into the glare of the lakeside afternoon. Seen through the sting of sun-tears the bridge between Asuada and Maldino Islands wavered in the heat, white cement floating over white dust, its shadow a black sword-cut against the ground. Santiago groped in the breast of his doublet for his sunglasses and the world regained its edges: the background of red-roofed tenements stacked up Maldino's hill, the foreground of the esplanade's railings marking the hour with abbreviated shadows, the bridge, the empty air, lying in between. The not-so-empty air. Even through dark lenses Santiago could see the mirage rippling above the lakebed, fluid as water, tempting as a lie, as the heat raised its ghosts above the plain. Beyond stood the dark hills that were the shore once, in the days when the city was islanded in a living lake; hills that were the shore still, the desert's shore. They looked like the shards of a broken pot, like paper torn and pasted against the sun-bleached sky. The esplanade was deserted and the siesta silence was intense.

"There's Bernal," Luz murmured in Santiago's ear. "Thirsty for blood."

She sounded, Santiago thought, more sardonic than a lady should in her circumstance. He had been too shy to look at her as she walked beside him down from Asuada Island's crown, but he glanced at her now from behind his sunglasses. She had rare pale

17

eyes that were, in the glare, narrow and edged in incipient creases. A dimple showed by her mouth: she knew he was looking. He glanced away and saw Bernal and his seconds waiting in the shadow of the bridge. Ahead, Sandoval and Orlando and Ruy burst out laughing, as if the sight of Bernal were hilarious, but their tension rang like a cracked bell in the quiet. Santiago wished he was sophisticated enough to share Luz's ironic mood, but he was too excited. He had the notion that he would do this hour an injustice if he pretended a disinterest he did not feel.

Sandoval vaulted over the low gate at the end of the esplanade, dropping down to the steps that led to the bridge's foot. Orlando followed more clumsily, the hilt of his rapier ringing off the gate's ironwork, and Ruy climbed sedately over, waiting for Luz and Santiago to catch up. Luz hitched up the skirt of her lace coat to show athletic legs in grimy hose, but allowed Ruy and Santiago to help her over the gate. The gate's sun-worn sign still bore a memory of its old warning—deep water, drowning, death—but it could not be deciphered beneath the pale motley of handbills. One had to know it was there, and to know, one had to care.

An intangible breeze stirred the ghost lake into gentle waves.

Bernal and Sandoval bowed. Their seconds bowed. To Santiago the observer, who still trailed behind with Luz, they looked like players rehearsing on an empty stage, the strong colors of their doublets false against the pallor of the dust. Bernal drew his rapier with a flourish and presented it to Ruy to inspect. The bridge's shade gave no relief from the heat; sweat tickled the skin of Santiago's throat. Sandoval also drew, with a prosaic gesture that seemed more honest, and therefore more threatening, than Bernal's theatricality, and Santiago felt a burst of excitement, thinking that Sandoval would surely win. Wouldn't he? He glanced at Luz and was glad to see that the sardonic smile had given way to an intent look. Belatedly he took off his sunglasses and her profile leapt out in sharp relief against the blazing lakebed beyond the shade.

The blades were inspected and returned to their owners. The seconds marked out their corners. The duelists saluted each other, or the duel, and their blades met in the first tentative kiss. Steel touching steel made a cold sound that hissed back down at them from the bridge's underside. The men's feet in their soft boots scuffed and patted and stirred up dust that stank like dry bones.

Santiago was there to watch and he did, but his excitement fragmented his attention, as if several Santiagos were crowded behind a single pair of eyes, watching everything. The fighters' feet like dancers', making a music of their own. The men's faces, intent, unselfconscious, reflecting the give and take of the duel. The haze of dust, the sharp edge of shade, the watery mirage. The rapiers hissed and shrieked and sang, and in the bridge's echoes Santiago heard water birds, children on a beach, rain falling into the lake. For an instant his attention broke quite asunder, and he felt blowing through that divide a cool breeze, a wind rich with impossible smells, water and weeds and rust. The duelists fell apart and Santiago heard himself blurt out, "Blood! First blood!" for scarlet drops spattered from the tip of Sandoval's sword to lay the dust. Bernal grimaced and put his hand to his breast above his heart.

"It's not deep?" said Sandoval worriedly.

"No, no," Bernal said, pressing the heel of his hand to the wound.

"Fairly dealt," Santiago said. He felt he was still catching up to events, that he had nearly been left behind, but no one seemed to notice. A grinning Ruy clapped his shoulder.

"A good fight, eh? They'll be talking about this one for a season or two!"

"Talking about me for a season or two," Luz said.

Ruy laughed. "She wants you to think she's too modest to take pleasure in it, but her tongue would be sharper if we talked only about the fight, and never her."

Luz gave Santiago an exasperated look, but when Sandoval came to kiss her hand she let him. But then, she let Bernal do the same, and Bernal's bow was deeper, despite the pain that lined his face. There was not much blood on the ground, and what there was was already dulled by dust.

"Does it make you want to fight, Santiago?" Ruy asked.

Yes? No? Santiago said the one thing he knew was true. "It makes me want to feel the rain on my face before I die."

"Ay, my friend! Well said!" Ruy slung his arm around Santiago's neck, and Santiago laughed, glad to be alive.

———

He held the crucible steady with aching arms as the molten glass ran over the ceramic lip and into the mold. The heat from the glass scorched his arms, his bare chest, his face, drying him out like a pot in a kiln. He eased the crucible away from the mold and set it on the brick apron of the furnace, glass cooling from a glowing yellow to a dirty gray on its lip, and dropped the tongs in their rack with suddenly trembling hands. The glassmaker Ernesto leaned over the mold, watching for flaws as the small plate began to cool.

"It will do," he said, and he helped Santiago shift the mold into the annealing oven where the glass could cool slowly enough that it would not shatter. Santiago fished a bottle of water from the cooler and stepped out into the forecourt where the glassmaker's two-storey house cast a triangle of shade. It was only the day after Sandoval's duel and Santiago did not expect to see any of that crowd again, not so soon. Yet there Ruy was, perched on the courtyard's low northern wall, perfectly at ease, as if he meant to make a habit of the place.

"I was starting to think he would keep you working through siesta."

Santiago shrugged, refusing to make excuses for either his employer or his employment. Ruy was dressed with the slapdash elegance of his class, his doublet and shirt open at the neck, his light boots tied with mismatched laces. Santiago was half-naked, his bare skin feathered with thin white scars, like a duelist's scars, but not, emphatically not. Still, Ruy had come to him. He propped his elbows on the wall and scratched his heat-tightened skin without apology.

"What do you have planned?" he asked Ruy, and guessed, safely, "Not sleep."

Santiago expected—he hoped—that Ruy would grin and propose another adventure like yesterday's, but no. Ruy looked out at the northern view and said soberly, "Sandoval was going to spend the morning in the Assembly watching the debates. We're to meet him at the observatory when they break before the evening session."

The debates. Santiago swallowed the last of his water, taking pleasure from the cool liquid in his mouth and throat, and then toyed with the bottle, his gaze drawn into the same distance as Ruy's. Because of the fire hazard Ernesto's workshop had an islet to itself, a low crumb of land off Asuada's northern rim. From here there was nothing to see but the white lakebed, the blue hills, the pale sky. Nothing except the long-necked pumps rocking out there in the middle distance, floating on the heat mirage like dusty metal geese, drawing up the water that kept the city alive. For now. Perhaps for not much longer, depending on the vote, the wells, the vanished rains. The empty bottle spun out of Santiago's tired hands and clattered to the baked earth beyond the wall. Ruy slipped down, one hand on his rapier's scabbard, to retrieve it. One drop clung to its mouth, bright as liquid glass in the sunlight, and Santiago had a glancing vision, a waking siesta dream of an earthenware pitcher heavy with water, round-bellied, sweating, cool in his hands. The plastic bottle was light as eggshells, an airy nothing after the crucible and glass.

"Thanks," he said, and shaking off the lure of sleep, he dropped the bottle in the re-use box and gathered up his clothes.

<hr />

The observatory crowned the higher of Orroco's two peaks, gazing down in academic tolerance at the Assembly buildings on the other height. More convenient for Sandoval than for his friends, but such was the privilege of leadership. Santiago felt no resentment as he made the long, hot walk with Ruy. He was glad of the company, glad of the summons, glad of the excuse to visit the observatory grounds. Too glad, perhaps, but he was old enough to know that he could have refused, hung up his hammock for a well-earned sleep, and it was that feeling of choice, of acting out of desire rather than need, that let him walk as Ruy's equal. Their voices woke small echoes from the buildings that shaded the streets, the faint sounds falling about them like the dust kicked up by their feet. Even the short bridge between Asuada and Orroco was built up and in the evenings the street was a fiesta, a promenade complete with music, paper flowers, colored lanterns, laughing girls, but now even the shady balconies were abandoned. These days the city's inhabitants withdrew into their rooms like bats into their caves, hiding from the sun. There was an odd, stubborn, nonsensical freedom to being one of the fools who walked abroad, dizzy and too dry to sweat, as if the heat of afternoon were a minor thing, trivial beside the important business of living.

"Why does Sandoval attend the debates? I didn't think . . . "

"That he cared?" Ruy gave Santiago a slanting look. "That we cared? About the Assembly, we don't. Or at least, I don't. They talk, I'd rather live. No, but Sandoval's family holds one of the observer's seats and he goes sometimes to . . . Well. He says it's to gather ammunition for his lampoons, but sometimes I wonder if it's the lampoons that are the excuse."

"Excuse?"

"For doing his duty. That's the sort of family they are. Duty! Duty!" Ruy thumped his hand to his chest and laughed.

Santiago was—not quite disappointed—he decided he was intrigued. He had not thought that was the kind of man Sandoval was.

Sandoval himself, as if he knew he had to prove Ruy wrong, had gathered an audience in the shady precincts of the observatory's eastern colonnade. He mimicked a fat councilor whose speech was all mournful pauses, a fussy woman who interrupted herself at every turn, one of the famous party leaders who declaimed like an actor, one hand clutching his furrowed brow. Santiago, having arrived in the middle of this impromptu play, couldn't guess how the debate was progressing, but he was struck more forcibly than ever by the great wellspring of spirit inside Sandoval that gave life to one character after another and made people weep with laughter.

"And where is he in all of this?"

Santiago turned, almost shocked. He would never have asked that question, yet it followed so naturally on his own thought he felt transparent, as if he had been thinking aloud. But Luz, who had spoken, was watching Sandoval, and by her manner might have been speaking to herself. Santiago hesitated over a greeting. Luz looked up at him, her face tense with a challenge he did not really understand.

"Isn't that what actors do?" he said. "Bury themselves in their roles?"

"Oh, surely," she said. "Surely. Here we see Sandoval the great actor, and in a minute more we'll see Sandoval the great actor playing the role of Sandoval the great actor not playing a role. And when do we see Sandoval, just Sandoval? Where is he? Buried and—"

Luz broke off, but her thought was so clear to Santiago that she might as well have said it: dead. Worried, confused, Santiago looked over her head to Ruy, who shrugged, his face mirroring the eternal puzzlement of men faced with a woman's moods. Sandoval's admirers laughed at something he said and Luz gripped Santiago's arm.

"It's too hot, I can't stand this noise. Let's find somewhere quiet."

She began to pull Santiago down the colonnade. Ruy pursed his lips and shook his finger behind her back. Santiago flashed back a wide-eyed look of panic, only half-feigned, and Ruy, silently laughing, came along.

The observatory was one of the oldest compounds in the city, built during the Rational Age when philosophers and their followers wanted to base an entire civilization on the mysterious perfection of the circle and the square. Life was too asymmetrical, too messy, to let the age last for long, but its remnants were peaceful. There really was a kind of perfection in the golden domes, the marble colonnades, the long white buildings with their shady arcades that fenced the observatory in, a box for a precious orb. Perfection, but an irrelevant perfection: the place was already a ruin, even if the roofs and walls were sound. As they left Sandoval and his admirers behind, the laughter only made the silence deeper, like the fragments of shade whose contrast only whitened the sunlight on the stone.

Luz led them across the plaza where dead pepper trees cracked the flagstones with their shadows, through an arched passage that was black to sun-dazzled eyes, and out onto the southern terrace. Even under the arcade there was little shade. The three of them sat on a bench with their backs to the wall and looked out over the islands with their packed geometry of courtyards and plazas and roofs, islands of order, of life, scattered across the dry white face of death. Ruy and Luz began to play the game of high places, arguing over which dark cleft on Asuada was Mendoza Street, which faded tile roof was Corredo's atelier, which church it was that had the iron devils climbing its brass-crowned steeple. Santiago, tired from his work, the walk, the heat, rested his head against the wall and let his eyes stray to the lake and its mirage of water, the blue ripples that were only a color stolen from the merciless sky. Suddenly he found the city's quiet dreadful. It was like a graveyard's, a ruin's.

"Why do they bother with a debate?" he said. "Everyone already knows how they're going to vote. Everyone knows . . . "

Luz and Ruy were silent and Santiago felt the embarrassment of having broken a half-perceived taboo. He was the outsider again, the stranger.

But then Luz said, "Everyone knows that when they vote, however they vote, they will have voted wrong. To stay, to go: there is no right way to choose. They argue because when they are angry enough they can blame the other side instead of themselves." She paused. "Or God, or the world."

"Fate," Ruy said.

"Fate is tomorrow," Luz said.

"And there is no tomorrow," Ruy said. "Only today. Only now."

Santiago said nothing, knowing he had heard their creed, knowing he could only understand it in his bones. The lake's ghost washed around the islands' feet, blue and serene, touching with soft waves against the shore. A dust devil spun up a tall white pillar that Santiago's sleep-stung eyes turned into a cloud trailing a sleeve of rain. Rain rustled against the roof of the arcade. White birds dropped down from the high arches and drifted away on the still air, their wings shedding sun-bright droplets of molten gold. Sleep drew near and was startled away by Luz's cry. Some scholar, despairing over his work or his world, had set his papers alight and was casting them out his window. The white pages danced on the rising heat, their flames invisible in the sunlight, burning themselves to ash before they touched the ground.

———◦———

The day of the vote was an undeclared holiday. Even the news station played music, waiting for something to report, and every open window poured dance songs and ballads into the streets. Neighbors put aside their feuds, strangers were treated to glasses of beer, talk swelled and died away on the hour and rose again when there was no news, no news.

Sandoval, trying as always to be extraordinary, had declared that today was an ordinary day, and had gone with Ruy and Orlando and some others to the swordsman Corredo's atelier for their morning practice. Santiago, summoned by Ruy, entered those doors for the first time that day, and he was not sure what to feel. While Sandoval strove to triumph over the day's great events by cleaving to routine, Santiago found it was impossible not to let his first entry into the duelists' privileged realm be colored by the tension of the day. And why shouldn't it be? He looked around him at the young men's faces, watched them try to mirror Sandoval's mask of ennui, and wondered if their fight to free themselves from the common experience only meant they failed to immerse themselves in the moment they craved. This *was* the moment, this day, the day of decision. And yet, Santiago thought, Sandoval was right in one thing: however the vote went, whatever the decision, life would go on. They would go on breathing, pumping blood, making piss. They would still be here, in the world, swimming in time.

"You're thinking," Ruy said cheerfully. "Master Corredo! What say you to the young man who thinks?"

"Thinking will kill you," said the swordsman Corredo. He was a lean, dry man, all sinew and leather, and he meant what he said.

"There, you see? Here, take this in your hand." Ruy presented Santiago with the hilt of a rapier. Santiago took it in his burn-scarred hand, felt the grip find its place against his palm. The sword was absurdly light after the iron weight of the glassmaker's tongs, it took no more than a touch of his fingers to hold it steady.

"Ah, you've done this before," Ruy said. He sounded suspicious, as if he thought Santiago had lied.

"No, never." Santiago was tempted to laugh. He loved it, this place, this sword in his hand.

"A natural, eh? Most of us started out clutching it like—"

"Like their pizzles in the moment of joy," Master Corredo said. He took Santiago's strong wrist between his fingers and thumb and shook it so the sword softly held in Santiago's palm waved in the air. After a moment Santiago firmed the muscles in his arm and the sword was still, despite the swordsman's pressure.

"Well," said Corredo. He let Santiago go. "You stand like a lump of stone. Here, beside me. Place your feet so—not so wide—the knees a little bent . . . "

Ruy wandered off, limbered up with a series of long lunges. After a while the soft kiss and whine of steel filled the air.

By noon they were disposed under the awning in Corredo's

courtyard, drinking beer and playing cards. Santiago, with a workingman's sense of time, was hungry, but no one else seemed to be thinking about food. Also, the stakes were getting higher. Santiago dropped a good hand on the discard pile and excused himself. He would save his money and find a tavern that would sell him a bushel of flautas along with a few bottles of beer. Not that he could afford to feed them any more than he could afford to gamble with them, but he had heard them talk about spongers. He would rather be welcomed when they did see him, even if he could not see them often.

And then again, the holiday atmosphere of the streets made it easy to spend money if you had it to spend. In the masculine quiet of Corredo's atelier he had actually forgotten for a little while what day it was. The vote, the vote. Red and green handbills not yet faded by the angry sun fluttered from every doorjamb and drifted like lazy pigeons from underfoot. Radios squawked and rattled, noise becoming music only when Santiago passed a window or a door, and people were still abroad in the heat. One did not often see a crowd by daylight and it was strange how the sun seemed to mask faces just as effectively as evening shadows did, shuttering the eyes, gilding brown skin with sweat and dust. Santiago walked farther than he had meant to, sharing the excitement, yet feeling separate from the crowd, as if he were excited about a different thing, or as if he had been marked out by Sandoval, set aside for something other than this. Life, he thought: Sandoval's creed. But wasn't this life out here in the streets, in these conversations between strangers, in this shared fear for the future, for the world? Didn't blood beat through these hearts too?

The heat finally brought Santiago to rest by the shaded window of a hole-in-the-wall restaurant. Standing with his elbows on the outside counter, waiting for his order, he ate a skewer of spicy pork that made him sweat, and then cooled his mouth with a beer. The restaurant's owner seemed to have filled the long, narrow room with his closest friends. Santiago, peering through the hatch at the interior darkness, heard the same argument that ran everywhere today, a turbulent stream like the flash flood from a sudden rain. Life's no good here anymore, but will it be any better in the crowded hills, by the poisoned sea, down in the south where the mud and rain was all there was?

"But life *is* good." No one heard, though Santiago spoke aloud. Perhaps they chose not to hear. His order came in a paper box already half-transparent with oil stains and he carried it carefully in his arms. The smell was so good it made him cheerful. All the same, when he returned to the atelier he found that as impatient as he had been with the worriers outside, he was almost as irritated by the abstainers within. They seemed so much like stubborn children sitting in a corner with folded arms. Like children, however, they greeted the food with extravagant delight, and Santiago found himself laughing at the accolades they heaped on his head, as if he had performed some mighty deed. It was better to eat, he thought, and enjoy the food as long as it was there.

Like normal people, they dozed through the siesta hours, stupefied by heat and food. Santiago slept deeply and woke to the dusky velvet of the evening shadows. With the sun resting on the far hills the bleached sky regained its color, a blue as deep and calm as a song of the past, a blue that seemed to have been drawn out of Santiago's dreams. They went out together, yawning and still pleasantly numb with sleep, into the streets where a hundred radios stamped out the rhythm of an old salsa band. It was impossible not to sway a little as they walked, to bump their shoulders in thoughtless camaraderie, to spin out lines of poetry at the sight of a pretty face. "Oh, rose of the shadows, flower in bud, bloom for me . . . " It was evening and the long, long shadows promised cool even as the city's plaster and stone radiated the last heat of the day. It was evening, the day's delight.

"So who is going to ask first?" Orlando muttered to Ruy. Ruy glanced over his shoulder at Santiago, his eyebrows raised. Santiago smiled and shook his head.

"We won't need to ask," Ruy said. "We'll hear, whether we want to or not."

But who in all the city would have thought they needed to be told? Holiday had given way to carnival, as the radios gave way to guitars in the plazas, singers on the balconies, dancers in the streets. It was a strange sort of carnival where no one needed to drink to be drunk. The people had innocent faces, Santiago thought, washed clean by shock, as if the world had not died so much as vanished, leaving them to stand on air. But was it the shock of being told to abandon their homes? Or was it the shock of being told to abandon themselves to the city's slow death? Santiago listened to an old man singing on a flat roof high above the street, he listened to a woman sobbing by a window, and he wondered. But no, he didn't ask.

They wound down to Asuada's esplanade where the dead trees were hung with lanterns that shone candy colors out into the dark. The sun was gone, the hills a black frieze, the sky a violet vault freckled with stars. The lakebed held onto the light, paler than the city and the sky, and it breathed a breath so hot and dry the lake's dust might have been the fine white ash covering a barbecue's coals. There were guitars down here too, and a trumpet that sang out into the darkness. Sandoval took off his sword and began to dance. Sweat drew his black hair across his face as he stamped and whirled and clapped with hollow hands. Ruy began to dance, and Orlando and the rest, their swords slung down by Santiago's feet. He ached to watch them, wished he with his clumsy feet dared to join them, and was glad he had not when Luz spotted him through the crowd. She came and leaned against his side, muscular and soft, never quite still as the guitars thrummed out their rhythms. Santiago knew she was watching Sandoval, but he did not care. This was his. A paper lantern caught fire, and when no one leapt forward to douse it the whole tree burned, one branch at a time, the pretty lanterns swallowed up by the crueler light of naked flame. It was beautiful, the bare black branches clothed in feathers of molten glass, molten gold. The dance spread, a chain of men stamping and whirling down the lakeshore. In the shuffle of feet and the rustle of flames, in the brush of Luz's hair against his sleeve, in the rush of air into his lungs, Santiago once again heard that phantom rain. It fell around him, bright as sparks in the light of the fire, it rang like music into the memory of the lake. It was sweet, sweet. Luz stirred against his arm.

"Are you going, Santiago? When they stop the pumps, are you going to go?"

He leaned back against the railing, and smiled into the empty sky, and shook his head, no.

COLD WATER SURVIVAL

November 11:

Cutter is dead and I don't know what to feel. Andy is crying and Miguel is making solemn noises about the tragedy, but I think they're acting. Not their grief—that's real—but their response to it. I think they're just playing to what's expected out there in the world. I can't, and I don't think Del can either. I've seen the shining in his eyes, and it isn't tears. There's a kind of excitement in the air, the thrill of big events, important times: death. It's a first for all of us. For Cutter too.

———◆———

[The viewer of the digital video camera is like a small window onto the past, shining blue in the dull red shade of my tent.]

There's a sliver of indigo sky, and the white glare of snow, and the far horizon of ocean like a dark wall closing us in. There are the climbers, incongruous as candy wrappers in their red and yellow cold-weather gear. But they're like old-time explorers too, breath frosting their new beards and snow shades hiding their eyes. [Only because I know them do I recognize Cutter in yellow, Del in red.] Their voices reach the small mic through gusts of wind so strong it sways the videographer [me], making the scene tilt as if the vast iceberg rose and fell like a ship to the ocean swells. It doesn't. Bigger than Denmark, Atlantis takes

33

the heavy Antarctic waves without a tremor. But this is summer, and we haven't had any major storms yet.

I can hear them panting through my earbuds, Cutter and Del digging down to firm ice where they can anchor their ropes. Rock can be treacherous; ice more so; surface ice that's had exposure to sun and wind most of all. They hack away with their axes, taking their time. Bored, the videographer turns away to film a slow circle: the dark line of the crevasse, the trampled snow, the colorful camp of snow tents, disassembled pre-fab huts, crated supplies, and floatation-bagged gear. I remember with distaste the dirty frontier mess of McMurdo Station, an embarrassment on the stark black-white-blue face of the continent, but I can sympathize, too. The blankness of this huge chunk of broken ice sheet is daunting. It's nice to have something human around to rest your eyes on.

Full circle: the climbers are setting their screws. They aren't roped together, the ice is too untrustworthy. The videographer approaches the near side of the crevasse as they come up to the far lip, ready to descend. Their crampons kick ice shards into the sunlight: the focus narrows: spike-clad boots, ice-spray, the white wall of ice descending into blue shadow. The climbers make the transition from the horizontal surface to the vertical, as graceless as penguins getting to the edge of the water, and then start the smooth bounding motion of the rappel. The lip of the crevasse cuts off the view. [A blip of blackness.] A better angle, almost straight down: the videographer has lain down to aim the camera over the edge. The climbers bound down, the fun of the descent yet to be paid for by the long vertical climb of the return. The playback is nothing but flickering light, but in it is encoded the smell of ancient ice, the sting of sunlight on the back of my neck. I must have sensed those things, but I didn't notice them at the time. I didn't notice, either, that I only watched the descent through the tiny window of the camera in my hand.

They're only twenty meters down when Cutter's screws give way. *Shit*, he says, *Del*— And he takes a hack with his axes, but the ice is bad and the force of his blows tips him back, away from the wall—his crampons caught for another instant, so it's like he's standing on an icy floor where Del is bounding four-limbed like an ape, swinging left on his rope, dropping one ax to make a grab—and the camera catches the moment when the coiling rope slaps the failed screw into Cutter's helmet, but he's falling anyway by then. Del looses the brakes on his rope and falls beside him, above him, reaching, but there's still friction on his rope and anyway, no one can fall faster than gravity. *Cutter*, says the videographer, and the camera view spins wide as she finally looks down with her own eyes. The camera doesn't see it, and I don't now except in memory. The conclusion happens off-screen, and we, the camera and I, are left staring at the crevasse wall across the way.

And so it's only now, in my red tent that's still bright in the polar absence of night, that I see it—them—the shapes in the ice.

———

November 12:

We spent the morning sawing out a temporary grave, and then we laid Cutter, shrouded in his sleeping bag, into the snow. It was a horrible job. Cutter, my friend, the first dead person I'd

35

laid hands on. It should have been solemn, I know, and I have somewhere inside me a loving grief, but Christ, manhandling that stiff broken corpse into the rescue sled, limbs at all the wrong angles and that face with the staring eyes and gaping shatter-toothed mouth. Oh Cutter, I thought, stop, don't do this to me. Stop being dead? Don't inflict your death on me? On any of us, I guess, himself included. I hated to do it, but the others aren't climbers, so it was Del and me, all too painfully conscious of how bad the ice could be. We made a painstaking axes-and-screws descent, crampons kicking in until they'll bear your weight, not trusting the rope as you dig the axes in. In spite of everything, it was a good climb, no problems at all, but there was Cutter waiting at the bottom for us. His frozen blood was red as paint on the ice-boulders that choked the throat of the crevasse.

It was so blue. Ice like fossilized snow made as hard and clear as glass by the vast weight and the uncountable years. An eon of ice pressed from the heart of the continent, out into the enormous ice sheet that is breaking up now, possibly for the first time since humans have been around, and sending its huge fragments north to melt into the oceans of the world. Fragments of which Atlantis is only one, though the only inhabited one. Like a real country now, we have not only a population but a graveyard, a history, too.

And an argument. Andy made her case for withdrawal—playing the role, I thought, that began with her tears—but none of us, not even her, had thought to call in the fatality the day it happened. "Why not?" I asked, and nobody had an answer for me. "Why didn't you?" said Miguel, but I hadn't meant to accuse. I had wanted someone to give me an answer for my actions, my non-action. Not reporting the death will mean trouble and we're already renegades, tolerated by the Antarctic policy-makers only because no one has ever staked a claim on an iceberg before. We set up McMurdo's weather station and satellite tracking gear and promised them our observations, but we aren't scientists, we're just adventurers coming along for the ride. And now Cutter's dead, out here in international waters, and though I guess the Australians will want some answers at some point—I know his parents will—Oz is a long way away. I almost said, Earth is a long way away. Earth is, dirt is, far from this land of ice and sea and sky.

[Camera plugged into laptop, laptop sucking juice from the solar panels staring blankly at the perpetual sun.]

I watch the fall, doing penance for my curiosity. My own recorded breath is loud in my earbuds. The camera's view flings itself in a blurry arc and then automatically focuses on the far wall. Newer ice, that's really compacted snow, is opaquely white, glistening as the fierce sun melts the molecular surface. Deeper, it begins to clarify, taking on a blue tone as the ice catches and bends the light. Deeper yet, it's so dark a blue you could be forgiven for thinking it's opaque again, but it's even clearer now, all the air pressed out by millennia of snow falling one weightless flake at a time. Some light must filter through the upper ice because the shapes [I pause] are not merely surface shapes, but recede deep into the iceberg's heart.

Glaciers (of which Atlantis was one) form in layers, one season's snow falling on the last, so they are horizontally stratified. But glaciers also move, flowing down from the inland heights of the continent, and that movement over uneven ground breaks vertical fault lines like this crevasse all through the vast body of ice. So any glacial ice-face is going to bear a complex stratigraphy, a sculpting of horizontal and vertical lines. This is part of ice's beauty, this sculptural richness of form, color, light, that can catch your heart and make you ache with wonder. And because it is the kind of harmony artists strive for, it's easy to see the hand of an artist in what lies before you.

But no. I've seen the wind-carved hoodoos in the American southwest and I've seen the vast stone heads of Rapa Nui, and I know the difference between the imagination that draws a figure out of natural shapes and the potent recognition of the artifact. These shapes [I zoom 20%, 40%] in the ice have all the mystery and meaning of Mayan glyphs, at once angular and organic, three-dimensional, fitting together as much like parts in a machine as words on a page. What are they? I've been on glaciers from the Rockies to the Andes and I've never seen anything like this. My hands itch for my rope and my axes. I want to see what's really there.

November 13:

I wondered if Del would object to another climb—he came up from retrieving Cutter stunned and pale—but the big argument came from Miguel who talked about safety and responsibility to the group. I said, "Have you looked at the pictures?" and he said, "All I see is ice." But Miguel's a sailor, one of the around-the-world-in-a-tiny-boat-alone kind, and ice is what he keeps his daily catch in. Andy said he had a point about safety, if things go really wrong we're going to need one another, but she kept giving my laptop uneasy looks, knowing she'd seen something inexplicable.

I said, "Isn't this why we're here? To explore?"

"What if it's important?" Andy said, changing tack. "What if it really is something? The scientists should be studying it, not us."

"Ice formations," Miguel said. "How important is that? It's all going to melt in the end."

"Are we always going to argue like this?" This from Del. "If we're going to quit, then let's get on the satellite phone and get the helo back here to pick us up."

"I'm just saying," Miguel said, but Del cut him off.

"No. We knew why we were doing this when we started. I hate that Cutter's dead, but I wouldn't have come to begin with if we'd laid different ground rules, and if we're going to change now I don't want to be here. I've got other things to do."

I backed him up. This was supposed to be our big lawless adventure, colonizing a chunk of unreal estate that's going to melt away to nothing in a couple of years—not for nationalism or wealth—maybe for fame a little—but mostly because we wanted to be outside the rules, on the far side of every border in the world. Which is, I said, where death lies, too.

Taking it too far, as usual. Andy gave me another of those who-are-you looks, but I fixed her with a look of my own. "Get beyond it," I said. "Get beyond it, or why the hell are we here?"

And then I remembered why these people are my closest friends, my chosen family, because they did finally give up the good-citizen roles and tapped into that excitement that was charging the air. Most people would think us heartless, inhuman, but a real climber would understand: we loved Cutter more, not less, by moving on. Going beyond, as he has already done.

So Del and I roped up again and went down.

———

[The images come in scraps and fragments as the videographer starts and stops the camera.]

The angle of light changes with the spinning of the iceberg in the circumpolar current. For this brief hour it slices into the depths of the crevasse, almost perfectly aligned with the break in the ice. So is the wind, the constant hard westerly that blows across the mic, a deep hollow blustering. Ice chips shine in the sunlight as they flee the climber's crampons kicking into the crevasse wall. The tethered rope trails down into the broken depths. Everywhere is ice.

[blip]

The crevasse wall in close up. Too close. [The videographer leans out from a three-point anchor: one ax, two titanium-bladed feet.] Light gleams from the surface, ice coated in a molecule-thick skin of melt water, shining. All surface, no depth. *Shit*, the videographer [me] says. *Look*, the other climber [Del] says. The camera eye turns toward him, beard and shades and helmet. He points out of the frame. A dizzying turn, the bright gulf of the crevasse, the far wall. More shapes, and Christ they're big. The crevasse is only three meters wide at this point, and measuring them against a climber's length, they're huge, on the order of cars and buses, great whites and orca whales.

[blip]

A lower angle. [Pause, zoom in, zoom out.] These shapes swirl through the ice like bubbles in an ice cube, subtle in the depths. Ice formations, Miguel said. Ice of a different consistency, a different density? Ice is ice, water molecules shaped into a lattice of extraordinary strength and beauty. The lattice under pressure doesn't change. Deep ice is only different because air has been forced out, leaving the lattice pristine. So what is this? The camera's focus draws back. They're still there, vast shapes in the ice. The wind blusters against the mic.

[blip]

The floor of the crevasse—not that a berg crevasse has a floor. There's no mountain down there, only water 3 degrees above freezing. But the crack narrows and is choked with chunks of ice and packed drifts of snow, making a kind of bottom, though a miserable one to negotiate on foot. The camera swings wildly as the videographer flails to keep her balance. Blue ice walls, white ice rubble, a flash of red—Cutter's frozen blood on an ice tusk not too far away.

[blip]

A still shot at last. A smooth shard of ice as big as a man, snow-caked except where Del is sweeping it clear with his ax handle. *It could be*, he says panting, *or part of one*. My own voice, sounding strange as it always does on the wrong side of my eardrums: *So it broke out when the crevasse formed?* Del polishes the ice with his mitts. The camera closes in on his hands, the clear ice underneath his palms. It *is* ice. The videographer's hand reaches into the frame to touch the surface. Ice, impossibly coiled like an angular ammonite shell.

41

November 15:

Del and I hauled the ice-shape up in the rescue sled as if it was another body, but by the time we had it at the surface the constant westerly, always strong, was getting stronger, and Miguel was urgent about battening down the camp. We'd been lazy, seduced by the rare summer sun, and now, with clouds piling up into the blue sky, we had to cut snow blocks and pile them into wind breaks—and never mind the bloody huts that should have been set up first thing. Saw blocks of styrofoam-like snow, pry them out of the quarry, stack them around the tents and gear, all the time with the wind heaving you toward the east, burning your face through your balaclava, slicing through every gap in your clothes. The snow that cloaks the upper surface of the berg blows like a hallucinatory haze, a Dracula mist that races, hissing in fury, toward the east. It scours your weather gear, would scour your flesh off your bones if you were mad enough to strip down.

The bright tents bob and shiver. McMurdo's satellite relay station on its strut-and-wire tower whines and howls and thrums—Christ, that's going to drive me mad. Clouds swallow the sun, the distant water goes a dreadful shade of gray. And this isn't a spell of bad weather, this is the norm. Cherish those first sunny days, we tell each other, huddled in the big tent with our mugs of instant cocoa. Summer or not, this gray howling beast of a wind is here to stay. Andy uplinks on her laptop, downloads the shipping advisories, such as they are for this empty bit of sea. There are deep-sea fishing boats out here, a couple of research vessels, the odd navy ship, but the Southern Ocean is huge and traffic is sparse. We joke about sending a Mayday—engine failure! we're adrift!—but in fact we're a navigation hazard, and the sobering truth is that if it came down to rescue, we could only be picked up by helicopter: there's no disembarking from the tall rough ice-cliffs that form our berg-ship's hull. And land-based helos have a very short flight range indeed.

Like most sobering truths, this one failed to sober us. Castaways on our drifting island, we turned the music up loud, played a few hands of poker, told outrageous stories, and went early to bed, worn out with the hard work, the cold, the wind. And for absolutely no reason I thought, with Del puffing his silent snores in my ear, We're too few, we're going to hate each other by the end. And then I thought of Cutter lying cold and lonesome in the snow.

·—•◦•—·

November 16:

Another work day, getting the huts up in the teeth of the wind. Miguel, sailor to his bones, is a fanatic for organization. I'm not, except for my climbing gear, but I know he's right. We need to be able to find things in an emergency. More than that, we need to keep sane and civilized, we need our private spaces and our occupations. We also need to keep on top of the observations we promised McMurdo if we want to keep their good will—more important than ever with Cutter dead—which was my excuse for dragging Andy away from camp while the men argued about how to stash the crates. Visibility wasn't bad and we laid our first line of flags from the camp to the berg's nearest edge. Waist-high orange beacons, they snapped and chattered in our wake.

Berg cliffs are insanely dangerous because bergs don't mildly dwindle like ice cubes in a G&T. They break up as they melt, softened chunks dropping away from the chilled core, mini-bergs calving off the wallowing parent. All the same, the temptation to look off the edge was too powerful, so we sidled up to it and peered down to where the blue-white cliff descended into the water and became a brighter, sleeker blue. The water was clearer than you might suppose, and since we were on the lee edge there wasn't much surf. We looked down a long way. Andy grabbed my arm. "Look!" she said, but I was already pulling out the camera.

———

[Tight focus only seems to capture the water's surface. As the angle widens the swimming shadows come into view.]

Deep water is black, so the shapes aren't silhouettes, they're dim figures lit from above, their images refracted through swirling water. Algae grows on ice, krill eat the algae, fish eat the krill, sharks and whales and seals and squids and penguins and god knows what eat the fish. God knows what. The mic picks up me and Andy arguing over what we're seeing. They move so fluidly they must be seals, I propose, seals being the acrobats of the sea. Could be dolphins, Andy counters, but when the camera lifts to the farther surface [when I, for once, take my eyes off the view screen and look unmediated] we see no mammal snouts lifting for air. Sharks, I say, but sharks don't coil and turn and dive, smooth and fluid as silk scarves on the breeze, do they? Giant squid, Andy says, and the camera's focus tightens, trying to discern tentacles and staring eyes. Gray water, blue-white ice. Refocus. The dim shapes are gone.

November 17:

The huts are up and we sent a ridiculously expensive email to our sponsors, thanking them for the luxuries they provided: chairs, tables, insulated floors—warm feet—bliss. Andy uploaded our carefully edited log to our website while she was online, saying that Cutter had been hurt in a climbing mishap and was resting. We'd agreed on this lie—having failed to report his death immediately, there seemed no meaningful difference between telling his folks days or months late—but once it was posted I realized, too late, what we were in for. Not just hiding his death, but faking his life, his doings, his messages to his family. "We can't do this," I said, and Andy met my eyes, agreeing.

"Too late," Del said.

"No," Andy said. "We'll say he died tomorrow."

"We can't leave now," said Miguel. "We just got set up."

"We can't do this," I said again. "Him dying is one thing. Faking him being still alive is unforgivable. Andy's right. We have to say he died tomorrow."

"They'll pull us off," said Del.

"Who will?" I said, because we're not really under anyone's jurisdiction. "Listen, if his folks want to pay for a helo to come out from McMurdo—"

"We're too far," Andy said, "it'd have to be a navy rescue."

"They can get his body now or wait until we're in shouting distance of New Zealand," I said. "If we upload the video—"

"We can't make a show of it!" Miguel said.

"Why not?" Del said. "It's what people want to see."

"We can send it to the Aussies," I said, "to show how he died. It was a climbing accident, no crime, no blame. If they want the body, they can have it."

Del was convinced that someone—who? the UN?—was going to arrest us and drag us off for questioning, but I just couldn't see it. Someone's navy hauling a bunch of Commonwealth loonies off an iceberg at gunpoint because a climber died doing something rash? No. The Australians wouldn't love us, god knows Cutter's parents wouldn't, but nobody was going to that kind of effort, expense, and risk for us.

"So why the fuck didn't you say so two days ago?" Del said to me.

"Well," I said, "my friend had just died and I wasn't thinking straight. How about you?"

———————

[The camera's light is on, enhancing the underwater glow of the blue four-man tent.]

The coiled ice-shape gleams as if it were on the verge of melting, but the videographer's breath steams in the cold. The videographer [me] is fully dressed in cold-weather gear, a parka sleeve moving in and out of view. The camera circles the ice-shape in a slow, uneven pan [me inching around on my knees] and you can see that the shape isn't a snail-shell coil, it's more like a 3D Celtic knot, where only one line is woven through so many volutions that the eye is deceived into thinking the one is many. The camera rises [me getting to my feet] and takes the overview. There, not quite at center, like a yoke in an egg: the heart of the knot. What? The camera's focus narrows. In the gleaming glass-blue depths of the ice, an eye opens. An eye as big as my fist, translucent and alien as a squid's. The camera's view jolts back [me falling against the tent wall] and only the edge of the frame catches the fluid uncoiling of the ice shape, a motion so smooth and effortless it's as though we're underwater. The camera's frame falls away, dissolves, and then there's only me in the blue-lighted tent, me with this fluid alien thing swirling around me like an octopus in a too-small aquarium, opening its limbs for a swift, cold embrace—

[And I wake, sweating with terror, to see Del twitching in his dreams.]

November 18:

Cutter died again today. We sent the video file (lacking its final seconds) to our Australian sponsors, asking them to break the news to Cutter's family. Andy wrote a beautiful letter from all of us, mostly a eulogy I guess, talking about Cutter and what it was like to be here now that he was dead. She did a brilliant job of making it clear that we were staying without making us sound too heartless or shallow. So this is us made honest again, and somehow I miss Cutter more now, as though until we told the outside world his death hadn't quite been real. I keep thinking, I wish he was here—but then I remember that he is, outside in the cold. Maybe I'll go keep him company for a while.

[The laptop screen is brighter than the plastic windows of the hut, the image perfectly clear.]

The camera jogs to the videographer's footsteps, the mic picks up the styrofoam squeak of snowshoes. There's the team on the move, two bearded men and a lanky woman taller than either, in red and blue and green parkas, gaudy against the drifting snow. The camera stops for a circle pan: gray sky, white surface broken into cracks and tilting slabs. Blown snow swirls and hisses; a line of orange flags snaps and shudders in the wind. The videographer [me] sways to the gusts, or the ice-island flexes as it spins across its watery dance floor. Full circle: the three explorers up ahead now, the one in green reaching into the snow-haze to plant more flags.

[blip]

Broken ice terrain, the sound of panting breath. Atlantis as a glacier once traveled some of the roughest volcanic plains on the planet, and these fault-lines show how rough it was, the ice all but shattered here. You have to wonder how long it's going to hold together. *Hey!* The explorer in blue gives a sweeping wave. *You guys! You have to see this!* Shaky movement over tilted slabs of ice, a lurch—

[blip]

A crevasse, not so deep as the one near camp, with the shape of a squared-off comma. In the angle, ice pillars stand almost free of the walls. Blue-white ice rough with breakage. Slabs caught in the crevasse's throat.

[Miguel, watching at my shoulder, says, "That's not what we saw. You know that's not what we saw!"]

⁕

November 20:

Miguel keeps playing the video of today's trek. Over and over, his voice shouts *You have to see this!* through the laptop's speakers. Over and over. Del's so fed up with it he's gone off to our hut and I'm tempted to join him, but it's hard to tear myself away. Andy isn't watching anymore, but she's still in the main hut, listening to our voices—hushed, strained, hesitant with awe—talk about the structures (buildings? vehicles? Diving platforms, Andy's voice speculates) that the camera stubbornly refused to record. At first I thought Miguel was trying to find what we saw in these images of raw ice, but now I wonder if what he's really trying to do is erase his memory and replace it with the camera's. I finally turned away and booted my own computer, opening the earlier files of the first ice-shapes I found. Still there? Yes. But now I wonder: *could* they be natural formations?

Could we be so shaken up by Cutter's death that we're building a shared fantasy of the bizarre?

I don't believe that. We've all been tested, over and over, on mountains and deserts, in ocean deeps and tiny boats out in the vast Pacific. Miguel's told his stories about the mind-companions he dreamed up in his long, lonely journey, about how important they became to him even though he always knew they were imaginary. I've been in whiteouts where the blowing snow deludes the eyes into seeing improbable things. Once, in the Andes, Cutter and I were huddled back-to-back, wrapped in survival blankets, waiting for the wind to die and the visibility to increase beyond 2 feet, and I saw a bus drive by, a big diesel city bus. I had to tell Cutter what I was laughing about. He thought I was nuts.

So we've all been there, and though we all know what kinds of crazy notions people get when they're pushed to extremes—I've heard oxygen-starved climbers propose some truly lunatic ideas when they're tired—we aren't anything close to that state. Fed, rested, as warm as could be expected . . . No.

But if we all saw what we think we saw, then why didn't the camera see it too?

———

[Bubbles rise past the camera's lens. The mic catches the gurgle of the respirator, the groaning of the iceberg, the science fiction sound effects of Weddell seals.]

The camera moves beneath a cathedral ceiling of ice. Great blue vaults and glassy pillars hang above the cold black deeps, sanctuary for the alien life forms of this bitter sea. Fringed jellies and jellies like winged cucumbers, huge red shrimp and tiny white ones, skates and spiders and boney fish with plated jaws. Algae paints the ice with living glyphs in murky green and brown, like lichen graffiti scrawled on a ruin's walls. Air, the alien element, puddles on the ceiling, trapped. The water seems clear, filled with the haunting light that filters through the ice, but out in the farther reaches of the cathedral the light turns opaquely blue, the color of a winter dusk, and below there is no light at all. Bubbles spiral upward, beads of mercury that pool in the hollows of the cathedral ceiling, forming a fluid air-body that glides along the water-smoothed ice. It moves with all the determination of a living thing, seeking the highest point. [The camera follows; bubbles rise; the air-creature grows.] The ceiling vault soars upwards, smeared with algae [zoom in; does it shape pictures, words?] and full of strange swimming life [are there shadows coiling at the farthest edges of the frame?], and it narrows as it rises to a rough chimney. Water has smoothed this icy passage, sculpted it into a flute, a flower stem . . . a birth canal. The air-body takes on speed, rising unencumbered into brighter and brighter light. The upward passage branches into tunnels and more air-bodies appear, as shapeless and fluid as the first. Walls of clear ice are like windows into another frozen sea where other creatures hang suspended, clearer than jellyfish and more strange. And then the camera [lens streaked and running with droplets] rises from the water [how?], ascending a rough crevice in the ice. The air-bodies, skinned in water—or have they been water all along?—are still rising too, sliding with fluid grace through the ice-choked cracks in the widening passage. [The videographer sliding through too: how?] The host seeks out the highest places and at last comes up into the open air—ice still rising in towering walls but with nothing but the sky above. Gray sky, blue-white ice, a splash of red. What is this? Fluid, many-limbed, curious, the water-beings flow weightlessly toward the splash of scarlet [blood]. They taste [blood], absorb [blood], until each glassy creature is tinted with the merest thread of red.

[And I close the file, my hands shaking as if with deadly cold, because these images are impossible. I'm awake, and my camera shows battery drain, and none of us, not even Andy, came prepared to dive in this deadly sea.]

———

November 22:

Miguel watched the impossible video and then walked out of the tent without a word. Andy sat staring at the blank screen, arms wrapped tight around her chest. And after a long silence, Del said calmly, "Nice effects." I knew what he meant—that I was hoaxing them, or someone was hoaxing me—but I can't buy it. Even if any of us had the will we don't have the expertise. We're explorers, not CG fucking animators. And who made us see what we saw in that inland crevasse? Who's going to make the evidence of that disappear on the one hand, and then fake a school of aliens on the other?

"Aliens," Andy said, her face blank and her eyes still fixed on the screen. "Aliens? No. They belong here. They're the ones that belong."

"Hey," I said, not liking the deadness in her tone. "Andy."

"Screw this," Del said, and he left too.

———◦═•═◦———

Miguel's not in camp. It took us far too long to realize it, but we spent most of the day apart, Andy in her hut, Del in ours, me in the big one brooding over my video files. We left the tents up for extra retreat/storage/work spaces and Miguel could have been in one of them—Andy assumed he was, since he wasn't in the hut they share—but when Del finally pulled us together for a meal we couldn't find him. And the wind is rising, howling through the satellite relay station's struts and wires—wires that are growing white with ice. The wind has brought us a freezing fog that reeks of brine. If it were Del out there I could trust him to hunker down and wait for the visibility to clear, but does Miguel the sailor have that kind of knowledge? We all did the basic survival course at McMurdo, but the instructors knew as well as Del and I that there's a world of difference between knowing the rules and living them. The instinct in bad weather is to seek shelter, and god knows it's hard to trust to a reflective blanket thin enough to carry in your pocket. But it's worse not to be able to trust your comrade to do the smart thing. We're all angry at Miguel, even Andy. He's put us all at risk. Because of course we have to go and find him.

November 24:

We're back. McMurdo's relay station is an ice sculpture and our sat phone, even with its own antenna, isn't working. I don't know what we're going to do.

We went after Miguel, the three of us roped up and carrying packs. Our best guess was that he'd gone back to the crevasse where we saw, or didn't see, the buildings, structures, vehicles— whatever they were in the ice. So we followed the line of orange flags inland. Standing by one you could see the next, and barely discern the next after that, which put the visibility roughly at 6 meters. But with the icy fog blasting your face and your breath fogging up your goggles, the world contracts very quickly to within the reach of your arms. Walking point is hard, but it's better than shuffling along at the end of the rope, fighting the temptation to put too much trust in a tiring leader. I was glad when Del let me up front after the first hour. Andy, who has the least experience with this kind of weather, stayed between us, roped to either end.

A long hike in bad weather. The sun, already buried behind ugly clouds, grazed the horizon, and the day contracted to a blue-white dusk. We huddled in a circle, knee-to-knee, with our packs as a feeble windbreak. I fell into a fugue state. The blued-out haze went deep and cold and still, like water chilled almost to the point of freezing. The wind was so constant it no longer registered; the hiss of it against our parkas became the hiss of water pressure on my ears. And the whiteout began to build its illusions. Walls rose in the haze, weirdly angled, impossibly over-hung. Strange voices mouthed heavy, bell-like, underwater sounds. Something massive seemed to pass behind me without footsteps, its movement only stirring the water-air like a submarine cutting a wake. No different than the bus I saw on that Andean mountain, except that Andy jerked against me while Del muttered a curse.

And then the ground moved.

Ground: the packed snow and ice we sat upon. It gave a small buoyant heave, making us all gasp, and then shuddered. A tremor, no worse than the one I'd sat through when I was visiting Andy in Wellington, but at that instant all illusion that Atlantis was an island died. This was an iceberg, already melting and flawed to its core, and there was nothing below it but the ocean. Another small heave. Stillness. And then a sound to drive you insane, a deep immense creaking moan that might have come from some behemoth's throat. I grabbed for Del. Andy grabbed for me.

The ice went mad.

We were shaken like rats in a terrier's mouth. The toe spikes on someone's snowshoes, maybe my own, gouged me in the calf. I didn't even notice it at the time. We lurched about, helpless as passengers in a falling plane, and all the time that ungodly noise, hugely bellowing, tugged at flesh and bone. I knew for a certainty that Atlantis was breaking up and that we were all already dead, just breathing by reflex for a few seconds more. I flashed on Cutter falling, knowing he was dead long before he hit the ground. I was glad we'd told his folks, glad Andy had sent that beautiful letter, eulogy for us all. And then the ice went still.

I lay a moment, hardly noticing the tangle we were in, my whole being focused on that silence. Quiet, quiet, like the final moment in free fall, the last timeless instant before the bottom. But it stretched on, and on, and finally we all picked ourselves up, still unable to believe we were alive. "Jesus," Del said, and I had to laugh.

We went on, me in the middle this time because of my limp, with Andy bringing up the rear. Tossed around as we had been, none of us was sure of our directions, and because of the berg's motion GPS and compass were both useless. Blown snow and fog-ice erased our footprints as well as Miguel's. In the end all we could do was follow the line of flags in the direction of our best guess and resolve that if it led us back to camp, we would turn and head straight back out again. I was feeling Miguel's absence very much by then, so much so that a fourth figure haunted the edges of my vision, teasing me with false presence. But maybe that was Cutter, not Miguel.

Flags lay scattered among huge tilted slabs of packed snow. We replanted the slender poles as best we could, and by this time I was starting to hope we *had* been turned around and were heading back to camp. If the berg-quake had scattered the whole line of flags they were likely to be buried by the time we turned around, and if they were, we were screwed. But we couldn't do anything but what we were already doing. We clambered through the broken ice field, hampered by the rope between us and already tired from the wind. Del got impatient and Andy snapped that she was doing the best she could. "You're fine," I said. "Del, ease off." He went silent. We re-roped and I took point, limp and all.

Spires of ice rose like jagged minarets above the broken terrain. Great pillars, crystalline arches, thin translucent walls. Scrambling with my eyes always on the next flag, I took the ice structures for figments of the whiteout at first, but then we were in among them and the wind died into fitful gusts. The line of flags ended, irredeemably scattered, unless this was its proper end and the former crevasse was utterly transformed. It was beautiful. Even exhausted and afraid I could see that, and while Andy shouted for Miguel and Del hunkered over our packs digging out the camp stove and food, I pulled out my camera.

———

[Digital clarity is blurred by swirling fog. Yet the images are unmistakable, real.]

Crystalline structures defy any sense of scale. This could be a close-up of the ice-spray caught at the edge of a frozen stream, strands and whorls of ice delicate as sugar tracery, until the videographer turns and gets a human figure into the frame. The man in red bends prosaically over a steaming pot, apparently oblivious to the white fantasia rising up all around him. The mic picks up the sound of a woman's voice hoarsely shouting, and the camera turns to her, a tall green figure holding an orange flag, garish among all the white and blue and glass. *Andy*, says the videographer. *Hush a minute, listen for an answer.* The human sounds die, there's nothing but the many voices of the wind singing through the spires. A long slow pan then: pillars, walls, streets—it's impossible not to think of them that way. A city in the ice. An inhuman city in the ice.

Movement.

The camera jerks, holds still. There's a long, slow zoom, as though it's the videographer rather than the lens that glides down the tilt-floored icy avenue. [The static fog drifting, obscuring the distant view.] Maybe that's all the movement is, sea-fog and wind swirled about by the sharp, strange lines of the ice-structures. [The wind singing in the mic, glass-toned, dissonant.] But no. No. It's *clarity* that swirls like a current of air—like a many-limbed being with a watery skin—gliding gravity-less between the walls, in and out of view. [Pause. Go back. Yes. A shape of air. Zoom. A translucent eye. Zoom. A vast staring eye.]

The camera lurches. The image dives to the snowshoe-printed ground. The videographer's clothing rustles against the mic, almost drowning her hoarse whisper. *We have to get out of here. Guys! We need to—*

We roped Miguel between Del and me, with Andy again bringing up the rear. It was an endless hike, the footing lousy, the visibility bad, all of us hungry and aching for a rest. Del tried to insist that we eat the instant stew he'd heated before we left, but I was seeing transparent squids down every street, and when Miguel stumbled out of the ice, crooning wordlessly to the wind even as he clutched at Andy's hands, Del let himself be outvoted. "This is how climbers die," he said to me, but I said to him, "If you're on an avalanche slope you move as fast and as quietly as you can, no matter how hungry or tired you are." Death is here: I wanted to say it, and didn't, and while I hesitated the silence filled with the glass-harmonica singing of the wind—with Miguel's high crooning, which was the same, the very same. So I didn't need to say it. We followed the broken line of scattered flags back to camp.

And now I sit here typing while the others sleep (Miguel knocked out by pills), and I look up and see what I should have seen the instant we staggered in the door. All of our gear, so meticulously sorted by Miguel, is disarranged. Not badly—we surely would have noticed if shelves were cleared and boxes emptied on the floor—but neat stacks and rows have become clusters and piles, chairs pushed into the table are pulled askew, my still camera and its cables are out of its bag my hands are shaking as I type this there's a draft the door is closed the windows weatherproofed I'm pretending I don't notice but there's a draft moving behind me through the room.

———

November 25:

I took my ax to the tent where we still kept the ice-shape Del and I brought up from the bottom of the crevasse. I was past exhaustion, spooked, halfway crazy. It was just a lump of ice. I took my ax to it, expecting it to bleed seawater, rise up in violent motion, fill the tent with its swirling arms. I swung again and again, flailing behind me once when paranoia filled the tent with invisible things. Ice chipped, shattered. Shards stung my wind-burned face. The noise woke Del in our hut nearby. He came and stopped me. There was no shape left, just a scarred hunk of ice. Del took the ax out of my hand and led me away, gave me a pill to let me sleep like Cutter. I mean, like Miguel. I'm still doped. Tired. I can feel them out there in the wind.

The relay tower is singing.

November 27:

The ice is always shaking now. New spires lean above our snow wall, mocking our defenses. Miguel cries and shouts words we can't understand, words so hard to say they make him drool and choke on his tongue. The wind sings back whenever he calls. The sat phone has given nothing but static until today when it, too, sang, making Del throw the handset to the floor. The radio only howls static. The fog reeks of dead fish, algae, the sea. Everything is rimed in salt ice. Andy hovers over Miguel, trying to make him take another pill: Del threatened him with violence if he doesn't shut up. I grabbed Del, dragged him to a chair, hugged him until he gave in and pulled me to his lap. We're here now, all four of us together. None of us can bear to be alone.

November 28:

A new crevasse opened in the camp today, swallowing two tents and making a shambles of the snow wall. Is this an attack? Our eviction notice, Andy says, humor her badge of courage. But I wonder if they even notice us, if they even care. Atlantis is theirs now, and I suppose it always has been, through all those long cold ages at the heart of the southern pole. Now the earth is warming, the ancient ice is freed to move north, to melt—and then what? What of this ice city growing all around us like a crystal lab-grown from a seed? If the clues they've given us (deliberately? I do wonder) are true, then they are beings of water as much as of ice. It won't happen quickly, but eventually, as the berg travels north out of the Southern Ocean and into the Atlantic or Pacific, it will all melt. Releasing . . . what? . . . into the warming seas of our world. Our world *is* an ocean world, our over-burdened continents merely islands in the vast waters of misnamed Earth. What will become of us when they have reclaimed *their* world?

Del and Andy, in between increasingly desperate attempts to bring our sailor Miguel back from whatever alien mindscape he's lost in, are concocting a scheme to get our inflatable lifeboat, included in our gear almost as a joke, down the ice cliffs to the water. Away from here, they reason, we should be able to make the sat phone work, light the radio beacon, call in a rescue. I have a fantasy—or did I dream it last night?—that the singing that surrounds us, stranger than the songs of seals or whales, has reached into orbit, filling satellite antenna-dishes the way it fills my ears, drowning human communication. I imagine that the first careless assault on human civilization has already begun, and that the powers—the human powers—of Earth are looking outward in terror, imagining an attack from the stars, never dreaming that it is already here, has always been here, now waking from its ice-bound slumber. It is we who have warmed the planet; we, perhaps, who have brought this upon ourselves. But brought what, I wonder? And when Andy appeals to me to help her and Del with their escape plan, I find I have nothing much to say. But I suppose I will have to say it before long: why should we leave—*should* we leave—just when things are getting interesting?

Get beyond it, I'll have to tell them, as I did when Cutter died. We have to look beyond.

In the meantime, though, I'll make a couple of backups, downloading this log and my video files onto flash drives that will fit into a waterproof container. My message in a bottle. Just in case.

BROTHER OF THE MOON

Our hero wakes in his sister's bed. Last night's vodka drains through him in sluggish ebb, leaving behind the silt of hangover, the unbrushed taste of guilt. He rolls onto his stomach, feeling the rumpled bed wallow a little on the last of the alcoholic waves, and opens his eyes. His sister sleeps with her curtains open. The tall window across from the bed is brilliant with a soft spring sunlight that slips past crumbled chimneys and ornate gables to shine on his sister's hands. She has delicate little monkey's paws, all tendon and brittle bone, that look even more fragile than usual edged by the morning light. Sitting cross-legged among the rumpled sheets, tough as an underfed orphan in the undershirt and sweatpants she uses as pajamas, our hero's sister is flipping a worn golden coin. She is a princess. Our hero is a prince.

The coin sparkles in a rising and falling blur. Our hero watches with bemusement and pleasure as his sister's nimble hands catch the coin, display the winning face, send it spinning and winking through sunlight with the flick of a thumb. Our hero's sister manipulates the coin, a relic of ancient times, with a skill our hero would never have guessed. It is the skill of a professional gambler who could stack a deck of cards in her sleep, which is mystifying. Our hero's sister is not the gambling type. Our hero clears a sour vodka ghost from his throat.

"You're up early."

The coin blinks at him and drops into his sister's hand. With her fingers closed around it, she leans over him and kisses his stubbled head.

"You snore."

"I don't," he says. "Are you winning?"

"It keeps coming up kings." Her monkey's hands toy with the coin, teasing the golden sunshine into our hero's eyes. "Who were you with last night?"

Our hero scrubs his tearing eyes with a fold of her sheet. The linen is soft and yellow with age and smells of his sister, comforting. "No one special. No one. I forget."

His sister's face is like her hands, delicate, bony, feral. Our hero thinks she's beautiful, and loves her with the conscious, deliberate tenderness of someone who has lost every important thing but one.

"How do you know I snore?" he says. "You're the woman who can sleep through bombs."

This is literal truth. When the New Army was taking the city and the two of them were traveling behind the artillery line, she proved she could sleep through anything. But she says, "Bombs don't steal the covers," and since our hero is lying on top of the blanket, fully dressed, with his shod feet hanging off the end of the bed, he understands that she was awakened by something other than him. It troubles him that he cannot guess what might have been troubling her. Or perhaps it is a deeper worry, that he can imagine what it might have been. He stretches out a hand and steals the coin from between her fingers. The gold is as warm and silky as her skin. The face of the king has been the same for five hundred years.

"Granddad," our hero says ironically.

His sister sighs and stretches out beside him, stroking his head.

"You need to shave," she says.

People have said they are too close. The new government has cited rumors of incest as one reason to edge our hero out of the public eye. The rumors are false, they have never been lovers. But perhaps it is more honest to say that if they are lovers, they have always been chaste. In any event, they are close. She rubs her palm back and forth across his scalp, and he knows how much she enjoys the feel of stubble just long enough to bend from prickly to soft, because he enjoys it so much himself. Her touch soothes his headache and he is on the verge of dropping off when a van mounted with loudspeakers rolls by in the narrow street below, announcing the retreat of the New Army—the new New Army, our hero thinks, remembering all the friends and rivals who have died—routed from the border in the south. The invasion has begun. Our hero squints to see the losing face of the coin against the mounting sun. The tree and moon of the vanished kingdom has been smoothed into clouds by generations of uncrowned monarchs' hands.

"One toss," our hero's sister says across the echoes of the retreating van. "If it comes up moons, I'll go."

A knot of dread squeezes bile into our hero's throat, but he does as she asks. She is the only person in the world he will obey, not because she rules him, but because he trusts her when he does not himself know what is right. This is often the case these days. Maybe there are no more rights left. Maybe there are only lesser wrongs. He props his head on his fist and flips the coin, catching it in his cupped palm. Moons. He makes a fist before his sister can see, and feels as if he is clenching his hand around his own heart. It's a dreadful duty, a calamity whichever one of them goes, but he would rather be lost than lose her. Before she can pry his fingers open, he tosses the coin high into the golden light and catches it again with a flourish.

"Kings," he says. She looks at him, stricken, heart-sick, and he is glad of his lie.

Walking north along the river our hero has the road to himself. No one will evacuate in the advent of this war. It is the last war, the death of the independent state, and in any case, Russia and the West have between them closed the borders: there is nowhere to go. Despite the years of infighting and politics, of failing idealism and the gradual debasement of his figurehead's throne, our hero still reflects with nostalgic pride on the romanticism and ruthless practicality of the mercenary army-turned-government he and his sister had fought for, legitimized, defended. They had been conquerors and puppets. They had driven the unlikely alchemy that transformed an imposed dictatorship into the last true democracy in the world. They had been used and pushed aside when they were no longer useful, but they had been loyal. This seems odd to our hero as he walks north along the blue river. He has always put his loyalty in the service of necessity, hidden it behind a guise of practicality, and now he has to wonder what moral force, what instinct of worth has shaped the meaning of need. What need—whose need—sends him north, leaving his sister behind to wait for the end alone? He loves her more than ever, and hates her a little for believing his lie and letting him go.

Walking in the sunshine intensifies his hangover thirst. He feels gritty and unkempt, with a sour gut and a spike through his temples, but his worn army boots hug his feet like old friends, and it is good to be on the move, good to have a destination and a goal. He hopes the security service doesn't give his sister too much grief when they realize he is gone.

There is little traffic after a year of oil embargoes. There are pedestrians, a few horse carts, peasants working their fields with mattock and hoe. Peasants who will watch the invasion on satellite feed, who will email reports to relatives in Frankfurt and London and Montreal, who will tell one another with pride and a languorous despair that they are sticking it out to the end. A young man wearing a billed cap with the logo of an American sports team dips his hand into the bag slung across his back and casts his seed with a sweeping gesture, a generous, open-handed gesture that answers the question *why* with a serene and simple *because*. He pauses between casts to raise his hand to our hero passing on the road. Our hero answers with an abbreviated wave and turns his head away, afraid of being recognized, afraid of being seen with tears in his eyes. Settling into the mud of the ditch between the river and the road lies the burned-out carcass of an army jeep, and there it all is, the present, the future, the past. A blackbird perches on the machine gun mount and sings its three note song. It is an image with all the solace of a graveyard.

Our hero walks off his hangover and an old vitality begins to well up through the sluggish residue left by weeks, months, of dissolution. He has relaxed into the journey, and the bolt of adrenaline he suffers when he sees the checkpoint ahead feels like a sudden dose of poison. His stride falters, losing the rhythm of certainty, but he does not stop or turn aside. The checkpoint has of course been sited to give the illegitimate traveler minimum opportunities for escape. He has papers, but he is afraid of being the victim of love or hate. He tells himself he is only afraid of being stopped, but does not believe his own lie.

The soldiers are young, volunteers in the new New Army, dressed in flak jackets and running shoes and jeans. One of them is a woman. She is younger than our hero's sister, with blond hair instead of black, brown eyes instead of blue, but she has a solemn, determined self-sufficiency our hero recognizes with a pang, though his sister is much more casual about her courage now. She is more casual about death, both our hero's and her own, and he suspects she has learned to think historically while he still sees the faces of the living and the dead.

Young woman, he thinks at her in a stern Victorian uncle's voice, *you are becoming historical*, which is a joke that would make her smile.

"Where are you going?" the young sergeant asks.

"North," our hero says.

"Away from the border."

This statement is indisputably true. The peacableness with which our hero answers the young people's hostility is not.

"Yes," he says mildly, "I have business there."

"Business." The sergeant's sneer is implicit behind the mask of his face. The bland, deadly façade of a brutal bureaucracy comes naturally to the nation's youth, they have been raised to it. It was the look of freedom that had been, briefly, imposed.

Our hero does not respond to the sergeant's echo. His mouth grows wet with a desire for vodka, and he has a fantasy, rich though fleeting, of walking into the shade of the soldiers' APC with his arm around the young woman's shoulders, hunkering down to pass a bottle around, to educate and uplift them with stories of the Homecoming War. That would be so much better than this. He unbuttons his shirt pocket and takes out his identity papers. The sergeant ignores them.

"We know who you are," he says. "What business can you have away from the capital at such a time?"

This is not an easy question to answer honestly. Our hero does not want to lie, yet claiming an urgent war-related mission in the face of no vehicle, no companions, no standing in the government, is impossible. After too long a silence, our hero says, "I am going to the old capital. It is my ancestral home. I will fight my war from there."

He looks deeply into the sergeant's eyes, and for a moment he thinks the old mystique has come alive, the old ideals of courage, nobility, adventure rising between them like a bridge of understanding, or of hope. But this young man was bred with disillusionment in his bones, and the moment dies.

"Give me your papers," the sergeant says with the blunt and sullen anger of disappointment. "I will have to call it in."

<hr />

As if she is summoned by his need, Colonel Vronskaya appears with a blast of fury for the recruits and a bottle for our hero. She embraces him with a powerful cushioned grip like a farmwife's, and then stands with her hands clenched on his shoulders to study him in the strong spring sun. She is not handsome at close quarters, Martiana Vronskaya. Her eyes are too close-set, too deep-set, too small for her flat, spider-veined face. Our hero leans into her regard, reassured by the familiar hard and humorous clarity of the old New Army, practical, piratical, and oddly moral in her amorality.

"Jesus fuck, you seedy son of a bitch," she says, shaking him. "This is the face we followed to victory?"

"Hell no," our hero says, "but it's the same ass."

"I wish I could say the same."

Vronskaya leads him to her car, a Japanese SUV rigged out in scavenged armor plate, and pulls a bottle of Ukrainian rotgut from a pocket of her bulging map case. They sit together on the back seat, passing the bottle between them as they talk. The river eases by, blue riffled by white around the ruins of a bridge.

"That river was like a sewer when we came. Shit brown," Vronskaya says, and our hero braces himself for some heavy-handed nostalgia. But his companion stops there, and he feels a youthful apprehension rising through him. He can feel her tension, and knows she is also braced for something hard. Thinking to make it easier on them both, he nudges her arm with the bottle and says, "You still shooting deserters these days?"

Vronskaya cuts loose with an explosive breath and says, "Hell no, we just kick their asses back to the front."

"It might be easier to tell them to sit down and wait."

"Fuck," Vronskaya says in agreement. She finally takes the bottle and drinks, passes it back. He drinks. She says, "Is that what you're doing? Looking for a good place to wait?"

"Pick your ground and defend it to the end."

"Lousy strategy, my friend. Lousy fucking strategy."

"You have a better one to offer?"

"No."

She drinks. He does. The rotgut burns going down, a welcome heat.

"Go ahead," he says. "Ask your questions."

"What," she says, "you think your crazy sister is the only one who remembers her babya's stories? Okay, okay." He had made a sudden move. "She's not crazy. She's not here, so she's not crazy. But don't tell me this isn't her idea."

"It isn't anyone's idea," our hero says, grandiose with vodka in his veins. "It's fate."

"Sure. Your fate."

"You'd be happy to see us both on this road? You want us both to die?"

"No." Vronskaya speaks with leaden patience. "I don't want you *both* to die."

Our hero slams out of the SUV, startling the checkpoint guards, startling himself. Mindful of weapons in nervous hands he smoothes his hands over his head, feeling the stubble pull at his sunburned scalp. Vronskaya heaves herself out of the car.

"Jesus fuck," she says, "you're serious. You're really going to do this thing."

"If you have any better ideas . . . " our hero says, too tense to give it the right ironic lilt.

"Sure I have better ideas. Fight and die with your old comrades instead of skulking off like a sick dog who's not allowed to die in his mistress's house."

"You never liked her," our hero accuses.

"No, I never did. Have you ever asked her what she thinks of me? Of any of us?"

"She loves you better than you know," he says, looking into Vronskaya's eyes.

"Me? The country, maybe, I'll grant you that. Me, she doesn't give a shit for, and never has. Or—" But Vronskaya's gaze slips aside.

Or you. But our hero knows that's not true, and knows that Vronskaya knows, so he can let it go. He says, "Will you believe me? This isn't her idea. I was the one who wouldn't let her go."

Vronskaya shrugs, sullen. "So you're the crazy one."

"Maybe. I've always been a gambler, and this is my game to play."

"It's not a game you can fucking win!"

"And yours is? Come on, Martiana, we've already lost. We lost before a shot was fired. You know it, I know it. Those damn kids know it, and so do the soldiers dying in the retreat, and so do the babyas waiting in the capital. We're losing. We've already fucking lost. East and West will meet at the river and swallow us whole." Our hero is shouting, hoarse with months, with years of frustration. Vronskaya, her driver, the checkpoint guards, are all listening with the shame-faced scowl of those caught with their worst fears showing. "We're fucked! We're doomed! *Tell me I'm wrong!*"

In the silence that follows, they can hear a trio of small jets roaring by in the southern sky. The West has promised no civilian populations will be bombed. Even if they keep that promise, everyone knows the Russians won't. Our hero squeezes the back of his neck, then lets his arms fall to his sides.

71

"I have one card to play, and I'm playing it. What difference does it make where I cash my chips?"

Vronskaya, long-time poker rival, long-time friend, gives him a mournful look and says, "It's bad to die alone."

But our hero won't be alone at the end.

The old capital perches on a high bluff, a forerunner of the northern mountains, like a moth on a wolf's nose. A wing-tattered moth on a grizzled and mangy old half-breed dog, more like, for the hillsides have been logged and grazed, and the ancient town has been starved down to its stony bones. But the river runs deep and fast in a curve around the old walls, white foam clean and bright around sharp-toothed rocks, and the castle high above the slate-roofed town still rears its dark towers against the sky. Sparrows and jackdaws make their livings there. The place might have been a museum once, but now it is not even a ruin, just an empty house with rotten foundations and a badly leaking roof. Our hero and his sister camped there for a time when the New Army was fighting to reach the modern city on the plain, and he remembers the ache of nostalgia, the romance of the past and the imperfect conviction that that past was his. But he had been younger then, and dangerous, and he could relish the pain.

The town is quiet. No loudspeakers here, just the murmur of radios and TVs through windows left open on the soft spring evening. It has taken our hero three days to walk this far, but the news is the same. Only the names of the towns marking the army's retreat have changed. His old comrades have managed to slow the invasion some, and along with the sting and throb of his blistered feet and the ache of his empty stomach he feels the burn of the shame he would not admit to Martiana Vronskaya, that he has been walking in the wrong direction. There must be some value to this last mad act. He must somehow make it so.

But how will he know if he has succeeded? The thought of dying in uncertainty troubles him more than the thought of death, and he pauses in his climb up the town's steep streets to sit at an outdoor table of a small café. His feet hurt worse once he is off them and he stretches his legs out to prop them on their heels. A waitress comes out and asks him kindly for his order. She is an older woman and he suspects her of having a son at the front: she is too forgiving of our misplaced hero. She brings him a cup of ferocious coffee and bread and olives and cheese. It all tastes delicious to our hero, and he looks up from his plate to tell his sister so, only to be reminded that she is not here. He wishes she was. He would like to see this small, cramped square through her eyes. She notices things: the sparrows waiting for crumbs, the three brass balls above an unmarked door, the carved rainspout jutting a bearded chin over the gutter. These things would tell her something about this neighborhood, this town, this world. To our hero, they are only fragments of an incomprehensible whole. The world is this, and this, and this. It is never complete. It is never done.

Oh God, our hero thinks for the first time, I do not want to die.

His feet hurt worse after the rest and plague him as he climbs the steep upper streets to the castle door. It is an oddly house-like castle, with no outer wall, no courtyard, no barbican and gate. The massive door, oak slabs charred black by the cold smolder of time, stands level with the street, and the long stone of the sill has been worn into a deep smiling curve by the passage of feet. Generations of feet, our hero thinks, an army that has taken a thousand years to pass through this door. The gap between door and sill is wide enough for a cat, but not a child, let alone a man. The sun has fallen below the surrounding roofs and the light has dimmed to a clear, still-water dusk. The stone is a pale creamy gray. The sky is as far as heaven and blue as his sister's eyes. Our hero, hoping and fearing in equal measure, turns the iron latch and discovers, with horror and relief, that the door is unlocked. The great wooden weight swings inwards with a whisper of well-oiled hinges, and the boy sitting before the small fire in the very large hearth at the far end of the entrance hall calls out, "Grandfather! He's here!" as if our hero is someone's beloved son returning home.

He has no idea who these people are.

The old man and the boy share a name, so they are Old Bradvi and Young Bradvi. They stare at our hero with the same eyes, bright and black and flame-touched, like the tower's birds. Our hero has heard the jackdaws returning to their high nests, their voices unbearably distant and clear through the intervening layers of stone. He remembers that sound, the mournful clarity of the dusk return, and misses his old friends, the lover he had embraced in a cold, cobwebbed room, his sister. He misses her so intensely that her absence becomes a presence, a woman-shaped hole who sits at his side, listening with her eyes on her hands. The boy explains with breathless faith that he and his grandfather have been waiting since the invasion began.

They live in the town. "My mother is there, in our house, watching the television, she wouldn't come, but we have been here all the time."

All the time our hero has been walking, this boy and his grandfather have been here, waiting for him to arrive. Despite himself, our hero feels a stirring of awe, as if his and his sister's despair has given birth to something separate and real.

Old Bradvi says, "Lord, we knew you would come." He makes tea in a blackened pot nestled in the coals, his crow's eyes protected from the smoke by a tortoise's wrinkled lids. In the firelight his face is a wizard's face, and our hero feels as though he has already slipped aside from the world he knows, as though he has already stepped through that final door. When the boy takes up a small electronic game and sends tiny chirps and burbles to echo up against the ceiling, this only deepens the sense of unreality. Or perhaps it is a sense of reality that haunts our hero, the sense that this is the truest hour he has ever lived. The old man pours sweetened tea into a red plastic cup and says, "Lord, it is better to wait until dawn."

Who is this man? How does he know what he knows? Our hero does not ask. Reality weighs too heavily upon him, he has no strength for speculation, and no need for it: they have all been brought here by a story, lured by the same long, rich, fabulous tale that has ruled our hero's life, and that now rules our hero's death. At least the story will go on. Stories have no nations, only hearts and minds, and as long as his people live, there will be those. He drinks his tea and listens beyond the sounds of the fire, the game, the old man's smoker's lungs, to his sister's silent voice.

Late in the night he leaves the old man and the sleeping boy to take a piss. Afterward, he wanders the castle in the dark, finding his way by starlit arrow slits and memory. It is a small castle made to seem larger than it is by its illogical design. It seems larger yet in the darkness, and our hero's memory fails. He stumbles on an unseen stair and sits on cold stone to nurse a bruised shin. He wants to weep in self-pity, and he wants to laugh at the bathos of this moment, this life. He curses softly to the mice, and dozes for a moment with his head on his knee before the chill rouses him again. He climbs the stair, and realizes it is the stair to the tower. The floors are wooden here and there is a cold, complex, living smell of damp oak, bird shit, feathers, smoke. He crosses to a window, his muffled steps rousing sleeping birds above his head, and squeezes himself onto the windowsill. There are few streetlights in the town below, but there are windows bright yellow with lamplight or underwater-blue with TV light. There are lives below those sharp, starlit roofs. There is history out there in the cold, clean air. And there is the moon, a rising crescent that hangs in the night sky no higher than our hero's window, as if it means to look at him eye to eye. A silver blade, a wink, a knowing smile, close enough to tempt his reach, far enough to let him fall if he tried.

Sitting above the town with no company but the moon and the sleeping birds, our hero feels alone, apart, and yet a part of all those lives, all that history taking place right now, here and everywhere, with every beat of every heart. The paradox of loneliness is a black gulf within him, a rift between the broken pieces of his heart. The moon casts his shadow into the room behind him, and there, in the moonlit dark, the shadow of his sister's absence puts her arms around his neck and lays her cheek against his stubbled head, and he turns and leans his face against her breast, wraps his arms about her waist, and finally weeps.

When the stars fade and the frost-colored light of day begins to seep back into the world, the old man brings the knife, and the deed is swiftly done.

It is the jackdaws that wake him. They have drifted down from the rafters and stand about, peering at him with cocked heads, discussing in hoarse and thoughtful tones whether he is alive or dead. Dead, he tries to tell them, but his throat remembers the iron blade and closes tight on the word. What is this? he wonders. Is he still dying? But he remembers the knife, the sudden icy tear, the taste of blood, the drowning. Air slides into his lungs at the thought, tasting of dust and feathers. What is this? Is he alive? He sits, clumsy with cold, and the birds sidle off, muttering and unafraid. Their claws make a clock's tock against the floor. Our hero's shirt is stiff and evil with blood. What, then, is this running through his veins?

He is too bewildered to feel afraid.

At first he cannot see the changes, and he thinks that he has failed, though how he could have failed and yet be alive escapes him. The dissonance between possibility and impossibility is too intense, he is numb and not, perhaps, entirely sane. He stumbles down the stairs, the same spider-haunted stairs, while the daws leave by the windows. They laugh at him as they go, he has no doubt: birds have a black sense of humor. He blunders his way through the half-remembered halls, gets lost, laughs out of sheer uncomprehending terror. When he finds the entry hall, there is a fire burning on the vast hearth, a whole log alight, filling the fireplace with snapping and dancing flames, but he does not pause. The door is wide open, and the air is bright with morning light, although the sun is still below the roofs of the town.

There are bells ringing somewhere below, a shining tin-tanning of bronze, such a happy sound that our hero pulls off his blood-soaked shirt so as not to sully the good day. He walks bare-chested into the town, and no one stares or looks aside, although the streets are almost crowded. The people are not so happy as the bells; many seem as quietly, profoundly bewildered as our hero feels. He stops a woman about his own age, a woman with soft fair hair tousled across her face, and asks what has happened.

"What do you mean?" she says. "Everything has happened. Everything!"

"O God," an older woman says beside them. "O God, do not abandon us. O God, preserve us."

A man across the narrow street is cursing with a loud and frantic edge to his voice. He seems to be haranguing his car which is parked with two wheels up on the pavement, and which is no doubt out of gas after all these months of the embargo. Our hero supposes that the invading armies are near, perhaps at the fragile old walls of the town, and so, although there is something odd about the man's defunct automobile, he continues on down the hill toward the river where he might be able to see what there is to see.

But there are other odd things, and gradually they begin to distract him from the shock of being alive. The streets are wider as they near the archaic boundary of the old wall, and the pavements here are lined with strange statues. Wrought-iron coaches with weighty and elaborate ornaments, brass lions with blunt, dog-like faces and curling manes, horses with legs like pistons and gilded springs. The people clustered around these peculiar artworks are predictably confused, but there are others in the streets who walk with shining eyes and buoyant steps, and some of these people, too, seem odd to our hero. Their clothing is too festive, their hair is strung with baubles, their faces are at once laughing and fierce. One bearded man catches our hero's eye and bows. He sweeps off his jacket, blue velvet stiff with gold braid, and offers it to our hero with another bow. "My lord," he says, and when our hero takes what is offered, the man spreads his arms with a wide flourish, as if to present to him everything: the people, the town, the world.

And then our hero sees, as if before he had been blind. The tired old houses propped up by silver-barked trees hung with jewel-faceted fruit. The banners lazily unfurling from lampposts that have moonstones in place of glass. The violets shivering above the clear, speaking stream that runs down the gutter, between the clawed feet of the transformed cars. It is the new world, the ancient world, the world that had faded to a golden dream on the losing face of his sister's hoarded coin. It is the world he died for. He has come home.

It is still a four-day walk back to the new capital, and though it seems both illogical and unfair, our reborn hero's feet still throb and sting with blisters in his worn-out army boots. He is warm enough in his old jeans and the blue velvet coat, despite the clouds that roll in from the east, but he walks with a deep internal chill that only deepens the closer he gets to home. He should have kept his ruined shirt to remind him that there is no such thing as a bloodless victory, a bloodless war. The invaders had penetrated too deeply to be shed with the nation's old skin. Like embedded ticks engorged with suddenly poisoned blood, they—men and women of the East and the West, their weapons and machines—have suffered transformation along with the rest of them, and though harmed, they have not been rendered harmless. There are monsters in this new world. He sees one slain, a tank-dragon with bitter-green scales, a six-legged lizard with three heads and one mad Russian face, in the fields near where he had met the checkpoint guards and Martiana Vronskaya on his way north just a few days ago. Perhaps some of these confused and scrabbling warriors are those same young volunteers with their flak jackets and jeans. The jeans have not changed, nor the fearful determination, but the short spears with the shining blades are new. New, and as old as the world. Our hero leaves them to their bloody triumph on the flower-starred field, and like the veteran he is, continues on his painful way.

The new capital has changed more than the old, its modern buildings wrenched into something too much stranger than their origins. Our hero suspects this will never be an easy place to live, not even the old quarter where his sister lives. Here, 18th Century houses have melted like candlewax, or spiraled up into towers like narwhal tusks and antelope horns, crumbling moldings and baroque tiles bent and twisted out of true. Our hero cannot tell if this new architecture is better or worse than the old, uglier or more beautiful. He is only frustrated that the landmarks have changed, and that he cannot locate the house is that once he could find blind drunk and staggering. It seems bitterly unfair. He circles the half-familiar streets, until finally a doorway catches his eye, a pale door like a tooth or a pearl, with above it a wholly prosaic glass-and-iron transom in the shape of a fan. He knows that transom, and now that he is looking, he recognizes a brass-capped iron railing, a graffitoed slogan barely legible among the creeping blue flowers on the pavement at his feet. Tears of gratitude sparking hot and wet in his eyes, he turns the corner and walks to the second door.

His key still works, despite the rubies bursting like mushrooms from the crazed paint on the door. He enters the old-house quiet, breathes in the intimately remembered smell of dry wood and cabbage and sandalwood incense, climbs the crooked, creaking, fern-and-trumpet-vine stairs. He knocks on his sister's door, and she opens it, and she is just the same.

THE RESCUE

She woke at the bottom of a well.

A squared-off well, strangely bright and lined with tiles, and with a painted door far overhead. Far, far overhead. She lay for a long time contemplating that door—it was so bright in the well she could see the flaws in the cream paint—until her other senses began to wake. She was lying as she must have fallen when they threw her in, with her head and shoulders on the floor and the rest of her body stretched up one wall . . . Gravity reasserted itself, spinning the well like a gimbal so that for an instant she was pressed like a squashed fly against the ceiling before it settled and she was lying on the floor. The floor of a room with tiled walls, and a window in the wall above her head, and a door a long way away. She went on looking at the door between her bare feet, blinking occasionally to mark the time. Gravity came and went. Finally she thought to test it, and raised her hand before her eyes.

Raised her hand . . .

Raised her hand, after a vast gulf of time, and left it floating in the air a while until she had encompassed what she saw. Not her hand (bony? small? chapped?) but a wool mitten strapped about the wrist and palm with dirty bandages. Was it cold? It began to seem to her that it was; that her bare feet were icy and the tiled floor beneath her was pressing a hard chill into her flesh through her clothes. While she was making these discoveries, her hand had drifted out of sight. She raised it again, with less lag time but more effort, and saw that the mitten was green.

She rubbed her face with it, and felt the fraying wool catch on new scabs, felt the sting of the scratches, and remembered clawing at her skin to release the insects tormenting her under the surface. Drugs, she thought. (Thought was slow. She went on lying there, looking at her hand, her toes, the door.) Drugs. Withdrawal from drugs: that was the bugs. Drugs: bugs: a rhyme. And this immense lethargy: that was drugs, too: a sedative. And this slow awakening: that was the sedative wearing off.

Now then. Here was a question. Where did the sedative come from?

The realization was like a second awakening: she was in a hospital room, bare of furniture and fixtures but unmistakable for its tiles and its sickly paint. Struggling with the weight of her limbs, she hauled herself up to sit against the wall, hugging her knees, trying to listen past the thudding of her heart and the ringing in her ears. Silence. That was wrong; that wasn't the hospital she knew. The color of the paint on the door was wrong, too, cream instead of green. Everything was wrong—broken tiles—cold radiator—old mittens instead of restraints—

And she remembered being taken out of her cell by a male orderly. She remembered it vividly and all of a piece: his soft, stupid face; his hard hand on her arm; her arm bare under the sleeve of her scanty smock. She had been drugged no more than usual, had been left alone for several days, had almost recovered herself. Had known that the appearance of a male orderly in the women's ward was a dreadful sign.

She couldn't really remember the passage through the

hospital, it was a pastiche of all her other trips through the halls, the unlocked and relocked doors, but she remembered being taken out into the courtyard. It was the kitchen yard, with the laundry steaming away on one side and the ambulances parked along the wall by the tradesman's entrance. It had been cold. She had been surprised by the cold, having forgotten the seasons, and she wore nothing but her smock. The air was shocking on her shaved scalp, her bare feet and legs. Her attention had been caught by the clouds of steam from the laundry, the steam of her own breath, the billowing exhaust from the big olive-green car idling by the kitchen door. *They're taking me away*, she thought without hope as the orderly handed her over to the two men in uniform. But the men in uniform, holding her by her arms, took her across the yard, past the laundry—through the wet clouds reeking of lye—and out a small door to the back of the hospital grounds, and then she knew for sure.

The wintry ground hurt her feet. Frozen grass gave way to frozen twigs and pebbles and leaves as they entered the bare-branched wood. She balked, and they hit her without waiting for a struggle. One hard punch on the back of her neck, and she could still feel the cruel ground scraping her feet as they dragged her to the ready-dug grave under the trees. They dropped her on her knees; she caught herself with her hands on the lip of the grave. There were roots protruding from the rough clay walls, black roots, brown clay. Her breath still steamed. There was a shot, two shots. A hard hand again on her arm, the hard ground again beneath her feet . . .

And a hospital room. And drugs. And bugs beneath her skin. Was this a rescue?

It was difficult—the gimbal that had spun the room was now inside her skull, spinning her brain—but she got herself onto her feet, and rather than dare the open floor she slid her shoulder against the wall, one corner and another, feeling the rough places in the tiles snag her sweater (sweater? over orderly's pants?) until she achieved the door. It had a round handle. The mitten slid and slid. She knew it was locked. She tried both hands and the mechanism rattled and the door opened a crack. She pried it open with her mittened fingertips. A long hospital corridor stretched before her, very long, very empty, lit only by a window at the far end. It was silent, and cold, and she could hear the emptiness echoing throughout. An empty hospital.

Was this a rescue? Or what was this?

<hr />

The cold grew worse as the sedative wore off. She huddled on the floor with her shoulder propped against the wall, trying to minimize her contact with the icy tiles. She had periods of lucidity when she knew she should escape. To stay when the door stood wide open was the worst kind of self-betrayal; it made her the canary who clings to its perch when the cage door is left ajar. But she had been drugged for a long time, and imprisoned for a long time too, and achieving even enough lucidity for that recognition took everything she had. The insects did not come back, but she had moments of severe dislocation when up became sideways and even so familiar an object as a door became merely a plane, a color, an angle, without meaning or name. Clinging to her sense of self was all she could do, and she did it for hours, unmoving, staring out the door and down the endless hall.

The light changed. Dusk filled the air with a tangible blue.

The empty hospital was not as silent as she had thought—perhaps the ringing in her ears was easing off. Sounds echoed down the empty hall, sounds she might have called footsteps or voices except that one never heard just one footstep, or a voice that said half a word and fell silent. *Be*— And the clink of a hypodermic syringe dropped into a steel dish, a sound she knew too well. Sometimes one of the voices would seem to speak its syllable directly into her ear—*Fa*— and she would wonder if she could still be sane after all the drugs, all the "treatments" that had no aim that she had ever seen but to drive her mad. She had never known anything worth betraying, and they had seldom asked her that kind of question. They had often not asked her any questions at all, but they had told her, endlessly, about her rebellious nature, and how disloyalty was a disease. But they had not cared about that either. She was a hostage for her family's good behavior—she had always known that—and they had only tormented her because she was there, and that was what they did there.

The footsteps were back. Not just one at a time, now, but a whole chain of them, one after another, tap, tap, tap. She had been listening to the phantom noises so long she was slow to realize these footsteps must come attached to actual feet walking up a flight of stairs—she could hear the echo. Then she heard a door open, and a yellow light fell across the middle of the empty hall. The light slid about so smoothly on the gritty floor that it surprised her. It was like oil, a pool of golden oil running down the hall that as a consequence had a definite tilt to it, so that she was sitting at the foot of a slide, or the base of a chute with the oil sliding down. The light sliding down. Footsteps tapping. A mental effort forced her perceptions back into their right order, and then he was at the door, shining his flashlight in her eyes.

"You're awake," he said, and dropped the light so it no longer blinded her.

She blinked tears out of her eyes—her pupils were sluggish and she was dazzled—and saw, before anything else came clear, the stiff shapes of the epaulets on his shoulders. He was in uniform. She scrabbled away from him. Her heels caught in the cuffs of the too-long pants. She got herself into the corner somehow, and wondered with a pounding heart what good she thought that was going to do.

"It's all right," he was saying, "be calm, I'm not here to hurt you. I got you away from those men, remember? You're not going to be shot. You're all right. You're all right."

He set the flashlight on its end so it made a circle of brightness on the ceiling and illuminated the room as a lamp might. While her eyes adjusted, he took off his officer's cap and smoothed his hand over his cropped hair. There was something familiar about the gesture, something that caught at her memory like a hook, and she had a flash of riding in a car, the backseat of a car, with that head in profile against the windscreen.

"Are you cold?" he said. "I'm sorry I had to leave you so long, I have to be careful not to be missed. There's some soup heating downstairs. I brought you up here so you wouldn't hurt yourself, they must have given you the devil's own cocktail of drugs, but you look like you're doing better now. Would you like some hot soup? How do you feel?"

"What is this place?" She had to force her voice to make any sound above a whisper. "Why am I here?"

"It's just for a little while," he said. "Until you're better, and the hunt dies down. Then we can see about getting you out."

Out of here? Out of the country, she supposed.

"You shot those men," she said.

"I hope it won't be too long," he said. "We had a good organization, but it's a bit disarranged just now."

"You shot those men."

"Our usual system had a bit of a breakdown."

"They were wearing the same uniform."

He looked down, and as if he had just discovered it in his hand, rubbed the shiny bill of his hat and put it on. It changed his face, making it dangerous and hard.

"They were killers," he said. "Would you like some soup?"

He had made a snug place downstairs, in a windowless room like a secretary's anteroom that could only be reached through another room. There was a canvas camp bed with rough wool blankets, a table against the wall and a single chair, and a cubbyhole with a toilet and sink.

"There's water," he said, "I jimmied the main valve. But the tank takes a while to fill."

There was a camp stove on the table that he warmed a tin of soup on, and afterwards a saucepan of coffee that he poured into a thermos bottle for her to drink later. There was something about the way he moved, the way he hung his hat on a spindle on the back of the chair, that made her think he had used this room before. Other rescues? He pulled the jar of instant coffee from a box under the table, and before he pushed the box back out of the way she saw the spines of several books. This was his place; she became convinced of it, watching him move. He had made this place for himself, a secret place, a place to hide. Yet there he was, in his neat brown uniform, his pistol holster as well-polished as his shoes, his hair freshly cropped and his face as clean-shaven as a monk's. She could not make sense of it, it was too disjunctive. An officer in Internal Security hiding in an empty hospital. An officer in Internal Security hiding her.

"I'll come back when I can," he said. He left her with the flashlight and the camp stove, but took away the matches and the fuel.

She spent a long time, more than a night, wrapped in rough blankets and dreaming violent, extravagant dreams. She was often nauseous, plagued by itches and pains, and constantly sweating; she thought the vomiting and the sweating and the dreams were all parts of the same thing, her system purging itself of her long incarceration. Three years? It had been spring when she was arrested, so it was almost three years, or almost four. She thought almost four. In the hospital—the other hospital—it had been better to lose her sense of time, to make every day one day, because she could survive one day in that place, but not years. Nobody could live for years that way and stay sane. If she had been sane when she went in. She thought she had been; she was pretty sure.

But if she was sane now, then this hospital was haunted.

There were always noises; the silence of the place was compounded of sounds, small, stealthy, edge-of-hearing sounds. An old building succumbing to damp: wood creaked, plaster flaked, linoleum peeled away from the floor. Air ticked its way through the pipes, too, and echoed her as she retched, helpless and aching, her stomach empty even of bile. But as she lay there in her woolen cocoon, sometimes a voice would speak over her, a single syllable—*Su*—that would jolt her awake. There was no question it was a voice, not a building sound. The footsteps might have been something else; the quiet click of a door closing might have been just that, a door swung by a draft. But she heard a gurney wheeling down a corridor, its wheels needing oil and its tires sticking to the floor. She heard the quiet, soothing murmur of a woman's voice, a nurse's, flowing on and on like a tap left running, no words, just the sound of comfort. Comfort, only it went on and on, until she had to wonder what procedure it was that was taking so long, what suffering the voice was trying to subdue. And then there was the scream.

She had drunk rusty water from the tap and managed to keep it down. She drank some of the coffee, tepid and sweet with evaporated milk, and kept that down as well: one thermos lid, she didn't want to push her luck. Daylight had been filtering in from the next room for some time, probably hours, and she switched the flashlight off, though its batteries were almost dead. *Ho*— said the voice in her ear. She imagined a magnetic recording tape unwound from its spool and scissored into confetti. The voice didn't frighten her, but it oppressed her a little; it was so present, and it robbed her of some much-needed privacy. She resented it, resented all the hauntings, because she was fairly certain they came from inside her head. She would have preferred ghosts, would certainly have preferred the ghosts of this place, because they could not have had anything to do with her. So she was thinking, when the scream happened. It leapt out at her from mid-air—that was what it felt like. It was *there*, in the room, loud and clear and sudden, and suddenly gone, bitten off as short as any of the broken words. But a scream, shocking as any scream always is.

"Leave me alone!"

Her voice, after vomiting, after long disuse, was nothing but a scrap of itself. Even from the inside it seemed much weaker than the voice that spoke the bits of words, the voice that screamed. Her mouth stretched and she put her hands to her face as if she was going to weep, but she couldn't. She didn't have that much feeling left, or maybe she was saving her self-pity for larger things. She gave up the attempt and climbed off the cot, taking the blankets with her. The floor was cold and dirty under her feet, and she had the cunning idea of using the mittens as socks. They had been too big for her hands and fit her feet well enough, though the empty thumbs looked absurd, like monkey toes. She shuffled into the outer room and peered out the window. It was a safe window, according to her rescuer, looking not on a street, but on the hospital's central courtyard.

From this view, the hospital was clearly deserted. The flagstones were almost buried under weeds and trash, and saplings of a few years' growth were forcing their way up from the larger gaps. The brick walls were blackened as if by fire, and there were broken windows and sagging gutters. Windows and doors on the ground floor had been boarded shut. Seeing that, she wondered how he came and went—how he had got her inside. It seemed as though she had materialized here, like a ghost. That was the first time it occurred to her to wonder if she was dead.

The outer room led to a narrow hallway, the sort of hallway

that kinks and bends its way through the interior of a building, contorting itself so that most of the rooms it services have some access to natural light. She shuffled her way around some of the corners. It was dark, sometimes very dark, most of the doors were closed. She opened several; the ones that looked out on the street were boarded up. She was standing at one of these, her cheek pressed to the plywood, listening for the sound of a car, a bird, a living voice, anything of the outside world, when she heard the footsteps tapping again. Leather soles on dirty linoleum, tap, tap, tap. *Wa—* said the voice, making her jump. *It's him,* she thought, and though she should have been afraid of him, and was, she was overcome by such a longing not to be alone that she shuffled back to the hiding place. They met in the outer room where the window was. He had just looked into the inner room.

"Where were you?" he said in a voice that matched his uniform.

She had mocked the men who arrested her, she remembered that. She remembered being whimsical and brave.

"Looking," she said in her rag of a voice. "Where were you?"

He looked at her. His eyes were so hard, so well-defended, they gave an impression of darkness, but in the light of the window she saw they were gray. She saw that his whole face was a deception: a priest's face pretending to be an officer's. None the less frightening for that.

"Running," he said, and as he said it she could see the quick motion of his chest beneath his coat.

"Why?" she said.

He looked at her—had never stopped looking at her—and then gave a start, as if the hospital's voice had spoken its syllable in his ear instead of hers. He turned into the inner room, and as she followed him, went on into the lavatory where he turned the tap at the sink and held his hands under the flow. There was blood on his hands; the water was red with more than rust as it swirled down the drain. She retreated to the cot and pulled the mittens off her feet, pretending to herself that she hadn't seen.

He had brought the fuel tank back, the matches, and a tin of soup, some tins of meat, half a loaf of bread. He opened one of the tins and gave her a crude sandwich before he reassembled the stove and set the soup to heating. The warmth of the small gas flame was tangible even from her corner. It made her feel the cold. He set the chair in the middle of the room, between her and the table, and wolfed down his own sandwich.

"Eat," he said, "you'll get sick if you don't."

She could smell the bread and meat in her hand. "Are they after you?"

He got up to stir the soup. She could hear the sound of the spoon scraping the bottom of the pot. One spoon, one bowl, one mug. One chair. She hadn't looked at the books yet.

"Will they catch you?"

He moved so suddenly she thought he had been scalded, burned. But he only turned about the room—not pacing—he made the hard, fast turns of an animal in a cage. She recognized the movement, felt it in memory, recorded in her bones. But the door was open.

He made three turns of the room, then went back to the stove and poured half the soup into the mug, which he brought to her. He was breathing quickly again, or still.

"Eat this, at least," he said. "You're half starved."

She took the mug in the hand that did not hold the sandwich. "Who did you kill?"

Leaving the stove burning for the sake of the heat, he poured the remaining soup into the bowl and drank it without troubling with the spoon. She was too fascinated by his hunger to be bothered about her own.

"Who did you kill?"

He sat in the chair with his head bowed and the bowl in his hand, sucking broth off his lips. His eyes looked at nothing.

"Can I go?" she said.

He just breathed. She wondered if he was sleeping with his eyes open; if he was as starved for sleep as he was for food.

"If you're caught, they'll kill me. And you'd be safer if I go."

" 's just a snoop," he said. His words were so slurred that at first she could not understand him. "A snitch. They're always being killed." He made a visible effort, wiping his hand across his eyes before he looked at her again. "Eat something. You'll be sick if you don't."

She held the sandwich out to him. "You eat it. I couldn't keep it down."

He got up and she was sorry she had offered: she had only wanted to shut him up, the way he clung to one thought was unnerving, but she didn't want him to come so close. It was like feeding the bears at the zoo—she remembered that from her childhood—the dreadful mingling of pity and fear. He took the sandwich as neatly as the bears did, though with no hot breath across her hand, and sat back down on the chair to eat it.

"If you let me go," she said, "you wouldn't have to risk coming here."

"It's not a risk," he said with his mouth full. There was as much soldier in him as priest. "This is the safest place I know."

That he had to kill a man, and run . . . ?

"But I want to go," she said, and for an instant was the little girl begging to leave the zoo and go home.

He finished the last bit of the sandwich and sat as he had before, leaning forward, head bent, eyes looking through the floor. She could see him work his tongue around his mouth and swallow. *He's thirsty and doesn't even know it,* she thought, and drank some soup out of sympathetic reflex.

"You can't go yet," he said, and for a moment she thought that was all he was going to say. But he made another effort, drawing himself upright and glancing at her before he let his gaze drift to a corner of the room. "I'm not keeping you here. But if you go now . . . your hair . . . I don't have any clothes or papers for you yet." Another effort. "If you go on the street like that you'll be picked up immediately, and they'll shoot you as soon as they know who you are. But if you wait a while . . . You need to grow out your hair, or they'll ask questions no matter how good your papers are. And I can't do that yet, the papers, it's all too unsettled."

"When . . . " she said, but she couldn't finish. He was killing informers. She was afraid the answer would be *Never.*

But he said, "Soon," as if it didn't really matter.

He fell asleep in the chair. It was a straight-backed, armless, wooden chair, and she watched with a kind of fascination as he leaned forward, slowly, slowly, never quite bending at the waist, never quite falling to the floor. She sipped the cooling soup and stroked the stiff stubble on her scalp, and had a hard time thinking about the practicalities of her situation. He was so strange, and his presence so thoroughly filled the room. *Su*— the hospital's voice said. He sat bolt upright and stared about him, his eyes fixed and wild, still mostly asleep. He terrified her. She slipped out of the cot and said softly, "Lie down. Lie down."

She wasn't sure that he heard her, or even registered her presence, but he did lie down. He even took off his belt and holster and jacket, hanging them over the back of the chair, before he did. She stood in the corner watching him pull the blankets across his chest and fall instantly asleep again. After several minutes, she eased herself over to the chair, pulled her knees up against her chest, and watched him sleep. The buckle of his gun belt prodded her in the back.

Ta— the voice said, and his eyelids twitched with his dreams.

He left when it was still dark. When the light came she took his stash of books into the outer room and sat under the window, reading. Birds came and went in the abandoned courtyard, pigeons and sparrows that knew no seasons, browsing for food among the weeds. They made good companions for her; she was browsing more than reading, and his books were all pastoral novels, sunlit and serene. She could tell his favorite passages by the dog-ears and the cracks in the spine, and they were all panegyrics on the quiet beauties of the countryside. Pages of deep blankets of snow muffling the warm cottages; pages of burning autumn leaves and rustling bracken; pages of those first tender budding leaves of spring. She remembered him desperate for food and sleep, and thought of him now, desperate for this: escape, quiet, peace. Did they all, all those deadly men in their brown uniforms, long for this? Did every one of them—spying, threatening, killing—dream of lying down under a flowering hedgerow and sleeping with the music of the birds in his ears?

Ho— said the voice. She had the feeling of someone reading over her shoulder and closed the book. Pity and fear, she thought. The poor bears in their cage must have suffered the same longing. *A—*

"Hush," she said.

But the ghosts, if ghosts they were, only seemed to gain vigor, as though they drew energy from her presence, or from his coming and going. She heard with such perfect clarity the rattle and slosh of a janitor mopping the floor outside that she could not forbear from getting up and opening the door, as though she might catch him in the act. But there was no ghostly form, no shadow, no mist. Just the sound, and that cut off abruptly a moment later, as though that fragment of tape had run its course. There seemed no more point to it than there was to the bits of words that fell about her ears, and she had a sense, not of a haunting, but of random pieces of the past being shaken out of the walls like dead moths being shaken out of a spiderweb by a breeze.

He came back and found her dozing over one of his books. She woke afraid, having felt him standing over her in her sleep. She looked up—he seemed immensely tall—and he bent and took the book out of her hands. All the other books were scattered around her on the dirty floor; she remembered something she had known once, that books, especially other people's books, were to be treated with more respect. Like other people's property, other people's privacy. He stood there in his uniform that had no respect for either, and she looked up at him in her guilt and waited for the hammer to fall. But he only knelt and picked up the other books, one at a time, brushing off the covers and tucking them carefully in the crook of his arm. He was very close; she could see the lines at the corner of his eye, the knot of muscle in his jaw. "I'm sorry," she said, and froze him with a touch on his arm.

Where did it come from, that human impulse? It was like a relic from the past, a fossil from a former age. Maybe it was just another ghost of this place, another moth, dead and dry, shaken loose by the breeze of his passing. He picked up the last book and carried it with the rest into the inner room.

He carried her food in his briefcase, and today she caught sight of the papers inside. What could they be about? she wondered. Whose life, whose captivity, whose death? But then she forgot about them at the wholly unexpected sight of an orange. An orange! It was a very orange orange, and even in the gloom of the windowless room it seemed to glow. The oils of the zest filled the air with a sharp, sweet scent as he peeled it. She watched his hands with close attention—she on the cot, he on the chair in the middle of the room—as he loosened the rind with his thumbs. It was a thick rind and it came away in three big sections that he fitted together like bowls and set beside him on the floor. Then he divided the orange, prying it into halves. He reached out to hand her one of these; she craned off the edge of the cot to receive it. He, who had probably seen many oranges over the years, ate his one section at a time, neatly, his eyes abstracted. She ate hers like a savage, biting into the whole half at once, filling her mouth with the juice. It stung the sores on her gums, but that wasn't what brought tears to her eyes. She felt as though she had tasted nothing, smelled nothing, seen no color, for the whole term of her incarceration. When she was done she sucked the juice off her fingers, and tasted book-ink as well as orange.

"Here," he said.

She looked up. He was offering her his last few sections of orange. She shied away, shook her head, confounded.

"Take it," he said. "I can always get another."

She had thought he was feeding her, his captive, his chore. She had not thought they were sharing. She did not know how to respond.

He got up and came over to put the sections in her hand. "You need it more than I do," he said, and turned to the stove to heat up a tin of beans.

"Why—" she said, and stopped to wonder why it had taken her so long to think of the question.

He opened the tin, shook the beans into the pot, lit the stove.

"Why are you doing this?"

He put the pot on the stove, gave the beans a stir.

"Why do you do this? You're an officer. You killed men in your own service to save me. There must be a reason why."

"Because it needs to be done," he said without turning.

"But you joined the service. You must have applied, trained. You must have wanted to be an officer."

"And that's why I need to do it." He tapped the spoon against the side of the pot and turned to face her. "You haven't asked me about your family."

This was clearly a riposte, a blow exchanged for her blow. It was well aimed. She dropped her gaze and turned her face away.

"Your brother deserted, fled the country. Your father refused to do his part in your brother's recapture, but they caught him anyway. He was shot trying to escape, or just shot, it makes no difference, and your father's in jail. So you'd failed in your role, you see? You were supposed to buy their good behavior, and you failed. That's why you were to be shot. It was a punishment for failure."

She stared at him and cried, "But is that really how they think?"

"Of course." He turned back to stir the beans.

She went on staring at the brown expanse of his back. "So why don't you think that way?" she said at last.

"But I do think that way," he said. "Everywhere but here, I do. That's why they won't catch me, you see. Because I'm loyal everywhere but here."

With nothing to say, she ate the rest of the orange.

They shared the pot of beans, she eating from the mug with the spoon, he, from the bowl with scraps of bread. He washed everything in the sink in the lavatory, then made a pot of instant coffee with the rusty tap water. And then he just sat in the spare wooden chair, being disloyal.

The scream came again, loud and intimate and bitten off as before, and she woke knowing that was what had awakened her, though she had only heard it in her sleep. She had told herself that the ghosts could not frighten her, but now she lay in a knot of blankets with her heart beating fast and her lungs starved for air. He had left her at twilight, and when she opened her eyes and saw the faint light filtering through from the outer room she thought he had just gone. But no, she had been asleep for hours, she could remember her dreams. *Go—* the voice said, and she remembered her brother was dead.

Part of the hospital had been burned—she supposed that was why it had been condemned—and sometimes she heard the insinuating whisper of the long-dead flames. She heard them now, and felt a roughness in her throat, and was compelled to get up and make sure it was only a ghost-fire, not a real one. She was alive enough to feel a horror of burning. She had got only as far as the outer room when the sound stopped. *Ru—* the voice said in her ear. Sick and groggy from the hurried awakening, she shuffled on cold feet to the window. Dawn was just starting to lighten the air, and it seemed as though only the air was brightening; the sky and the well of the courtyard were black. While she stood there, pulling at a blanket so that it hung more evenly about her shoulders and thinking that her sore throat must be the beginning of a cold, a light appeared in one of the windows across the way. It illuminated nothing but the filthy glass of the window, made a fleeting lighthouse sweep and was gone. So that was where he got in, she thought. And then she thought: suppose it was not he? Suppose he had been followed? Suppose he had betrayed her.

The corridor was pitch black once she had turned the first corner. She thought with longing of the open wards upstairs, the wide hallway that led from one end of the wing to the other. This floor was a maze, a convolution of the dark. *Li—* said the voice in her ear, and she had a moment of panic that she could not get away, even from this. Her groping hand found a doorjamb, a doorknob. She opened the door—it whispered across the gritty floor—and crept inside the lightless room.

She forgot what she was afraid of. Hiding seemed to make its own reasons, its own fear. She huddled inside the door, listening, as she scarcely had before, to the hospital's emptiness. A single step outside the door, the distant dripping of a rusted pipe, a child's voice raised in complaint and cut off, always cut off. The rattle of a curtain drawn on its metal rings, she knew the sound, a worn curtain drawn briskly, brusquely, to hide the gruesome procedure, the suffering, the corpse. She knew the sound, and knew that it was with her in the room, behind her in the dark.

A rusted flake of the past, a nothing, a ghost. She turned, with her back pressed to the door so as not to lose her bearings—in the perfect darkness there was no direction, no distance, no boundaries to the room. If it was a room. It was as dark as the inside of her skull. And the haunting did not stop with that sound, the harsh scrape of curtain-rings on a metal rod. There was the intermittent whine of breath, caught in pain and released in a whimper that tries not to be heard, a thin, stifled *ah!* And other breathing, harsher, the breath of exertion. And other sounds, damp sounds, and a soft, muffled crunch, the sound of kitchen shears severing a chicken's wing.

She turned back to the door and fumbled it open, stepped out into the equally black hall. One step, and she was enveloped, immersed, in the folds of a curtain. *Ah—!* said the voice, and the curtain, thin and damp, pressed close to her face, her mouth, and her arms, even her shins. She jerked back. It clung. She put out her hands, prying away from her mouth and nose, feeling the impossible pressure, the restraint. She pushed hard, made her fingers into claws, and tore through, and ran in the dark to the open door of the room and the window that was growing light, and found him waiting for her there.

———————

The lavatory had no mirror, but she knew, by the change of texture under her palms, that her hair was growing in. No longer than his, perhaps, but the stiff stubble had changed to a close cap of fur. Too short still, and she knew they would be looking for her, but how long . . . ? She asked him: "How long will I have to stay here?"

"It isn't safe yet. They're looking hard, because of the men who were killed."

The men he had killed.

He seemed to have recognized the quality of her hunger, and had brought her an apple and a thick-skinned winter carrot, which he cut into thin, uniform slices with a large pocket knife. She had not forgotten the day he had come with blood on his hands, and watched his hands, the knife, with a chill under her skin. But she could smell the apple like a draft from the pages of one of his books.

"You must have other safe houses," she said, forcing her gaze away. "Your friends . . . "

"Friends?" He pronounced the word oddly, as though it were new to him.

"Your organization."

He did not look up, though the apple was sliced and pared, the carrot cut into fingers thinner than hers. Misgiving shook her.

"You said . . . you had a system. You said . . . an organization . . . "

He wiped the knife, folded it and put it away.

"Well, don't you? Someone to get me a, a wig, and clothes, and—papers—you said—"

He looked at her at last. "I can find those things. When they are not watching me so closely."

A white flame ignited in her skull. "You don't have any friends, do you?"

He looked away, stood with his empty hands at his sides.

"Do you? No organization, no system. Just you, hiding in this room."

He had a statue's eyes, cold and blind. "I signed the order," he said.

The order . . . for her rescue? She couldn't make sense of it, of him. The white flame guttered into confusion.

"I signed the order," he said, "and then I came here. To think. It's the only place safe enough to think in. And I thought: it's supposed to be a hospital. I thought: it's supposed to be for healing the sick, for giving peace to the troubled. And I thought: death is a kind of peace. But still, I thought. Still. I can't help but think there are other kinds of peace. And it wasn't your fault, in the end. Your brother, your father. It wasn't your fault they didn't care enough in the end. So then I came to wish it was undone. And I did what I could, to undo it."

She sat in silence, piecing together the meaning of all this. The order, she thought. The order he had signed was to have her killed. And the hospital he was talking about wasn't this one, but the one in which she had been a prisoner. Peace to the troubled. This place, those books. Peace to the troubled. He was insane.

She hardly knew whether the pity she felt was for him or herself, but it was as intense in this moment as grief.

"But you can still help me," she said, more in response to this last realization than to what he had said. "You can still get me clothes, and papers. You can still . . . " Her voice failed on a breath of tears. "You can still . . . let me go."

"It isn't safe yet," he said, and stirred, the statue come back to some semblance of life. "Not yet. Maybe in the spring."

Spring, she thought, when the tender leaves were budding in the pastoral woods, in some chapter of a book.

"That would be . . . nice," she said raggedly, carefully. "Maybe then we . . . could go into the country. When the flowers are blooming. In the spring."

His face softened, the strain in his body eased. He smiled—but it was as though his mouth was unaware of the blank despair in his eyes, the collapse of his mind. He turned and placed the apple and carrot slices in the bowl.

"Here," he said. "It will do you good."

She took the bowl, and coughed.

COUNTRY MOTHERS' SONS

Now we live on the edge of the bombed quarter of the Parish of St. Quatain in the City of Mondevalcón. The buildings are crooked here, tall tenements shoved awry by the bomb blasts and scorched by the fires. At home in our valleys we whitewashed the houses every spring, even the poorest of us, brightening away the winter's soot. Here, for all the rent we pay, the landlords say they are too poor to paint, and we live in a dark gray soot-streaked world, leaning away from the wind and the dirty rain. Spring comes as weeds sprouting in the empty lots where no one has yet begun to build. Build what? We are outside the rumors, we who only moved here after the war. My village was only a hundred miles away, but I am a foreigner here. Stubbornly, like most of us, I am still in my heart a native of my village; I only happen to live in this alien place.

Elena Markassa lives high at the top of a creaking staircase, in her "tower," she says, where she can look far out and down. They are bright rooms, though cold and restless with the wind that sneaks in through the broken and never-mended panes. But the rest of us live lower down, out of the reach of the sun, so we often gather there, wrapped in our sweaters and shawls. Lydia Santovar huffs and puffs after the climb, but Agnola Shovetz and I are mountain women and too proud, even carrying a sack of potatoes between us. Elena Markassa never leaves her flat, she's an antiquated princess in her gloomy tower waiting for her perennially absent son to come home.

We all have absent sons.

"These boys!" Agnola Shovetz says with a toss of her hands and a note of humor in her voice, but Elena Markassa's broad face is heavy as she brings the flour tin from the pantry. We are making peroshki today, a long and fussy chore demanding company.

"They need work," Lydia Santovar says.

"My boy works," Agnola Shovetz says, ready for a mild quarrel.

"I don't mean that kind of work. Waiting tables! I can't blame my boy, even grown men take what they can find these days, but what kind of work is that for a man? And all for a pocket of small bills. I hardly saw a coin from one end of the month to the other, back home. Who needed it? We worked the land, and it gave us what we needed. The apple trees and the barley fields and the cows: there was always something that needed doing at home. That was work, all of us together, building up the farm. That was where the wealth was, and you always knew where the boys were . . . "

At home. Is this all we talk about? Home. The war took it away from us, or took us away from it. The land we all thought eternal, ruined or lost, simply lost, as if the mountains had closed in, folding the valleys away out of reach. It's true, the word conjures our small house with the walls of plaster over stone, and the icon of St. Terlouz growing dark as an eclipsed sun over the hearth. But it's also true that when I hear that word I think of Georgi out on the mountain slopes, running through the streams of moonlight that splash through the spruce boughs and shine off the patchy remnants of snow. How he could run! Not a handsome man, my Georgi, and with a shy, hostile look with strangers, as if he were poised between a snarl and a fast retreat, but oh, to see him moving across the steep meadows, dancing from rock to rock above the backs of the scurrying sheep. Our son moves a little like that, so that it hurts sometimes to see him hemmed in by all these stony walls. *Mountains, buildings,* my boy says to me, *it's all rock, mama. Either way, it's only rock.*

It isn't the buildings, his father would have said. It's the walls.

Lydia makes a well in the mound of flour on the table and I start cracking eggs while Elena fills the big kettle at the tap.

"This morning," Elena says, pitching her voice over the rush of the water, "I had to hear from my neighbor across the hall on the other side, she looks over the roofs going down to the harbor. She says all last night she heard the boys out on the roof, drinking, fighting, God knows what they get up to—"

"My boy's not a fighter," Agnola says.

"Whatever they do," Elena says, "this morning the roofs were covered with dead birds. Feathers like a ruined bed, that's what my neighbor said, and the birds all lying there like a fox went through the henhouse, dead."

"They keep hens on the roof over there?" Lydia says. Her strong arm is pumping as she beats the eggs into a yellow froth.

"Not hens," Elena says. "Pigeons, seagulls. Should I know? City birds. Nobody keeps hens here."

"People keep doves," Agnola says. She has a worried look, always on the verge of hunger.

"Not for eating," Elena says authoritatively. Perhaps living in her tower has made her an expert on the city's heights. "They're racing pigeons, for sport."

"We used to snare wood doves and cook them into pies," Agnola says.

"You can't eat city birds," Lydia says. She's a little short of breath. "No better than rats, with what they eat."

"It's the *dead* birds I'm talking about." Elena bangs the kettle down on the stove and turns to us. "Of course I had to hear it from my neighbor. *He* comes home almost at dawn, when all night I hardly slept for wondering where he is, and 'Where were you?' I say, but it's 'Mama, I have to go to work, do I have any clean socks?' "

"Oh, but my boy's just the same," says Lydia. "They're all the same, aren't they, Nadia?"

They look at me, because they think my boy is the ringleader, the troublemaker, the one whose role in life is to lead the innocent astray. But what can I say? That, no, unlike their boys he tells me everything, sitting on the edge of my bed in the dark?

The clouds blew away before midnight last night, and the moon shone so bright the birds mistook it for day. Down below, far below the height of rooftops on the hill, the harbor looked like a circle of sky, black water and moon sequins embraced by a lunar crescent of headlands. The water trembled under the wind that cleansed the air of its night smokes, and the birds confused by the brilliance of the moon lifted their wings, half aloft as the sea air flowed over and around them. Multitudes of pigeons on the roof leads leaned silently into the wind, bright eyes colorless, ruffled feathers like pewter. They stood in ranks like a congregation waiting for the hand of God to part the curtain of sky and sweep them away to another world; city doves, gray as the pavements, waiting for the right hand of God. And all around, like lumps of creosote on chimneys, finials on church spires, heat-slumped lightning rods and weather vanes frozen by the cold light, perched the owls.

If you move slow enough, not stalking-slow, but easy, you have to have some humor about it, be a little careless—but if you're easy you can walk right among them. They're used to people, it's like feeding them in the square, except they're so still, in a trance, soft around your feet. In the cold you can feel the warmth of them against your ankles, the soft feathers of their breasts.

I can feel it. I can see the sleepy shutter-blink of their eyes as they stare out to sea, bemused, be-mooned.

The boys climb the roofs as if tenements were mountain peaks and they were wolves climbing into the thin air to serenade the moon. And what happens to the hundreds of souls under the roofs when the roofs are no longer roofs, the buildings no longer buildings but hills, and the streets are only ravines, black with moon-shadow? What happens to all the dreamers when our boys are alone with the birds on the high hills? Do we dream beneath their feet like the dead dream, locked in the solid earth?

The boys stood on the steep roof slope, feet warmed by pigeons and faces icy in the wind. The pigeons with their wings half spread, and maybe the boys, too, with their arms thrown wide, so many saints on so many crosses of moonlight, waiting for the right hand of God. And the owls, their yellow eyes the only color in the world, lifting free from chimney and spire, more silent than the blustering wind.

And you'll never know, mama, you'll never know how it is to see the plunge, the hard short fight, the feathers flying like confetti

at a wedding, and feel the hot bloody claws clench your arm.
They're so strong. They're so strong.

But I do know. You can't tell your son that, not when he's sitting on the edge of your widow's bed with his young blood running so hot and fast in his veins. But I know. I can see it still, and breathe the cold air that pours like slow water off the edge of the snowfields. Spring in the valleys, but winter on the heights, so cold there is ice in the air to catch the light of the moon. The waning snow is so white it turns the rest of the mountain to shadow; and the broke-neck grouse, wings wide and head lolling below a halo of scattered feathers; and my Georgi, a shadow, with only his eyes bright with moon. Is that why I left the mountains? Not because there was nothing left but scarred fields and a gutted house, nothing for my son but the choice between brigandry and hunger. But because as long as I am here, or anywhere else, I can see my husband there, as if I had to leave before he could come home from the war.

But the women, my country friends, are looking at me, waiting for an answer. "Yes," I say with just the right sort of sigh, "these boys, they're all the same." And I reach for a potato and a paring knife, taking my share of the chore.

———

When you're trudging through the gray streets, with maybe a shopping basket in one hand, an umbrella in the other, bumping along with all the other umbrellas on the way to market to buy vegetables off a truck without even a crumb of good dirt in sight—when you're walking the daytime streets, you'd think there's only two kinds of animal in the world: the pigeons and the cats. Maybe if you look hard you see the little house sparrows, brave as orphans snatching up what the pigeons are too slow to grab, and the seagulls lording it up on the gutters and the gable ends; and there are cormorants down in the harbor, drying their wings like so many broken umbrellas on the pilings; and of course there are the poor city dogs, tugged about on leashes when they're not trapped inside; and rats you only ever hear scrabbling in the walls. But the city belongs to the pigeons and the cats, like rival armies in a battle as old as the city, and this city is very old. Very old.

Somehow, it's the pigeons that believe themselves in the ascendant, though you'd think it would be the cats, arrogant with their armament of teeth and claws. But it's the pigeons who bustle around like women on market day, keeping a sharp eye out for a good bit of gossip and a bargain, while the cats slink about on the edges of things, holding themselves equally ready for a fast retreat or a lightning raid. Only at night, when the pigeons hide from the dark and the streets are quiet, do the cats quietly take command.

Mondevalcón is a snarl of streets, a tip-tilted tangle running across the hills that rise between the harbor and the high black mountains inland. Even with the new electric streetlights going up there is a lot of darkness here at night, and of course the streetlights are going up first among the palaces on the hill and the docks down by the water. In between, where most of us live, there is still darkness, deep as the sea. Only sometimes the moon slips in, canny and elusive as the little gray tabby that comes to my balcony for her saucer of milk or her bit of egg every morning. Yes, moonlight comes like a cat, easing silently down one street angled just so, skipping across the battered roofs, running rampant in the bombsites, then darting, sudden and bright, down an alley so narrow you would have sworn it hadn't been touched by natural light for a thousand years. And one night the foxes from the wild mountains followed the moon into town.

You should have seen them, mama! my son says in the dark of my curtained room. I can hardly see him for the darkness, just the shape of a gesture or the glint of an eye, but I can smell the sharp sweat of him, still more boy than man, and the fruit tang of the liquor he shares with his friends. I hear, too, the wild energy that still has him it its grasp. He won't sleep until it lets him go, so I prop a second pillow under my head and listen. *You should have seen them*, he says.

Cats are solitary creatures and seldom gather, so it's a curious thing when they do. They came so quietly, as if they gathered substance out of the night air, appearing like the dew on the cobblestones of the street, on wide marble steps and the lofty pediments of the grand old buildings, the banks and palaces and guild halls, that survived the war. There is one wide avenue on the seaward face of the Mondevalcón hill, Penitents Climb, that rises, steep and nearly straight, from the harborfront to Cathedral Square. It runs on from the square, the same wide street though its name has changed, down the back side of the hill, past the townhouses of the rich, and up again, past the train yards and coal depots and feedlots, and up still more into the harsh black rock country of the high mountains, shaded here and there by juniper and pine. This was the road the foxes took as they came dancing on their long black-stockinged legs, their grinning teeth and laughing eyes bright in the light of the moon. They were not silent. Like soldiers marching into town with a weekend leave before them, they stepped with a quick hard tapping of claws and let out the occasional yelp, or a vixen scream to tease the lapdogs barking and howling from the safety of their masters' houses, and so their coming was heralded.

The cats waited where Penitents Climb runs into the square. The bombed cathedral stood in its cage of scaffolding, as if it were half a thousand years ago and it was being raised for the first, not the second, time. The cobblestones, where light once fell from jewel-toned windows, were dark, and the square, domain of pigeons in the daylight, was a black field waiting for battle to be joined. How did the boys find themselves there, so far from their usual harborside haunts?

We followed the moon, my sons says, though perhaps they only followed the cats.

The silent cats. In the moonlight you could see the wrinkled demon-masks of their small faces when they hissed, the needle-teeth white, the ears pressed flat, and the eyes. Eyes black in the darkness, black and empty as the space between the stars. Even in the colorless light of midnight you could see all the mongrel variety of them, small and dainty, long and rangy, big and pillow-soft in the case of the neutered toms; and the coats, all gray, it's true, but showing their patches, their brindles, their stripes. All the cats of the city, alley cats and shop cats and pampered house cats, thousands of cats, as many and as silent as the ghosts of the city's dead, so many killed by the bombs, and all gathered there to repel the invasion of the mountain wilds.

The foxes came skipping into the square, long tongues hanging as they drooled at the daytime scent of the pigeons. Is that what drew them down from the mountains? Or did they, like our mountain sons, only follow the moon?

Battle joined. One fox makes a meal of one cat, if the cat is surprised before it can climb. Foxes are long-legged and long-jawed, clever and quick, and born with a passion for mayhem. But for every fox there was a dozen cats or more, and a cat defending its nest of kittens is a savage thing, with no thought for its own hurt.

The foxes took joy in it, you could see that, the way they pounced four-footed or danced up on two. It almost seemed the cats were the wild ones. No fun in them, no quarter, no fear of death but no thought for anything else, either. Your heart could break for them when they died. You could love them for it, thrown broken-backed and bleeding from some grinning dog-creature's mouth, but they were fearsome, too, so many of them in such a bloodthirsty crowd. I could imagine them turning on us like that. One black she-cat turned such a face to me, with her white, white teeth and the eyes black as holes, that I was almost afraid, forgetting how small she was. Like a lioness.

And so they prevailed, the cats, though terribly many of them died. As the moon slipped away behind the black mountains the foxes seemed to lose the fun of the thing, or maybe it was only that the moon's setting called the signal for retreat. And so the sun rose, and the pigeons, never knowing the battle that was fought for their safety, gathered to hunt for crumbs on the bloodstained cobbles of the square.

<hr />

"And now there are police about asking questions!" Lydia Santovar says.

It is just the two of us today. Elena Markassa, up in her leaning tower, has pleaded a headache, and Agnola Shovetz is cleaning offices, to her chagrin, so Lydia has come to my small flat to make our pies. We have wrinkled apples from the winter store, rhubarb crisp and fresh with sour juice, and hard little raisins that look like nothing so much as squashed flies. This has a satisfying appearance of bounty spread out on my counters along with the sacks of flour and sugar and the tin of lard, something to take pleasure in, in the face of all our worries about money. Beyond homesickness, I am thinking more and more about our weed-choked fields and ruined barns back home. I have rented our pastures to the shepherds and that gives us our tiny income—that and my son's small wage from cleaning trolley cars—but oh, to have enough to hire a man to rebuild the house and plow the fields! Oh, to have a man, my man, back again! So I am not listening very closely to Lydia's tale.

"You have had a theft in your building, Lydia? I hope you lost nothing yourself."

"You aren't listening, Nadia Prevetz."

Well, this is true.

"It's the cats I'm speaking of. Surely you must have heard!"

What I have heard is what my son tells me, but nothing more, so to play it safe I say, "Someone has been stealing cats?"

Lydia looks at me strangely. Does she doubt my innocence, or my sense? "Killing them, Nadia. Someone has been killing the cats all over the city. The police say nothing, you know how they are, but everyone has been talking— But you must have heard this?"

I have a slice of apple in my mouth and can only shake my head no.

"Everyone says it is the work of a madman, or perhaps even a wicked gang, and now with the police everywhere asking about men seen out late at night, and in the newspaper today a letter about bringing the curfew back into force . . . Well, you can see what they think, that soon it won't be just cats but people that are getting killed."

"But surely . . . " I keep my eyes on my hands, the neat curl of apple peel sliding away from the knife. "Isn't it just as likely to have been animals?"

"That's what I say! It's just animals. Even if it is some gang of fiends."

It's clear what kind of newspapers Lydia reads. I bite my lip to keep from smiling. "What I mean to say is, isn't it likely that it was dogs or some such that killed the cats? I think a pack of dogs roaming the streets makes more sense than a gang of cat-murderers."

Lydia refrains from giving me another look. I can feel it, though her hands are as busy as mine.

"Maybe that's all it is," she says. "But the police are about, with their questions and their eyes, and I'm keeping my boy in at night until it all settles down."

"Well, you can try," I say, with the smile fighting free. Try to keep the young men indoors with spring on its way!

"Maybe you should try too," Lydia says, her voice sharp as my paring knife. "To be on the safe side."

Still she forcibly refrains from looking at me, and my smile dies.

For here is another memory of home, and one I wish I could forget. Why is it that I need to build my memories of our house piece by piece, like our bedroom so small that our marriage bed, too big to fit through the door, had to be built inside the room—that room, warm as a hen's nest in winter, with its white plaster walls and black beams and tiny two-paned window set to catch sunrise and moonrise in the east—I have to build it one eye-blink at a time, yet the bad memories leap sharp and wounding to the front of my mind. There is Georgi, with his hunted look and restless body, and there are the shepherds complaining of sheep dead in the sheering pen, and there is our son, so small and his eyes so wide, never understanding why these angry men have come to accuse his father . . . of what? Even they did not seem to know, except that we were the only people in the valley who did not raise sheep. My poor Georgi! I had to take them out and show them our goats, that I kept for milk and for the finer wool, and such a clamor did the does raise when they smelled the sheep blood on the men's clothes that the boy started to cry and the men went away ashamed. But by then Georgi was also gone, back up into the high trees. The best hunter in the valley—as if he had to demean himself by slaughtering sheep penned and helpless! It was two sheep dogs that went bad, the way they sometimes do, and leapt the fence to savage the sheep they were meant to be guarding. The dogs were shot, but no one apologized to my Georgi. I don't think he ever noticed, but I did, remembering how our little boy cried.

And now my boy, his father's son, refuses to stay inside on nights when the sky is clear.

I spend all day in the maintenance shed with the stink of oil

*and paint, mama, I wouldn't know if it was raining or snowing or
dropping fish from the sky except that the trolley cars come back
all covered with scales. I have to see the sky sometimes, don't I?
I'd go crazy! Listen, mama, don't ever let them lock me away. If
I wasn't a lunatic when I went in, I would be before I could come
out again.*

And why would anyone lock him away? But I can see his eyes
are dancing with mischief, he's only teasing his sad old mother,
and so I laugh with him about the fish. *But think, mama,* he says
solemnly, *those scales had to come from somewhere.*

Like the foxes did.

———◆———

Oh, these bright nights of spring! For the spring is well advanced
now, and for all I thought it would be invisible here in the midst of
the gray old city, there seems to be sweet new green everywhere.
Workers clearing the bomb sites must cut the wiry vines to free the
rubble, and even the heaps of wilting greenery show white trumpet
flowers still trying to open with the dawn. Every balcony has
sprouted an herb garden, rosemary already dressed in faded blue,
bergamot opening in orange and red, mint in vivid green despite
the soot that dusts everything indoors and out. And at night, when
the onshore wind drives the clouds onto the high mountain peaks
and the blazing moon robs the world of color, the tenements are
like cliffs seeming too sheer to climb but beckoning with tender
leaves in every cranny and on every ledge. And the cloud-heavy
peaks are still barren with snow.

*Do you remember, mama, how papa used to take us up through
the woods to the high meadows below the cliffs? He was always the*

one who saw them first. Do you remember? The way they would leap, you would swear, from nothing to nothing where the rock was so steep even stonecrop could barely cling. The way they would leap . . .

Do I remember? The steep meadows strewn with the earliest flowers, the yellow stars of avalanche lilies and the pale anemones too tender, you would swear, for the harsh high winds; and the black cliffs with their feet buried in the rubble of stone broken by ice in the winters when no one was there to see it fall; and the sharp-horned chamois like patches of dirty snow where no snow could cling, until they moved, leaping, as my son says, from nothing to nothing, or so you would swear. The chamois made my neat-footed goats look clumsy and earthbound, the tame and more than tame cousins condemned to valley life: debased. Or was that how I felt, trailing in the wake of my husband and my son, who seemed to have been born for the heights? But even they were banned from the steepest cliffs.

It was the challenge, mama. You don't know, you don't know . . .

The longing for the high places, the hot-blooded joy of risk.

The chamois came across the rooftops in the full noon of the moon. Did they ever touch the city ground? Perhaps they stepped from the mountain slope onto some steep outlying roof and leapt from there to the next, roof-edge to ridgepole, gutter to gable, never dropping to the mortal earth. I can see them under the moon, skirting the dome of some palace on the hill, leaping over skylights with a patter of hooves. I wonder what they thought, those people living in the topmost floors. Maybe they heard it as a sudden fall of hail. And then the airy descent to the window-box gardens, the heady herbs, the alarm of the reflection in the moonlit window glass, and the far greater alarm, the shock of prey, when the window slides up and the young man tests his weight on the high iron landing loosened by bomb blasts and eaten by rust.

You have to keep moving. It's the only rule: keep moving, and always go up instead of down.

The chase, the glorious moonlit chase. Buildings are crowded here on the seaward face of the Mondevalcón hill. They press upwards like trees starved for sunlight, confined by the streets that are so narrow, some of them, a strong boy can leap from gutter to gutter like a mountain chamois, that nimble goat with horns so sharp they can stab through a wolf's hide like a twin-bladed spear. So the chamois fled before the silent hunting pack, a light thunder of flinty hooves that drowned the quieter thump and pad of bare feet; running in fear, perhaps, but in challenge, too, the challenge their kind has always offered the would-be predators of the mountain heights. They fled across the hill and upwards, the way instinct led them, and the moon followed to its setting among the clouds trapped by the western peaks, and the late dew fell, the heavy dew of the ocean shore—

—and when we looked he was gone. Just gone. He must have fallen without a sound. We didn't know until we looked down and saw him on the street there, ten stories down.

Lydia Santovar's son. Lydia Santovar, my friend, who came from a village on the flat plain far inland, and whose son had never even seen mountains before the end of the war.

"It was the war," Elena Markassa says outside the church on the funeral day. "These poor boys, too young to fight—thank God!—but old enough to know what the fighting meant. And always with the threat of a bomb falling or the wrong partisan band coming through any day or night, the end of the world, for all a child knows, coming maybe today, maybe tomorrow or next week, next year. No wonder they grew so reckless. Poor boys!"

"They need their fathers," Agnola says, and we stand in silence a moment before going in, the three of us already in our widow's black, ready for a funeral any day, today or tomorrow or next week. A funeral every day.

My boy has come with me, as all the boys have, and I can feel him beside me as we stand and sit and kneel to the priest's sure direction. He is a reassuring presence, the solid living weight of him, and it is hard for a widow with an only child not to clutch him, not to scold in mingled relief and fear. But I can feel the restlessness in him. For the first time, I see his father's hunted look in his clear young face, the dark wariness that prepares itself for fight or flight at any moment. (Maybe today, maybe tomorrow . . . Elena's words haunt me, drowning out the priest.) What does this mean for him, for his future life? I watch the priest, I watch my friend Lydia, stony in her grief, but I see our mountain-shadowed home, the roofless house and weedy fields, the green pastures hemmed not by fences but by the dark mass of the trees. At the same time I see a doubled image, a shadow, the dark tenements hemming in the greening bomb sites, and I remember my son saying, *Mountains, buildings, it's all rock, mama. Either way, it's only rock.* But this place cannot be home to my Georgi's son. Surely this tragedy proves as much? No matter that the wilderness has followed us—followed him—into the city. Surely, to such a boy, such a man, the city can never be home. Yet, even as he ducks away from Lydia's accusing, tear-washed stare, my son refuses to admit we must go.

Well, it is my mistake. It was my doing that brought us here, fleeing the burnt house and the ex-partisans and the hunger. It is my fault. I have no one to blame but myself. Perhaps even this death should lie heavy in my hands.

———

The sun is shining above the inland peaks, the last long slant of sunlight before the mountain shadow comes, the last bright heat of the first warm day of spring, and we have made a feast of farewell. There are peroshki, of course, stuffed with potato and bacon, potato and sauerkraut, potato and onion, and drenched with melted butter. There are roast beets and sour cream. There is the stewed pork red with hot paprika, and the baked cockerel, and the leek and rabbit pie. There is soft white bread and bread as dark and thick as molasses, and hard cheese, and pink sausage reeking with garlic, and red sausage studded with black peppercorns, and butter packed in a little bowl of ice. There are pies, tart rhubarb and sweet apple, with crusts bubbled with golden sugar. And there is wine, the harsh, sour, country wine that is as familiar and as vital as the blood in our veins. The boys follow us, half unwilling, drawn as much by the smell of the food as by any sense of obligation to their fallen friend. He has been buried nine days, Lydia's son, and it is time to make his final goodbyes before he moves on.

We have spared no expense, and two black taxicabs carry us up to the cemetery gates and stand there while the drivers, bemused, help us unload our hampers. The city parishes have long since run out of room for their dead; the Mondevalcón cemetery stands high above the city, above even the palaces, on the first slope of the mountains. The grass is very green here, well fed and watered by the heavy fogs that haunt this coast, and there are flowers among the graves, roses and irises already blooming, and tiny white daisies scattered across the lawn. The black mountains rise above us in their scanty dress of juniper and pine; below us the city swells in a wave of dark roofs to the shining palaces with their towers and domes, and falls, roof piled against roof, to the blue water of the harbor; and beyond the dark headlands lies the sunlit blaze of the sea. There are seagulls crying, even this far from the water, and a clanging from the train yards, but there is still a great silence here, the enduring quiet of death and the open sky.

The three boys are abashed by the amusement of the taxi drivers (this farewell feast is a country rite, it seems, and the men make them feel so young), but they help carry the big hampers through the iron gates and down the gravel path we all trod nine days ago. The smell of the food follows us, mingling with the scent of cut grass, mouthwatering in the open air. Seagulls perch on monuments nearby, white as new marble on the grimy little palaces of death.

The boy's grave is humble, still showing dirt beneath the cut sod, with only a wooden stake leaning at its head. Lydia straightens this with a countrywoman's practical strength, as if she were planting a post for a new vine, while Elena Markassa, Agnola Shovetz, and I organize boys and hampers, and spread blankets politely between the neighboring graves. There will be a headstone in the fall, once the turned earth has settled; they don't know it yet, but the boys will be saving the money they have been spending on liquor and cigarettes to help Lydia pay for a good marble stone.

We spread the feast upon the blankets and the grass, open the bottles and toast the dead boy's name. Lydia tells stories of his none-too-distant childhood and the living boys seem to shrink in their clothes, becoming even younger than they are, until they are children again, enduring their mothers' company. They eat, guilty for their hunger; we all eat, and for us women, at least, there is a deep and abiding comfort in this act. There is no mystery here, and no great tragedy, just another family meal. We are all family now, with this spilled blood we share among us, and Lydia is at once ruthless and kind to the living boys, speaking bluntly about the life and death of their friend. There are four mothers here, and four sons, though one of them lies silent in his bed and leaves his plate untouched.

The sun makes a bright crown on the mountain's head, and then falls away, spilling a great shadow across the city as a vanguard of the night. We feel the chill even as the sunlight still flashes diamonds from the distant sea. The food has cooled, sparrows have the crumbs. The air is sweeter than ever with the smell of turned earth and new grass, and even the haze of coal smoke from the train yard adds no more than a melancholy hint of distance and goodbyes. The first stars shine out. The wine has turned sad in our veins. It is nearly time to shake out the blankets, stack the plates and pots and sticky pie tins, find the corks and knives and cheese rinds that have gone astray in the grass, and begin the long walk home.

My son stands and looks above the monuments with their

weeping angels to the mountains. They are very black now, clothed in shadow. He moves towards them, weaving among headstones and walking softly across the graves. I am struck again by how like his father he walks, that supple prowl, and in the fading light he looks older, almost a man, walking away from us, the mothers, old already in our widow's shawls. I watch him with a pang in my heart, as if to see him thus is to lose him, as I lost his father, who walked away one day and never came home. I will call him in a moment to come and help me fold the blankets. The other boys have also stood, watching with a bright attention that excludes their mothers, and soon they have followed him, vanishing among the tombs, leaving us in the ruins of our feast while the color drains out of the world, into the deep clear blue of the sky.

The moon is rising, out on the eastern rim of the world. The horizon gleams like a knife's edge, the ocean catching the light even before the moon herself appears. So beautiful, that white planet, that silver coin. They tell us she is barren, nothing more than rock and dust, but there must be something more, something that calls out to the heart. How else could she be so beautiful? How else could she exert such force over the oceans of the world, and the hidden oceans in our veins? She rises, and all my longing comes over me again. Maybe here, whispers my most secret hope. My Georgi has been lost for so long. But maybe here, at last, he will follow the moon's call to the eastern edge of the world, and find me once again.

We watch the moon rise, silent at last, while the boys wander out of sight among the graves. And as we sit here, wrapped in our nighttime thoughts, we hear the first voice lifted in a long lament. A voice to make a stone weep. Surely the moon herself would weep to hear such a cry! A rising and a falling note so long it seems it will never end, and then a silence so deep we can hear the grass rustling to the passage of the worms. And then the voice sings again, and is joined by another, and a third, in a chorus of grief, of longing, of love so wild it trembles always on the edge of death. They sing the moon up into the zenith, and fall still, so that the silence folds gently about us, as deep and as peaceful as the grave. The rustling comes again, so quiet you would swear it was beetles or mice, but then we hear the paws striking the gravel path, the huff of breath and the faint clicking of claws, as the wolves follow the moon's path into the city. We see them for only an instant, two shadows, three . . . four? . . . we sit a while, waiting to see if there are more to come. One more, is all I pray for. Oh please! Do I pray to God or the moon? One more of those quiet gray shadows come down from the mountains to pass among the graves. Please, let there be one more. But we are alone now, four widows with absent sons, and soon we must rise, and pack away the remains of our feast, and make our last goodbyes.

PROVING THE RULE

A busy pub at noon.

He had his pocket notebook out on the table and was flipping past old stories, scratching out unconfirmed facts and unusable quotes: the merest gesture toward work. Someone jogged his table, but he saw it coming and lifted his pint out of danger. He drank, licked his lip, set the glass warily down. Should have ordered food, he thought. The crowd at the bar was two deep and if he got up now he'd lose the table and the chair he was saving for her. If she didn't come he'd go hungry. But if he got up and she came? He went on leafing through the notebook, his head bent low.

She slipped inside like a draft through an open window. He would have sworn that he felt her, that he looked up an instant before she came into view. The crowd parted for her like curtains; she lit him up like a ray of light. Resenting it, he refused to stand, but bad manners failed to hide his open face, his pencil falling to the floor. She smiled, pleased to see him, and sat in the saved chair.

"What are you drinking?" she asked him.

"Bitter. You won't like it. Try the ale."

"All right. And food? Are you feeding me, too?"

He fed her cold game pie and apples and cheese. The apples were from somebody's cold store and under their wrinkled skins tasted of cider and old wood. They went well with the beer.

She had the knack of elegance. She was dressed well, of course, something simple in green wool that hinted at the coming spring, but that was just money. The mystery was the rest of her. The way she could hum with greed, wrinkle her nose when she took a bite, catch a drop of mustard with her tongue, and still be elegant, dainty and refined. That wasn't money, surely? Breeding, another woman of her class would say. But she was the daughter of a scandal and didn't know who her father was.

"You aren't listening," he said.

She took her time reeling her gaze in from the depths. She had darkish hair, paleish skin, eyes somewhere between gray and blue. Yet her gaze was definite. When she looked at you, you knew you were looked at.

"I am," she said. "Well, a little bit, I am."

"What did I say, then?"

She offered him a smile. "I'm inventing a riddle. The answer is 'magic', but I haven't got the question right yet."

"If it's the one about the racehorse trainer and the greyhound, I've already heard it."

She smiled again, but her mind was still somewhere else.

Piqued, he said, in accidental parody of a jealous lover, "If you don't want the work, just say so. We both know you only do it for fun."

"Fun? You mean, I don't do it for money."

"What for, then?"

"Well, it's what I do. History. Research. All the delicious books, yum, yum, and reading dead people's letters behind their backs. Lovely, malicious sense of power. Blackmailing ghosts. It's where my money really comes from, of course." She played at mischief with a straight face, her long-fingered hands fluttering in the air.

"All right," he said heavily to drag her back down to earth. "But really. Why?"

She looked at him with those pale eyes, her pupils so black they never seemed to reflect any light. "All for love of you, my hero. Tell me again what you need?"

Another beer, he thought. He flipped a page in his notebook so vigorously that the thin paper tore.

— ·•·•· —

For love of him? *Because it's my only talent, because it's the only thing that marks me as something besides my mother's daughter, because it's the only thing that's entirely mine.* But though Graham was her friend, he wasn't that kind of friend, so she didn't say it. She just took a little leather-bound notebook out of her purse and made notes, to mollify him, with her little gold pencil. He was writing a series of articles on immigration. While he was talking she jotted down a few citations, reminded herself of a private memoir that she had found in the family library; thought that she probably could have written the articles herself, and knew that she would never say so. Graham needed to work for a living. They could be friends for fifty years, she thought, and he would never reconcile himself to the fact that she did not.

No, she only needed to work to live. Because, because.

Her name was Lucy Donne. Her mother was beautiful, her grandfather was rich. She had been allowed to go to university—it was one of the done things these days—but there were no advanced degrees for women. One could study, write, publish, even tutor, but one could not lecture; one could never call oneself Professor Lucy Donne. She might have done anything, really, she had her mother's recklessness, but she had her grandfather's self-conscious pride as well. She would not trail in her mother's footsteps. Books would be her open doors. A drab compromise, she thought sometimes, though she tried not to think about it. She preferred the delicious books, the impossible hunt, the riddling obsession that kept her up late, night after night. Yum, yum . . . yawn.

The library was a rich man's pride, a set-designer's dream: a long room with a gallery and window bays, jewel-colored carpets and fat-legged tables and a globe clasped in a polished brass arm. It was real to Lucy, though, it was her province, her private realm. She knew about the mousetraps behind the bottom shelves, the silverfish like hungry beads of quicksilver, the dead moths that would fly again if you gave the curtains a good shake. She knew that in a cold winter the cavernous fireplaces could only warm the end bays, leaving an arctic space between them, and she knew that in a hot summer the very walls breathed sleep into the dusty, sun-shot air. Home.

The big clock with its gold and ivory face ticked down another hour. A brass-shaded lamp spilled its pool of light, but Lucy's mind had wandered off into the dark, and so did her books and papers, sprawling outside the lamplight. Her chin was in her hands, her elbows on the ink-splotched blotter. An hour ago she had still been chasing her quarry. Now she dreamed, tracing the route of past hunts across the map of knowledge in her mind. Landmarks, scraps of information, raised themselves up above the horizon and fell away. Yes, she knew this. Yes, she had been there. Most recently:

. . . in the "he's famous even if I don't care" category, the Marshal of Kallisfane (of ancient and dull renown) returned to the capital today after a refreshing month's holiday in the historic and terminally comfortless garrison of Denbreath. The garrison might have a greater appeal to this writer and several other ladies of her acquaintance (the Hon. Miss H. comes to mind!) if it still featured hot-and-cold running soldiers, but as the Denbreath Fortress was recently turned into a museum, one can only wish the Chief Exhibit joy of his new vacation spot . . .

Yes, and:

From our provincial correspondent: Two teachers at the Palton Grammar School were dismissed yesterday after a recent outbreak of hysteria among the students forced authorities to close the school. The school will reopen next week and school governors say they will not be bringing charges against the teachers, saying the two women demonstrated "poor judgment rather than criminal intent."

And what has the one to do with the other? Nothing at all, except that Palton is only ten miles from Denbreath as the crow flies. What tales did the teachers tell? What tales did the children claim to encounter on their way home from school? What would the crow see as it launched itself from the highest steeple in Palton and flew over the winter-dark woods of Breadon How?

Up over the haunted trees, up over the bare brow of the hill where the Cold Hounds were once said to lair, out along the stony ridge where Denbreath Castle sits as it has for six hundred years, a fortified shell for its silent master, the Exhibit, who is older still. The breeze carries the crow to the deep sill of an archer's window, where it folds its wings and cocks its head to stare inside. A stony room. A man, or the shape of a man, stiff as a mannequin waiting for the curators to put its armor on.

The clock clunked and whirred, preparing Lucy for the mellow gong of the hour. One, two . . . Lucy waited for the rest, but the clock had said its piece. She rubbed her face, made a token gesture towards putting her notes in order . . . impossible, it would take a week . . . she put out the lamp and went to bed.

She dreamed the dream in which her house dissolved into a muddled realm of college rooms and hospital corridors. There were a lot of doors, a lot of odd corners twisting the known world out of true. It got harder and harder to find her way, but the harder it got the closer she was to something important, some vivid presence at the heart of the maze. This anticipation was as familiar as the dream, but as the dreamer did not know she was dreaming she could not say, as she would when she woke, "Ah! *This* dream!" But she could recognize the feeling for what it was, and that recognition opened the final door. There were the heavy stones of the wall, the arch that opened out onto nothing but the air. There was the bright clear light, the taste of autumn, the memory of trees. And perhaps the dreamer woke a little in her dreaming, because when she saw the man who stood looking out on the world, she thought or said, "Maybe this time I will see his face. Maybe I will. I will."

An obvious dream; a biographer's dream. But there was nothing stale about the brightness of her will to turn him. Oh, she wanted to see! He knew she was there, he stirred. Her heart leapt. She would wake now, she always woke now and was now awake enough to know it. She held on to the dream with both hands.

And then it seemed that the dream turned and grabbed on to her. The brightness in the air was gone, there was only a warmth as oppressive as a stranger's breath. He stirred, and she no longer knew why she wanted to see his face. "Don't," she said, and the catch of sound in her throat drew her farther out of sleep.

The dream followed her.

He turned. He saw her, and she fled, a bird dashing across the room—the window was there again, his dark figure like a door—she fled, he plucked her from the air. She was a sand-colored dove between his hands, his flesh pressing her flesh as if he grasped her bare ribs, her naked arms. She cried out and woke.

She was still held.

She tore herself free from the bedclothes, flung herself from the bed to fall on her hands and knees. Awake, yes, and dreaming, yes, and still held. Her heart beat its wings. Sweating, trembling, she launched herself from the floor and caromed into the wardrobe across the room like a bird battering itself against a windowpane. Wood bruised flesh, a banged elbow barked, and she woke, finally, truly woke, with the wardrobe door swinging open and her nightgown clinging to her skin.

With a deliberate, practical gesture, Lucy reached out and swung the door closed. The latch *snicked*, and held.

Her room was dark except for the pale rim around the curtain's edge, and the house was quiet, although it seemed to Lucy that the reverberations of her thumps and cries still hung in the air. She stood and listened as if the house might mutter a response—

As if, far below, the street door might open and booted feet might begin to climb the groaning stairs.

She was found.

It was a dream, she told herself with the sweat still wet on her face. Only a nightmare version of a dream she had been dreaming since she was a little girl.

She had been hunting him since girlhood. She had finally come near enough to be noticed.

Him.

. . . the Marshal of Kallisfane (of ancient and dull renown) returned to the capital today . . .

The Marshal of Kallisfane, the Dead Lord, the Revenant, the Living Ghost, Empire's Bane: Him.

The Marshal of Kallisfane returned to the capital today.

She was found.

Lucy pried herself away from the wardrobe and crept up to the window. One finger opened a crack between curtain and frame. A gray dawn, the garden in the square still more turned earth than green, the windows in all the houses still dark. No deathless warrior on the pavement, no Nameless Regiment pulling up in big black motorcars. No one at all, in fact, except for a few sparrows and a cat digging in a flowerbed. Logic, late in waking, said that even if he had found her by some arcane process in her dream, a dream does not shout out a name and an address. Her heart was still thumping, her skin still clammy, and Lucy was not reassured. Sick with fear, she walked with increasing haste down the hall to the lavatory and vomited out the residue of the dream.

Pipes thumped when she flushed the toilet and sang when she ran water to rinse her mouth, guaranteed to wake half the household. But the prosaic was reassuring and nausea imposed its own earthy fatalism. If the Revenant really had found her where she lived then she was already doomed, and if he had not, then . . . Then she hardly knew what. The need to do something was beginning to assert itself, but what the something was, was still obscure. Bathe, Lucy thought, smelling the fear-sweat like bile on her skin.

She washed, found a skirt and jacket in sensible tweed, and put on the most sensible shoes she owned, which weren't very. Dull, ordinary, please-don't-notice-me clothes. She pinned up her hair, powdered her face—in the mirror her hands shook—put a few practical items in her pocket book. She paused on the landing, but there was no sound from behind the family's doors. Her mother's door. Would her mother still hold her after a bad dream, envelop her in warm silk and cigarette smoke and perfume?

Lucy shook herself back into motion. Down the stairs to the grand entry hall, and did she scurry across the marble floor, wrench open the bolts, flit like a sparrow out into the square? That was the motion of her heart, but she hesitated at the stained-glass window by the door, peering through a red rose into the square. A yawning domestic was airing a pair of leashed dogs. Still no living statue (ten feet tall? lichened armor? pigeon-stained helm?) and no ominous black cars. Do what, Lucy? Go where? Seized by a sudden impulse, she left the hall and struck out for the library.

No one had been in yet to open the drapes. She pulled them open as she walked down the main room, letting in daylight the same color as the dust she shook from the brocade. The farthest bay held her table like a ship in its berth, a ship still laded with the cargo of a years-long journey: books, clippings, diaries, letters; notes sorted and unsorted, re-sorted, scribbled over, lost. No one tidied Lucy's desk, Lucy least of all. The order was all in her head, a tangled complexity that, taken all in all, built a structure as simple as a tombstone. Lucy sifted through the top layer of papers, shifted a book from one stack to another, and failed utterly to discover the source of her panic. This was scholarship. It had only been a dream.

Then the panic said: *This is evidence.*

At first she read her notes over with an eye to organization, but she gave that up almost immediately. The clock chimed the half hour and her whole skin shivered. She crammed papers into whatever folder would hold them, shook out the books and scrabbled to gather up the snowfall of torn envelopes and old letters and receipts from the dressmaker with her elegant scrawl on the back. She liberated a large portfolio from an ancestor's anatomical sketches and tied her papers inside with a faded ribbon. She took up armloads of books and scattered them about the shelves, almost dancing as she moved in and out of bays, up and down the gallery stairs. It would take her days to find them all again, these books with their damning marginalia, but it would take a stranger weeks. Finally, swiftly, she disposed of the anatomical sketches behind a rank of foreign dictionaries, tore the blotter from her desk pad and tossed it burning into the fireplace, snatched up the heavy portfolio and her pocketbook and fled for the door.

Doing what, Lucy?

She seemed to be discovering that as it got done.

Going where, Lucy?

She would likely discover that as well.

But it was only a dream.

The same pub, too early for a crowd.

Resentful at being called away from his typewriter, Graham sat at a table under the small-paned window, scribbling on a tablet of ruled paper: real work this time, distilling interviews into news. The midmorning sun fought through thin clouds and thick, old glass to raise a gleam from the polished table. He didn't notice. He did notice the brewer's dray that creaked to a stop outside, its high sides painted with the brewer's slogan—Our Best Bitter is Better! Barrels rumbled off the tailgate, enormous horses stamped iron-shod feet, and he experienced one of those hiccups in time, a flash of his childhood when horses were everywhere and motorcars were rare. Change, he thought. Would we dread it so much if it didn't sneak up on us from behind?

"What do you do," she said, "if you have a story no one will believe?"

"Don't write it." He rescued his notes from the descending bulk of a leather-bound portfolio. The thump of its landing was lost in the grumble of barrel rims being rolled across the stone floor. "You could have asked me that over the telephone."

She sat down and drank from his glass. It was an unprecedented intimacy and he watched, astonished, the tilt of the glass and the long swallow. The bitter made her grimace even as she sucked the dampness off her upper lip. Oh, Lucy, he thought. What is this, now? A barman materialized, wiping his hands on his long white apron.

"Brandy, please," she said.

"She means the real stuff, Jock," Graham said. "In one of those fat glasses that spill all down your chin."

"A snifter, sir, yes, thank you, sir," said Jock, his accent refined to the point of sarcasm. But he came back with the brandy and another pint for Graham. Graham finished off the old pint and then looked at Lucy. She was shivering from too harsh a swallow—Our Best Brandy Isn't Better—and put the back of her hand to her mouth, a fascinating gesture, but they all were, her gestures like a private conversation between Lucy and herself, and she had such beautiful hands . . . Graham gave his second pint a wary look and pushed it away. Trouble, he thought. And then looked at her again and woke up to her pallor and bruised eyelids: trouble indeed.

"But what do you really do?" she said, and lowered her hand.

He had to retrieve her initial question. "Really don't write it. What would be the point?"

"What if people should believe it? What if they need to know?"

Graham hooted with laughter. "There is no such story. Listen, love, you can't tell the glorious public anything for their own good, not unless you're in advertising. One of the great mysteries of life. Tell them snake oil cures warts and they're happy to pay a shilling an ounce. Tell them the Country Hospital Fund requires property taxes to increase by a shilling next year and consider the outrage!" He drank from his beer, then remembered and set it aside.

"Maybe outrage cures warts," she said with a smile that made him feel she was looking at him for the first time.

"Maybe snake oil does. What's your story that no one will believe?"

"Maybe magic does."

"Cut a potato with a silver knife and bury it by the light of a full moon."

Her smile grew lighter, questioning.

"Magic," he explained. "To cure warts."

"Shhh." She reached across the table and touched her fingers to his lips. "Not so loud. He might hear you."

She wasn't smiling now. He knew what he was supposed to ask, but it took him a moment, seduced as he was by a touch that lingered after she had taken her hand away. What is this, Lucy? What the hell?

"Who might hear?"

She didn't answer him directly. "Do you believe in magic?"

"Do I believe in . . . are we talking philosophy? History? Curing warts?"

"Magic," she said, as if it were a perfectly sensible thing to say in an empty pub on a day in early spring. "Here and now, curing warts, whatever you like."

"No. Never tell me that's your story." His eyes wandered to the fat portfolio between them on the table. "What is that, dispatches from a thousand years ago? Or is all this just leading up to something else?"

"Magic is real. Here and now. And I can prove it."

She had a faint smile and a tension that dared him to take her seriously, but was she serious?

"You're dead right, chicken: nobody will believe you."

"But I can prove it. I can. And it's easy, anyone can do it who's ever read a newspaper, seen a newsreel at the moving picture show. Anyone who learned their history lessons at school."

"What?" This whole conversation was the set-up for an insult to his intelligence. "Can you possibly be talking about who I think you're talking about? That stuffed suit the royals haul out for parades! That dressmaker's dummy! That moth-eaten remainder from a waxwork museum! What the hell has come over you?" His gaze was caught again by her portfolio. "Oh, Lucy. Lucy, no. *This* is your life's work? *This* is what you've been chasing after all this time?"

She looked down as if she were surprised to see the battered folio case on the table. Her cheeks were flushed and her smile had fled; he felt a stab of shame, as if he'd been picking on the slow child at school; but all the same!

"Of all the dull corners of history you could have chosen," he said before he could change tack. "Well, all right. But please don't suggest the Marshal of Whatsisname is news. Really, old darling, believability is not the issue. Sheer, unadulterated boredom is the issue."

"Didn't you ever scare yourself with the stories when you were a child?" Her voice was quiet, and though there was a humorous quirk to her brows she didn't meet his eyes. "The end of an empire, the end of an age. The end of magic. And the one who did it just goes on and on . . . "

"I know. 'Don't stay out after dark, *he* might get you!' But that was just to make staying out after dark more fun." Studying her face, Graham found himself increasingly sorry for his scorn. She always looked delicate; at this moment she looked frail. "I still don't get what this is about? The story no one will believe?"

"Magic is still alive," she said, almost in a whisper. "And I can prove it."

"All right. What's your proof?"

"The Marshal of Kallisfane."

"But he ended it." He leaned forward, as if it was important to convince her. "He brought the dread empire down and put an end to magic. Hurray for the dawn of reason and the rule of law."

"A thousand years ago."

"Give or take."

"Then what's keeping him alive?"

"What . . . " Graham scratched his chin. He was on the verge of laughter, because though it was nonsense, it was clever nonsense. "Well, he's a remnant, isn't he? Sort of . . . a leftover. Wasn't it supposed to be the doing of it, whatever he did, that preserved him? Dried prunes, salt cod, the Marshal of Whatsisname?"

"Are you asking me, or telling me?"

"I am telling you," he said pompously, "what they taught us in school."

But the more he tried to jolly her out of it, the more solemn she became.

"That," she said with one of those direct, heartstopping looks, "is what he told someone a long time ago."

"There you are, then."

"And he's a reliable source, is he? Mister Newspaperman?"

"Oh, come on!" He was stung by her echo of his scorn. "It's clever, I grant you, but you don't think you're the first person ever to think of it, do you?"

"No," she said, her gaze falling again to her papers. "No, I don't."

"Even if it's a neat bit of logic, it doesn't go anywhere, does it? I mean, so what if he is . . . " (he felt like an ass for saying the word) " . . . magical. If he's the only magical thing in the world, what's it good for? He's an anomaly, the exception that proves the rule."

"That just means 'tests the rule'. The challenge to the rule. Did you know that?" This, apparently to the portfolio.

"And it's no kind of newspaper story," he forged on, though he was starting to hate the sound of his own voice. "You do know that, right?"

"Oh, yes. I know. Because no one will believe it, and no one will care."

"Well, listen . . . " By this time feeling like an utter shit. "There's nothing wrong with the idea. I mean, as an idea. Philosophy, history, all that. Very profound."

"Rest easy, my hero. I wasn't going to ask you to put it in your paper."

She smiled, finally, but she didn't quite met his gaze. And then before he knew it she was gathering up the weighty portfolio and bending down to kiss him, which she never did, a press of her lips to the corner of his mouth, a gesture as mysterious and expressive of any of hers, warm and sad and what? What is this, Lucy? What the hell *is* this?

But by the time it occurred to him simply to ask, she was gone.

———

Lucy had called up Graham with the vague notion of asking for help, or perhaps for less than that, for comradeship, a shoulder braced against her own. So his contempt stung, and confused her, too, because she could have argued against it, but what if he was wrong? What if the danger was real? It *was* real, it was the crooked backward course she had been plotting all this time. So if she was wrong, if she had been chasing nothing more than a scholar's delusion, then she was a fool, but she was safe. And if she wasn't wrong, then *he* was safe, because she had taken her proof away unshared. And wasn't it just a dream? She didn't know. She could not explain the certainty of danger, even to herself. She went home.

And walking from the bus stop (the bus easier than hunting for a cab so close to noon) she turned the corner into the square and saw him.

Him.

Benbury Square was really three squares nested one inside the other: the outer square of townhouses; then the square of cobblestone pavement fronting the houses; then the square of the central garden, hemmed in by palings and punctuated by trees. There were beds of turned earth, two benches awaiting this year's coat of paint, and a rounded patch of lawn already showing green. And on the lawn stood a man wearing a double-breasted overcoat of the sober, fashionless type favored by royalty. As Lucy had said to Graham, one saw this figure sometimes in the newsreels: herky-jerky frames of celluloid gray, at once luminous and drab, of the king opening the High Court or greeting a Special Envoy, with this stiff dark figure in the background. Stuffed suit, waxwork dummy, museum mannequin waiting for his armor. He stood so dreadfully still on the greening lawn. Watching Lucy's house.

Lucy drifted backwards, taking a glacial age to slip back

around the corner. She felt transparent as a ghost, as if her substance had been stripped by shock, leaving nothing but the damp gray chill of the day. She drifted, and even around the corner she could feel him, as if she were a compass and he, black as iron, were a magnetic pole. Still walking backwards, she was jostled by a passer-by, and suddenly the world leapt into existence: not a ghostly arena hushed with anticipation, but a living city, busy with pedestrians, motor cabs squawking their horns and delivery-van horses clattering on metal-shod hooves.

She ran until she could not breathe around the stitch in her side.

She rode a bus until the conductor turned her off at the end of its route, and then she rode another one.

She did not know where to go. The very concept of hiding was equivocal, denying as it did her passage from there to here. Hadn't her feet pressed all that ground? Didn't the tires of the bus? Wasn't there a trail?

Hadn't he, even he, left a trail?

The buses all seemed to turn her back towards the center of the city. After a bit she realized this was no arcane conspiracy, it was simply the logic of transportation: where else would the buses go? But getting off was hard. She looked anxiously through the dusty windows, expecting that stiff, dark, figure; or if not that, then the rumored black motorcars of the Regiment No One Ever Saw.

There were black cars, but they were only taxicabs. She hoped. She dared. She descended the high steps onto the curb and found herself in a neighborhood she knew, the politely shabby territory behind the national library, realm of scholars and writers, private libraries and obscure museums, bookstores and cafés. She was known here. She could not possibly go to ground here. But her feet were on pavement they knew, and they took her to one of the smaller train stations in the city where she bought a ticket for a slow suburban train leaving in half an hour.

Half an hour. A terrifying gulf of time.

She sat, her feet throbbing in her not very sensible shoes, and watched the suburban shoppers flock and scatter like pigeons. She eyed the crippled clock above the ticket booth that refused to move its hands any faster than a creep. She studied the Departures board, looking for the hundredth time for a train that left any sooner. Which means that she must have look at that one word a hundred times before she saw it. Palton. A country town, one stop among many, so why did it swim slowly up into her consciousness like a fish rising to the hook? Palton, Palton . . .

Palton, where only last week two teachers had been dismissed to cover up the "hysteria" amongst the students of a country school. Palton, that lay tucked under the haunted peak of Breadon How. Palton, that was only a crow's flight away from the castle at Denbreath.

It was like finding a path in the trackless wood. She had somewhere to go.

The last thing Lucy expected was to fall asleep on the train, but that was what she did, all but resting her head on the shoulder of the plump girl who had entered the compartment with a bevy of aunts just as the train pulled away. While they clucked over their parcels Lucy slipped gently into the murmur of voices, the swaying of the carriage, the rhythm of the wheels. Outside the window the city peeled away, diminishing into low brick districts, into gray waste grounds, into greening suburbs half-veiled by the engine's steam. The train's whistle shrieked at crossings and hooted for stations like a huge iron owl. Lucy half-slept while the train was in motion, half-woke when it crawled into one station and the next. The ladies left in a flurry of packages and she had the compartment to herself until a young man looked shyly in.

"Do you mind, miss?"

"No," she said. He had a plain, open face, and an old raincoat slung over an off-the-rack suit that gave an impression of untidiness despite the bright polish of his enormous black shoes. Perhaps it was just that men of a certain size shouldn't wear suits: he wasn't fat, but he was very large. He gave Lucy a nervous smile and tucked himself away behind a paperback book that looked small in his hands. She relaxed a little; yet as the train rolled on, she began to find the racketing rhythm of the wheels more implacable than soothing. *To Palton to Palton to Palton* and what was she going to do when she got there? Something, she thought with her hands clenched into sharp-knuckled fists. Something to oppose. Something to defy.

Unable to sit still, she got up and slid open the door to the corridor. The countryside spread over brown fields and grey-green trees to the dusky northern hills. The smoke of burning thatch rose to meet the end of the day, drawing down the clouds. Lucy leaned against the corridor window, feeling a hard, old-woman's sadness that seemed like the older sister to her fear, as if part of her knew that things weren't going to turn out well. To defy, yes, that seemed necessary. That did not mean that she, knowing what she knew, could hope to overcome. She thought of the books scattered throughout her grandfather's library. She thought of her grandfather, and her mother, and Graham. She thought of the hasty letter she had written, and of the papers she had abandoned to the care of the Left Luggage Office of Skillyham Station, and of the claim check that had gone into the post just as the train was called.

A woman swaying down the corridor to the end of the carriage excused herself as she bumped into Lucy. Lucy pressed herself aside, and through the window of the compartment's glass door she caught the eye of the large young man with the book, who was watching her as patiently and unfeelingly as the fox watches the brush pile, waiting for the hare.

———

My hero,

Here is the story no one wants to know:

218 years ago, the Marshal of Kallisfane founded Madrigal College's Chair of Imperial Studies, the only one in that subject in the university. Since the founding, there have been twenty-nine Fellows, as compared to an average of sixteen Fellows in the same period of time across all other subjects. Of those twenty-nine Fellows, only six in 218 years have died peacefully of old age. Three have simply disappeared—the rest have died of suicide, unexplained accident, or outright murder. Check the university records and local police blotters: this is fact. Also ask yourself: Why is there only one fellowship in Imperial History, when we are, today, living in the ruins of that empire? In the university, it is because every time another such fellowship has been proposed—even when the proposal

includes generous funding—the University Council has declined.
The only reason ever offered: such a chair already exists. Never mind
that six different colleges sport research chairs in Modern History.
There shall only ever be one chair in Imperial History, and the
scholars who hold that chair are more likely to die violently than if
they joined the army or worked in a mine . . .

They waited until she stepped off the train in Palton.

The large young man, with his book in his coat pocket, followed her onto the platform and was joined by an older man, thin enough to hide in his shadow, who materialized out of the engine's steam.

"Please, Miss Donne," said the older man as he took her elbow, "let's not have a fuss."

They didn't have a fuss. It was exactly as though she had been met by friends. The large young man took her pocket book and rifled through it, but he did it so calmly no one seemed to notice. The ticket collector took Lucy's ticket from his hand without a flicker and they walked out into the astonishing freshness of the spring evening. There was the cobbled street of the country town, the sketch of chimney pots against the violet sky. The air was impossibly sweet after the stuffiness of the train. Instinct made Lucy look up, but clouds hid the stars. Looking down she saw the massive shape of the long black car pulling up to the station door. There was something inevitable about that car, about the dusk, about the country quiet pouring in around the wail of the departing train. She drew a long breath with a strange kind of eagerness. Whatever else happened, she was going to *know*.

"That's right, Miss Donne," said the older man as he opened the rear door. "Nothing to be frightened of here."

———•◦•◦•———

. . . But it isn't only scholars he is keeping under his thumb. Seventy-two years ago the village of Galburgh in South Pevenshire was digging up a section of the commons at the edge of the village to widen a carriage road. In the course of the work they uncovered a stretch of old paving which, when it was taken up, proved to cover a spring that drained into the Macklebrook via an underground channel. There was some debate, reported in the parish records, as to whether to cover the spring and carry on with the road or to leave it uncovered and put it to some use. In the meantime, however, workmen who drank from the spring complained of dreams of such terrible import that one man joined an overseas missionary society and another committed suicide. The parish priest called upon the bishop for advice, but no church action was ever taken, for the simple reason that that was the month in which the Crown passed the Commons Development Act which allowed, and still allows, the sale of common land by parish councils for the "creation or development of such industries, enterprises, public buildings, etc, to the benefit of the township." The commons was bought, the spring was paved over, and a new village police station built on the spot. According to the Pevenshire newspapers of the time, the Marshal of Kallisfane was on hand for the new station's official opening.

Graham, the king overturned a common-use law of centuries' standing so that the Revenant could pave over a spring and put it under guard. And that is one of the most harmless stories that comes to mind . . .

The motorcar slid down narrow country roads, carrying Lucy into the night. Lucy's companion from the train shared the back seat with her, but with the darkness to hide his watchful gaze he was just the shy young man abashed by his own size, and then even less than that, as if he were absorbed into the car itself, just one more shade of dark. The air was chill, whistling with drafts, but it smelled warmly of tobacco and leather, leaf-mold and aging upholstery. Lucy was reminded of being chauffeured from school to her grandfather's country house, always knowing that the man behind the wheel reckoned she was no more than an excuse to take the new car, hand-built in her grandfather's own stable, out for a drive. She had never minded that feeling. It had been the real holiday between the heated friendships and rivalries of school and the equally perilous attentions of her mother, her cousins, her aunts. Tonight, as the wind whined in around the windows and the chill soaked through her sensible tweed, she felt as though she were wrapped in a ghost of that comfort. But while she acknowledged that ghost, she did not let it fool her. In the end, she thought, it was just the calm certainty of doom.

. . . for he is rarely inclined to hold his hand. Consider the fishers of Belmouth, who only two years ago complained of seals with human voices wrecking their nets and stealing their fish, but paying for their plunder with prophecy and song. The Marshal of Kallisfane, according to your very own newspaper, was granted use of the royal yacht for a late-autumn cruise ending

in Belmouth harbor. Captain Ellerby, master of the king's yacht, reported cloudless skies, light breezes, and an easy sail. That same day, the entire fishing fleet of Belmouth was lost in a freak storm. We will never know if it was because those fishermen were telling stories of talking seals, or if it was because of what those seals were saying. Every man off those boats is presumed drowned. Fifty-seven men . . .

The black motorcar of the Unnamed Regiment paused just long enough for an iron gate to swing open. They eased past a saluting sentry and onto a drive. It was late. They had traveled much further than Denbreath. Trees flickered in the edge of the headlamps' glow, then fell away into blackness and an impression of rough ground. The car's note deepened as it began to climb. Then even the ground fell away, and Lucy's heart stopped for an instant of disoriented terror—but they were not flying, only following the back of a ridge, its steep slope invisible in the dark. That moment of fear lingered, a quickening in her belly and a tightening in her flesh, prelude to the shock of arrival.

. . . And if even the list of the dead is still not enough to make anyone care—and Graham, I know hundreds of these stories— then consider our history. Consider the holy wars in which the ancient pantheon and its temples were thrown down. Thousands of priests hanged or burned, their congregations killed, persecuted, scattered, an entire faith relegated to a footnote in the history books, because we have no ancient history, no memory, and no

way to know what those priests once knew about the world or the magic the Revenant claims to have killed a thousand years ago.

He isn't a joke, Graham, he isn't a scarecrow stuffed with straw. He isn't even a walking corpse. He is a tombstone, and he has spent the last thousand years keeping magic in its grave.

My train is leaving, I must fly—

Lucy

Perhaps it was the starless night they had traveled through, perhaps it was the chill and the wood-rot smell of age, but Lucy was exquisitely aware of the stony weight of the castle that swallowed her up. She felt as if she had been eaten by a mountain, as if the dark were the perfect and immutable dark of a mine. And there was the silence, too, a deep, conscious, listening silence. Even her escorts seemed reluctant to intrude; they stepped softly, spoke in undertones to the men at the door.

What must it be like to work for the Undying, to run his bloody errands, to keep his house?

They ushered her through the great hall, shadowy as a cathedral, and down a back-eddy of a corridor to a chapel. In the corridors there were electric lights strung along the plastered walls, but in the chapel there were only banks of candles burning with a honey smell. Light and warmth hovered in the narrow room, complimenting rather than banishing the cold and dark. The high white walls were decked with brass memorial plaques, mirrors for the ranks of flame burning in their corner stands, and there were more plaques set in the floor. There were no pews, only a plain altar stone and the candles, and the Sacred Flame hanging on the end wall, a tapered silver oval like the point of a spear.

The room was so quiet Lucy could hear the rustle of the many candleflames, and the footsteps coming down the hall.

He still wore his overcoat, buttoned to show only his trouser hems and the neat square knot of his tie. His head was bare, his thick dark hair neatly combed, his face expressionless, lifeless . . . dead. Lucy thought his eyes were dark, but she found it impossible to meet them. She did not want to see them or be seen by them. Her heart beat with a trapped flutter, remembering the bird in her dream.

"Miss Donne," he said, "do you know why you are here?"

His voice shocked her: an ordinary baritone, a little rough, but without menace. No sullen echo of the grave.

"I dreamed . . . "

He waited for her to finish, as patient as the walls. The pause was so long it finally seemed that Lucy's fear had peaked, that she had breasted some steep rise and found herself still standing. She took what felt like her first breath since he entered the room and said, laying her cards on the table or throwing them to the wind,

"I have been studying you. I have researched you, I have learned . . . I have learned some of what you are . . . " Lucy tailed off again, this time with a blush. How childish that sounded! And how intimate, with an unwarranted, uninvited intimacy.

"And you dreamed," he said, inflectionless.

"I did not dream you outside my house," she said. *You*. That was the intimacy: saying not *him*, but *you*. You.

Lucy, is it only fear that makes your heart race?

He had stepped further into the chapel without her noticing. She drifted away from his advance.

"You looked for me. You found me." He began to unbutton his overcoat, standing before the altar, and Lucy realized there was something lying on the stone as if for consecration. She tore her gaze away, desperate not to have seen what she saw. The Marshal of Kallisfane shrugged his coat from his shoulders and bent to lay it on the floor, and Lucy closed her eyes, trembling in every bone.

This was beyond fear. This was the end of her life.

"Me, and some of what I am," he went on. "Tell me what you think you know."

And there it was, still, the magic of intimacy; of talking with him, her whole treasure store of knowledge rising in her mind. Who he was, who she was.

Lucy opened her eyes and accepted what she saw: the sword on the altar, the Marshal of Kallisfane laying his suit jacket, neatly folded, next to his coat on the floor. He looked smaller in his shirtsleeves, but she could see the muscles in his arms as he began to unknot his tie.

She was very conscious of her trembling body, her stuttering heart, the dizzying lack of air.

"I know that magic did not die with the Empire."

"True." He slipped his tie from his collar.

"I know . . . " Breath failed her. Her chest hurt, a widening pain from her breastbone to her shoulder blade, and for the first time she began to wonder if this was only fear. It felt as though he crowded all the air out of the room, pressed the blood out of her heart. Even the candles seemed to be growing dim. "I know you have been fighting all this time to keep magic out of the world. I know you have lied to us, and killed us, and led us by the nose."

"Go on." The tie went into one trouser pocket, cuff links into another. He began to roll up his sleeves, revealing powerful wrists and forearms shadowed with dark hair.

Lucy leaned against the wall. The pain pried into her shoulder, her wrist. I'm going to die, she thought, before he gets a chance to kill me.

"I know the worst lie you've ever told," she said.

"Tell me." He unbuttoned his collar and tossed it onto his coat. He looked completely human now, and Lucy could hardly bear to look at him.

"That you have no magic of your own."

He was finally still. "Why is that the worst lie?"

"Because you betray . . . you betray magic. The world, the gods, the Divine. You betray *us*. You lie . . . " She had no air left. The pain grew like a tree through her chest, down her arm.

"What do you imagine magic is, that you think I've done wrong in betraying it?"

"Life," she whispered. "You're the tombstone. You're the paving over the well."

"You know nothing of magic."

She looked at him past the sparkling darkness in her eyes and for an instant she was entirely *Lucy*, as if she had regained the fear-scattered pieces of herself just in time for the end. Her hand described a fluttering moth's circle in the air and she said faintly, lightly,

"Dying gives one a certain insight. So does living, I suppose. Perhaps I know something you don't."

"I have always considered the possibility," he said. He turned to the altar and with a movement devoid of ceremony he picked up the sword. Steel rang gently off the stone; light slid like water off the steel. "Tell me, Miss Donne. What did you hope to accomplish in Palton this afternoon?"

Palton? This afternoon? A lifetime ago.

"Breadon How. The Cold Hounds. I thought . . . "

"Yes?"

"I thought I . . . "

"You thought you could oppose me. You thought you could raise up some power I have kept buried for nine hundred years."

"No." Lucy's tears caught the light like the steel. "But I thought I had to try."

"Ah." It sounded oddly like satisfaction. He turned the blade in his hand as if he too wanted to see the candlelight run off its edge. "You aren't the first to think that."

"I know."

"The others all failed."

She knew.

He lifted the sword, a man in modern dress playing with an archaic toy—but he did not look ridiculous. He looked like himself. He looked like death.

"Does your heart pain you?"

"Yes." The pain *was* her heart, condensed into a pulsing star lodged against her spine.

"You might have succeeded at Breadon How, Miss Donne, although I think you would not have found the Cold Hounds comfortable allies. But you might well have awakened them. I believed it after dreaming your dream, and I think it even more

157

likely now. But you are wrong about one thing, and your heart, Miss Donne, is wiser than you. Your heart, so full of life, knows that I am not magic. I am the antithesis, Miss Donne. I am exactly what you called me: a tombstone. For I promise you, Miss Donne, if I had one glimmer of magic in me, I would have ended this curse of a life the instant I knew my emperor was dead."

"But you killed him?"

"My emperor, the last emperor. Yes, I killed him, but it was treachery, Miss Donne, not magic. And it was not life that he would have summoned if I had not stopped him, very far from life, that magic he would have raised. Oh, I won't call it death. Not life, not death: a denial of both. But you do not understand me."

"I want to. Tell me . . . " But the pain clenched, her pulse stumbled, racing at the edge of a fall.

"Ah, but it is not your understanding that I need. Put out your hand."

Lucy was aware of the sword he held as she was aware of her exhausted heart, her stuttering blood, but she had come too far for petty defiance. She held out her shaking hand and he pressed the sword's hilt against her palm.

"Take it," he said. "Hold hard."

Her hand clenched in instinctual response as he let go, so she did not drop it, but the point chimed when it struck the floor. The blade was heavy, the leather-wrapped grip warmer than her own chilled flesh.

The Marshal of Kallisfane knelt on the floor and began to unbutton his shirt.

"No," Lucy said.

He ignored this so completely the word might have been a burning wick, a drop of wax. He took the neck of his undershirt in both hands and tore it to bare his chest. He seemed to diminish at every stage, smaller and smaller, now showing bone as well as muscle beneath the pale skin.

"Just here," he said, pointing, as if she might have missed it, to the thick crosshatch of scars between his nipple and his breastbone.

Lucy used the sword's weight to drag herself away from the supporting wall, though her heart beat like a bird crushed between icy hands. Pain tasted like a new penny on her tongue.

"How many times . . . ?"

"Oh, many." He spoke as if he still stood over her, as if he were not half-naked on his knees. "Not always in search of death. Men have needed to test me, to be sure of who or what I am."

"And you want this?" The point of the sword jittered across a memorial stone, struck a spark from a date of birth.

"Call this," he said, "my test of you."

She put her free hand to her own breast, as though the pain she felt there was the pain of those terrible scars.

"Here," he said, and he lifted the sword, cutting his fingers on the edge as he aimed the point at his heart. "Lean your weight against the hilt, it needs no more than that."

The star behind Lucy's own heart bloomed in sympathy. She let go the hilt, and though he tried to hold the blade, it pulled itself out of his grasp, cutting his palm, ringing like a bell on the floor. Lucy fell to her knees. Her hand traveled the distance between her heart and his. She felt his scars, his warm and living skin.

"I pass your test," she whispered on the last of her breath. "I am not you."

Then there was no more light, no more air.

No more pain.

The envelope containing a left-luggage claim check was collected from the mailbox in the train station not long after the Palton train pulled away from the platform. It was sorted that day and delivered to Graham's flat the next morning at 10:12. Graham, however, was not there to receive it. He had interviews to conduct, an article to write, and an argument to have with his editor after he handed in his copy. He stopped for a drink and a bite to eat with some of his colleagues, and finally reached his flat around 9—early for him, but after the argument he was in an unsociable mood. So an early night for once, and for once, only the one drink. He unlocked the street door, fished his mail out of its box, and sorted through it as he climbed the stairs.

Lucy's handwriting stopped him cold three stairs below the landing.

Lucy, Lucy. He hadn't thought about her all day, and yet here she was. A drink of beer, a touch, a kiss. He could feel her mouth against the corner of his mouth, her lips warm and mobile, as if they shaped a thought even as she kissed him.

Graham shook himself, finished the climb to his flat and let himself inside. With Lucy's letter in his hand, he saw the place as he would if she were here: dusty, not too untidy, but uncared-for, unloved. Somehow all his things acquired a sepia tone, regardless of their original colors, as if a couch or a lampshade could fade like a plant for lack of attention. He turned on the desk lamp, which at least afforded kinder shadows, leaving the letters on the desk while he shed his coat and tie, pulled on a sweater, poured himself a drink. Only two for the night, so he was still ahead. Finally he sat, his desk chair creaking as he leaned back against the spring, and picked up her letter again. Her handwriting, elegant but hard to decipher, reminded him of her gestures, her hands.

He realized he was reluctant to open the letter. Love note, brush off, the research notes he was waiting for? He turned the envelope in his hands. Cheap, mass-produced, a far cry from the heavy rag of her usual stationary. He tapped it edge-on against his desk, feeling the shift of several folded sheets inside. Research notes, he decided, and did not know if he was relieved or—Well, but he did know, didn't he? Because he didn't believe in the love note, kiss or no kiss. He wasn't sure he believed in the kiss.

He took a drink, tore the envelope, shook out the letter and a claim check, a rectangle of red pasteboard that lay on his inky blotter, the only spot of color in the room. He let it lie, unfolded pages.

My hero, here is the story no one wants to know . . .

He read it once distractedly, remembering their conversation in the pub. His scorn, he remembered that, and her face, delicate and tired. He remembered that better than he remembered her words. *Proof*, she had said, and, *I can prove it.*

He threw the letter down, poured himself more whiskey, paced, muttering, around the room.

Then he read the letter again, forcing his attention onto the points that could be verified: parish records, newspapers, police reports.

He paced again, glass in hand. "I don't believe it." And, "Come on, Lucy! Magic isn't *news*."

An imagined Lucy said, "The systematic murder of university professors isn't news? The manipulation of the Crown to the detriment of rural villages isn't news?"

"I don't believe it. Not a word, Lucy. I don't."

But it could be checked. Some of it could be. University records, harbormaster's logs. He emptied his glass and started for the drinks cabinet, then changed course for the desk.

"What bloody train? Where the hell did you go?"

The claim check stared up at him. Left Luggage. Skillyham Station. Hours: 6 a.m.—Midnight.

He glanced at his watch, snatched up his coat and his keys.

———

Whirr, whirr, click.

"Benbury oh-oh-nine-three."

"Could I speak with Miss Lucy Donne?"

There was a pause, a most definite pause, and a deepening chill. "Who is calling, please?"

Something was wrong. "A colleague at the national library. We were doing some research together and she has some materials I need. If I could speak with Miss Donne . . . I know it's early . . . you can assure her I will be brief if she is otherwise engaged . . . "

Another pause. Then, ominously, another voice. "Sir, Miss Donne is not available. If you give me your name and a telephone number and address where you can be reached I will be sure to pass the message along."

Graham hung the receiver gently on its hook, breaking the connection. Then he set the telephone on the floor, where it kept company with his typewriter, his dictionary, his mug full of pencils. Lucy's papers covered his desk, sheet after sheet of foolscap, typewriter bond, notepaper and envelopes and scraps, a drifting sea of her handwriting that threatened to drown the desk. She kept meticulous record of her researches, but it was in no sort of order at all. And yet the sheer mass of it was compelling. Whatever one thought of old wives tales, the whispered glories of the magical past—and he had stored up a far-ranging argument on that score—it was difficult to deny that the Marshal of Kallisfane was actively at large in the world, working toward some goal.

Or did he have a goal? Could all of this be, what? The senile boredom of a very old man? The directed service of an agent of the Crown?

There were more possibilities the farther away he looked from Lucy's obsession with magic, but he couldn't deny the weight of her research. He wanted to argue it out with her. He wanted her to lead him through the chaos, form an argument, defend her conclusions—*convince* him if that was what was in the cards—but most of all he wanted her to be here. After a night of reading about death, disappearance, suppression, manipulation, he was all too ready to read bad news into that brief conversation with whomever it was that answered the telephone at Lucy's house. Especially that second voice asking his name, his telephone number, his address. Why his address, when there he was talking on the telephone? Was it because, with the newly automated exchanges, it was more difficult to trace a call? And do upper servants really "pass messages along"?

My train is leaving, I must fly—

Fly where, Lucy, damn you? And why?

Oh, Lucy, Lucy. What the hell am I supposed to do with all this?

What do you do if you have a story no one will believe?

The answer did not come so glibly this time. He sat with his elbows holding down a drift of paper and his hands clenched before his mouth. What do you do if you have a story you don't dare to tell?

"Because if you're right, Lucy . . . " If you're right about even half of this—forgetting the magic for a minute—don't you see what you have here? Not just the Revenant, but the police, the army, the church, the very Crown! And even if you ducked the whole boiling lot of them, who the hell else is there left to tell? The common people? The general public who go to church, who believe the police keep good citizens safe, who would be scared pissless if you told them you were bringing magic back into the world? The truth is, Lucy, you could publish a book and give it away on the street corners, and if the king said it was all for the good of the bloody realm, they'd believe him. They would say, thank you, Mister Revenant, sir, and toss the book on the fire, and you could kiss your hand to whatever it is you're looking for, justice or the cure for moral outrage, because you know what, Lucy? *They might be right.*

If magic is real. And if that's what the Marshal of Kallisfane has been doing: keeping magic out of the world all these years.

And if you're not just being a coward, Graham Isles, Mister Newspaperman.

My hero, here is the story that will destroy your life, your career, your every cherished illusion about yourself...

He bundled her papers back into the portfolio. Shaved, changed his shirt. Went to work.

He was not surprised to find a message waiting for him, directing him to his editor's office. Even if last night's dispute had not spawned fresh points of attack, he was late. He *was* surprised to find one of the crime reporters lying in ambush outside the editor's door.

"Just remember, Isles, you talk to me before you go anywhere."

"What?" Graham's attention was still more on Lucy than the world. "Go where?"

"Nowhere, until you talk to me."

Graham shut the office door in the man's anxious face.

"You took your time," his editor said. "Drowning your sorrows?"

"Research," Graham said shortly.

"Well, I've a bit more for you to do. Lucy Donne. You've heard, I suppose?"

Graham experienced the curious sensation of blood leaving his face as he went pale. A tightening, a cooling. "Heard what?"

"She went missing two nights ago. The family was keeping it quiet, figuring she'd turn up on her own, I suppose, but now the police have issued a bulletin. We've got a friend in CID who will tell us what comes of it—a dog's breakfast of bus conductors and ticket sellers so far—but no one's getting in to see the family. But you worked with her quite a bit, didn't you? Something in the way of being friends?"

"Something in the way." Graham worked his tongue in his dry mouth. "Do they think . . . What do they think?"

"Reserving their opinions for the moment, but you can suppose they lie somewhere between scandalous and dead. What do *you* think? You know her. Inside information will win your employer's approval, affection, and possibly a wee bonus on the side."

Graham saw that last scribbled line. *My train is leaving, I must fly*—Had she just played into the Revenant's hands, leaving everyone a trail that went nowhere? Or had she successfully escaped his notice—and gone where?

He shook his head. "Sorry, I don't have a clue. Actually," he added with perfect honesty, "I'm stunned."

"No boyfriends that you know of? No fights with the family? Storming off to leave them stewing and make the papers who cried havoc look like silly chumps when she comes home in perfect health?"

"That, no. I think she has a very high regard for her family, in her way." In her off-hand, defended, too-sensitive way.

"And no, er, lover's quarrel?"

His editor's feeble attempt at delicacy told Graham volumes about the rumors circulating in the newsroom this morning.

"Not a chance."

"No coppers here, son."

"I've bought her a drink or two, but that's as far as it ever went. Look," he said, a little desperate in the face of skepticism, "the last time I saw her she told me a story about the Marshal of Kallisfane. I mean . . . " He shrugged, put out his hands.

"A funny story?"

"Not particularly."

His editor nodded, accepting this as proof of the absence of romance. "Well, if you think of anything. In the meantime, what about getting in to see the family? As a friend and colleague, I mean. Offer them the resources at your disposal."

"Do you mean the paper's resources?"

"Well, we wouldn't mind posting notice of a reward for information received, especially if it came with an exclusive interview with the mother. That might open the door for you. Also keeping in mind that she did work for us, even if she was freelance and, well, an amateur. We owe her our support." This was said, not with self-righteousness, but with the tone of a newsman trying a subhead out loud.

Graham felt a quickening, the conception of an idea. "If I had a note on the publisher's letterhead?"

His editor scratched his chin and said he would see what he could do.

"Are there any more questions, Mr. Isles?"

Sir Roger Donne picked up the paper knife on his blotter and set it a little to one side. It was the ninth time he had made that gesture in the course of the interview and it was starting to obsess Graham. He made a mark beside eight other marks in his notebook.

"Sir Roger, you have been very forthcoming."

Though in fact, Lucy's grandfather had not said any more than a hundred other anxious relatives Graham had interviewed over the years. *She's a good girl, really. She'd never stay away if she could come home.* And sometimes they were right, and sometimes they were wrong, and the one was as likely to crush a loving family as the other. *We're just praying she's all right, wherever she is.*

"Then if that is all." Sir Roger put his hands on the edge of his desk, preparatory to rising.

"There is one other thing." Graham hesitated, as he had been hesitating all along. He felt a flash of empathy for Lucy, remembering again their last conversation: her tentative opening, his scorn.

Sir Roger frowned into the pause. "I hope, Mr. Isles, that you and your superiors are sincere in your offer of help. It would add enormously to the pain and distress of Lucy's mother if old scandals are raked up out of the past, and it would do no good whatsoever. I'm sure I can rely on you in this matter."

"No, it isn't that. I mean, yes, sir, you can rely on us to be discreet." Although if the old man thought the tabloids weren't going to disinter the scandal of Lucy's fatherless state, he was more naïve than Graham supposed.

"What, then?"

"Are you aware of the nature of Lucy—of Miss Donne's research?"

Sir Roger's scowl deepened. "I was under the impression, Mr. Isles, that my granddaughter was providing background material for your newspaper articles. Are you suggesting that her work for you put her in some kind of danger?"

"No! Absolutely not. I was referring to her own private research."

"Lucy is an amateur historian. An intelligent and erudite young woman. And I can assure you, sir, that her 'private research' has no bearing the case whatsoever. She reads books, sir! No young woman has ever disappeared because of reading books."

"Even if the books she reads lead her into a pursuit of the Marshal of Kallisfane?" Graham kept his eyes on his notebook, as if was just one more question to make a note of, but eventually he had to look up into Sir Roger's silence.

For the first time Graham saw some family resemblance between Lucy and her grandfather, a ghost of her fragility and pallor, a reflection of her steady, unreadable stare. Sir Roger lifted a hand, touched the paper knife. Pushed himself away from the desk and stood.

"Come with me."

Sir Roger took him to the library, and it was a long walk through grand rooms, useless unless you were giving a party for three hundred friends. The library would have seemed just the same, as empty as a stage between shows, except that Graham had seen Lucy handle books, had seen how they spoke to her hands as well as her mind. Thousands of volumes, and any one of them might have come alive to her touch, her fingers slipping through their pages as if paper were fur, as if books could purr. For every window bay they passed he felt a jolt of anticipation, as if she might be standing there perusing the shelves, but she never was. Her absence persisted all the way down the room.

The table at the end bore a desk lamp, a blotter pad, a box of paper, and a neat stack of books. This tidy set-up obviously had nothing to do with the mad profusion of Lucy's papers and

Graham gave it no more than a glance. He turned to Sir Roger, waiting for him to explain, but Lucy's grandfather gestured at the table.

"Here is my granddaughter's research, Mr. Isles. A perfectly unexceptional genealogical study of her grandmother's family. Please, have a look."

Graham picked up a book from the pile. It was a ledger, a handwritten parish register, a record of births and deaths. He gave the pages a desultory ruffle with a distinct feeling of heat growing beneath his collar.

"Take your time," Sir Roger said. "There are some notes there, too, which you are welcome to read. You see, I want you to be absolutely satisfied on this point, Mr. Isles, because when your article appears in the newspaper, I want there to be no doubt in anyone's mind that my granddaughter is a perfectly innocent young woman. Which you should already know as well as I, if your claims of friendship have not been grossly exaggerated for the sake of this intrusion into our private affairs."

The heat rose into Graham's face. "Are you suggesting that research into the Marshal of Kallisfane would *not* be innocent?"

Sir Roger rocked back on his heels. "I am telling you that this is all there is. Lucy did nothing to deserve her fate."

"What fate?" Graham said, anger giving his reporter self full rein. "Do you know what has happened to her? Do you know where she is?"

"No! Of course—"

"So what fate do you think she *would* deserve if she had been studying the Marshal of Kallisfane?"

Sir Roger's face was as red as Graham's. "This is an outrage! I let you into my home only because your superiors assured me of their desire to help us find Lucy—"

"Do you want to find Lucy?"

"Of course!"

"Then why are you lying?"

"Get out!"

"Why are you covering up for the Revenant?"

"Get out before I throw you out!"

The story about Lucy's disappearance ran without any mention of the Marshal of Kallisfane. Not because of any interference from on high, but because Graham had written it that way. It had seemed the only reasonable thing to do. His editor would never have agreed to print unfounded allegations of a public figure, and to found the allegations on Lucy's research, unconfirmed as it was, would have been at best premature. There is still time to tell that story, he said to himself. But it was harder to say it to Lucy as she stared at him from the printed page. The paper had copied a studio portrait that made her look like a woodland fawn.

Graham paid for an uneaten meal and took the paper home with him; another early night, though he made no resolutions about the whiskey waiting for him in his flat. He was turning his key in the lock of the street door when a friendly voice said, "Mr. Isles? I wonder if you could give us a moment of your time?"

He turned, his keys in his hand, just in time to see the black motorcar pulling up to the curb.

In the Castle of Kallisfane the silence persisted. It was impossible not to be conscious of it, of the way a footfall or a word only threw it into sharper relief. Impossible, too, not to think of museums, mausoleums, tombstones, tombs. And so Lucy did think of them, but they were not gloomy thoughts. She felt as light as a hummingbird among the mourning wreaths, a petal on the breeze. The fact that her heart skipped and bounded like a puppy tumbling down a flight of stairs, the fact that her breath came in sips and gasps, the fact that her hands were icy and her lips were halfway numb: these facts were simply irrelevant. She was alive, alive in the Marshal's stronghold, alive and on her way to talk to him again.

She had to sit on the stairs to rest halfway down. Her guide, the thin balding man who, in her other life, had taken her arm in a train station and warned her not to make a fuss, waited patiently, cleaning under his fingernails with the thumbnail on the opposite hand.

The castle was disappointing at first, as the oldest castles tend to be, being small and cramped and dim. But age exerts a subtle fascination, most of all in the ancient place that is still inhabited. Lucy the historian thought of the famous men, the legendary men, who had trod these floors, who had passed through these doors, who had ridden out from these walls to impose a new order on their collapsing world.

The Marshal's order, Lucy, don't forget. The Marshal's chaos, too.

The Marshal's library was a pokey warren of badly lit rooms, old castle offices knocked together with shelves built to fit the awkward walls, and books and papers crammed in every which way to fill the shelves. Lucy the book hound was drawn like a nail to a magnet, but the scholar in her was shocked, even offended. Did the Marshal of Kallisfane, the embodiment of living history, have so little respect . . . ? But then she remembered the dead and vanished scholars, herself included, and felt a little pulse in her gut that had nothing to do with her damaged heart. Of course he had no respect. Respect, for history and for historians, was the very last thing he would have.

He met her in the largest room.

"Sit there," he said, gesturing to a chair by the door. "It would be better for you if you don't come too close."

Lucy had to believe him, with her blood scampering through her veins, but it didn't trouble her. He took all her attention. Was this what it would be like to be in love? The shape of him, the glance of light across his shaven cheek, the arch of his brow. The movement of his chest beneath the shirt and jacket and tie. The lightless eyes that woke a tremor in her skin. Not love—fear, in fact—and yet . . . Was there something of desire, some kind of desire, here? Or was it only that deceptive intimacy of being here with him, of knowing the scars that lay behind the armor of his suit?

"I wish I knew your name," Lucy said, breathless and fey.

"That isn't necessary." He was dismissive, faintly ironic. For some reason it made her laugh.

"No, I'm just curious. But I do wonder why I'm still alive?" She had lost the rhythm of breathing and had to snatch after air when her words failed. "But maybe that doesn't matter either. Maybe I'm only curious, a curious ghost, you must know so many."

The Marshal of Kallisfane looked at her a moment, his eyes

black in shadow, then pulled a chair away from the desk under the window and sat down facing her from across the room. (The room darkly walled in books, with a too-small rug on the stone floor, a window cut through thick walls, a paraffin heater exuding its peculiar oily smell. Lucy would only notice these things later, when their memory cast a shadow on her mind.)

"You said a thing to me last night," the Marshal said. "You said magic was life and I was its death, keeping it out of the world. I wonder why you think you know this? I wonder how you could know."

"Then you're curious, too. Such curious hauntings . . . " More air, and a stab at humility: "I don't, of course," except she spoiled it with a shrug and a coiling gesture with her hand. "Well, maybe it came to me in a dream."

"Magic was life and death, once. We used to say, the fires of creation, the breath of the gods. They did, the wizards and the priests. I was only a soldier, of course, I made my sacrifices and held to my oaths, no more than that. Most of us were like that. Magic was part of the mysteries, part of the world. The Cold Hounds of Breadon How were no different than the ice storms that blow out of the mountains in the north. They were the same. Their victims were the same. Living and dying was what humans did. Life and death was a matter for the gods."

It *was* like love. Lucy lay back in her chair, pinning her pulse with a thumb on her wrist, watching his dry, spare mouth shape his words. Oh, to say *you* to this man. Oh, to hear him say *we* and *I*.

"Caedemus was insane, but only in the manner of his kind. Wizard, priest, emperor's son: the godfire was in him—like a disease, you would say now, but then it was expected, desired even, it was the mark that made him heir. Not that he had powers," the Marshal added distastefully. "He *had* nothing, none of them did. They were not gods, only men . . . and women, some of them, like you. You need to know this. You will need to understand."

Oh, to hear this man say *you*. Lucy's heart found its rhythm as it quickened.

"They had nothing—*he*—had nothing," the Marshal said, speaking still of the emperor he betrayed. "He was no more than a door through which magic could sometimes step into the world. And he knew it. Being a little madder than the rest, he saw it clear. And being a little madder than the rest, he sought to change that fact, to change himself, to change the world. To become magic. To transform the human world of living and dying into the world of the gods where life and death stand still, where life and death are one . . . The perfect world, he called it. I was a soldier. He was what he was: a wizard, an emperor, insane. I have never understood what he desired. But what he tried to bring into the world. What he tried to make of the world . . . "

Lucy was nothing but the sight of him, the sound of his voice. She hung suspended over his hesitation as if it were a chasm in the earth.

"I know what it would have made of the world, because I know what it made of me when I killed him. Death and life: death *in* life. Perfection. The tombstone you saw in your dreams. And that is what I have been keeping out of the world these endless years. That is what I have been keeping out of the human world. Myself, writ large."

She thought of him as he had been without his armor. She thought of him in the chapel, on his knees, her hand on the warm scars over his heart.

She thought of her studies. She thought of her letter to Graham. She thought of herself, and dared to ask, "The dreaming spring of Galburgh? The prophetic seals of Belmouth? Is that lifeless, deathless perfection?"

"It is magic."

"But then—"

"Is that," he said, "a gamble you would take if you were me?"

But Lucy's mind was already skipping down another path of logic. She laughed, incredulous, stunned. "Why, then you are a god!"

"No," he said, an absolute negation.

Lucy, not believing him, laid her fingers against her lips and stared.

"No." He rose, with the first restlessness she had seen in him, and then stood, self-restrained, as if pacing were too alien a concept—too human a concept—to pursue. "Believe me. Understand me. I am a tombstone, I am a closed door, nothing more."

"Keeping magic out of this world. Or . . . this other thing, this perfection."

"If they are not the same thing."

"If?" Lucy whispered, incredulous all over again. "If? Don't you know?"

"I have wondered," he said, and stopped. "I have wondered, from time to time."

Lucy went cold, and then more than cold, thinking of what he implied. To take on such a mission, such a burden—not only the long years, not only the murders, the lies, the kings held under his sway, but the destruction, the erasing from history of the whole world he had been born to—*and then to doubt.* The chasm between them was deep, and filled with hell, and in that moment, terribly, terrifyingly real.

"When one such as you comes along," he said to her, "an open door yourself, with a mind prying at every door I have ever closed, digging up every spring I have ever paved over, I do wonder."

"No, I . . . " Lucy's voice trembled with tears. "I only . . . "

"Wondered?" A perfection of irony. "You were only curious, I know. But perhaps you understand my dilemma now. To release what my emperor summoned would be to allow the end of everything, the end of life, an end without ending, an end with no hope of beginning, an end without even the hope of death. And yet. And yet."

"And yet," Lucy said—oh, to hear this man!—"And yet, what if what you are keeping out the world is life? 'The fires of creation, the breath of the gods.' "

"It is not such a terrible world, this world that I have made."

"No. It isn't, no. No, but . . . " Trembling on the edge of the abyss.

"But could it be better? But could it be that without magic it is as dead as that other world would be, as dead as I am, could it be?"

"But do you have the right to have made it anything at all?"

He stood with his back to the window, looking down at her with his lightless eyes, and she felt again the weight of the sword in her hand.

"No right," he said at last. "Only the necessity to save . . . Do you understand, Miss Donne? It was the necessity of the moment, the desperate need to stop my emperor before he brought about the ruin of the world. And I have been stopping him ever since."

"But not knowing!" she cried, and was not sure if she was crying out in empathy or argument.

"Ah, but you still do not understand me. He was an open door, once upon a time. Like any wizard. Like you, and all the other open doors I have closed. Even if it is magic that I have been keeping out of the world, to let it back in might be to let *him* come again, some time, in some form, when I am not there to stop it as I stopped him before."

"Do you mean his ghost or his idea?"

"Either!" He turned away from her, and by that she knew.

"If that sufficed to lay your doubts I'd be dead now."

"I am so tired!" His voice broke, he bent an arm across his chest as if to protect himself from further scars. "Gods give me aid, I am so tired."

Lucy hung on his silence, afraid, but it was the fear of awe at what he had given over into her hands. Finally she realized that the silence was hers. "What do you want me to do?"

⁕

The black car conveyed him to an anonymous building that was, if one unwound the tangle of streets, not far from the royal palace. A small, un-numbered door let him into a corridor lit by bare electric bulbs, stark and dim. Graham could feel his courage fading like old wallpaper, and it didn't help that his escort, a hulking young man with a face like a plowboy, moved him along by the simple expedient of stepping forward and assuming Graham would proceed to get out of his way. Graham proceeded, a wry internal voice telling him *you're in trouble now, mate* even as the sweat came out on his palms. Anger guilt fear . . . and Lucy. Lucy very much on his mind.

"Just here, Mr. Isles," said the oversized plowboy, rattling open an accordion-fold lift door. They went up, the lift bobbing and swaying in its shaft, and exited into a corridor where there were new runners on the floor and the light bulbs had frosted glass shades. Coming up in the world. The plowboy knocked on a door and pushed it open without waiting for an answer.

"Mr. Isles, you can't know how glad I am—how relieved I am to make your acquaintance. Thank the Divine you're here." Not a tall man, but a bulky one, his body fronted by a robust belly and his face obscured by jowls. Neither handsome nor famous, but Graham knew who he was, at least, he had a vague notion that crystallized as the man drew him into the room. Barrimond, senior bureaucrat, quiet power in the Ministry of State. Releasing Graham he smoothed his hand over the glossy hair painted over his scalp and offered Graham a drink. Nothing to be offended by there, and in fact Graham could have used one, but he didn't like the assumption that had the plowboy already clattering amongst a tray of decanters.

"No," Graham said with deliberate lack of courtesy. "Why am I here?"

A small pause, a look of calculation in the fat man's eyes. "Yes. Perhaps it is a trifle late for the amenities. I should apologize for sending an invitation you could not refuse—and yet—great heavens—here I am not even offering you a chair. Please." He gestured.

Graham sat where indicated. Barrimond sat behind his desk. The plowboy propped himself against the door. *All in our stations*, Graham thought.

"I'm glad to see you're a direct kind of man, Isles," Barrimond said, "though I should say I'm not surprised, having read so much of your work—read and admired, I should hasten to say. I also believe—indeed, I am relying on it—that you are capable of discretion, a much rarer thing in a newspaperman. I take this evening's article about poor Lucy Donne as an example in point, because you and I both know how much more you could have written."

"I don't know what you mean," Graham said, more or less automatically.

Barrimond looked at him, then bent to haul open a drawer in his desk. "I suppose that if I want directness from you I should be honest myself. Always the best policy, really, though I'm afraid I owe you a kind of an apology. Or rather, since we are being driven by necessity, not so much an apology as an expression of regret. Your privacy and your person have been a little impinged upon, but I trust it will be made clear how important—and really, we could have done much worse and been justified . . . " Having been talking with his hand in the open drawer, Barrimond now dragged out a heavy object and laid it on his desk. It was Lucy's portfolio, stolen from Graham's flat. "For example, we could have simply turned this, and you, over to the Marshal of Kallisfane. As I think you know."

There is something painfully ineffectual about sitting in the face of an outrage, so Graham stood, his pulse beating in his temple. But although he was angry—almost as angry as he was frightened—his thinking was clear and he knew he was only making a show. When the oversized plowboy stepped away from the door, Graham sat back down and raised his eyes from the portfolio to Barrimond's face.

"You might as well turn me over," he said, fairly calm. "Why not let the old man do his own dirty work? He certainly doesn't seem to mind."

"No, indeed," said Barrimond, though the plowboy made a noise suggestive of irony or dissention. "But this is a rather unusual case. I take it you have in fact read . . . ?" He patted the portfolio.

"Some of it," Graham said, as if he could at this stage still hedge his bets.

"A remarkable piece of work. Truly remarkable. Miss Donne must be an interesting young woman to know."

Graham felt his temperature rise, but he said nothing. He had no intention of discussing Lucy with this man. Barrimond, however, seemed bent on discussing Lucy with him.

"A highly interesting young woman, and in other circumstances, in another field, no doubt an asset to us all. But in this particular instance . . . No, I'm afraid our Lucy has been stirring up some murky waters. Very murky—and to be frank, extremely dangerous. I wonder if you would be glad to know she is still alive?"

Graham's heart seemed to shrink, leaving a dizzy cavern in his core. He still said nothing, but he doubted his reaction went unseen. Barrimond went on finger-tapping Lucy's portfolio, almost caressing it, but his eyes never left Graham's face.

"Yes. A relief to me too, of course, although something of a surprise. And I hope you understand me—it's crucial that you understand me—that although the *fact* that Miss Lucy Donne is still alive is a great relief to all of us, the *circumstances* are a matter of extraordinary concern, and not only for Miss Donne's sake—though she is not, I assure you, far from my thoughts at any time. No, the consequences for her . . . But then, you see, the consequences for us all . . . "

To Graham's relief, Barrimond finally took his hand off Lucy's portfolio, knotting his fingers together as if he physically captured his thoughts. "It occurs to me that I have skipped a crucial question. I asked you if you had read Miss Donne's research. I did not ask you if you believe it. Really a crucial question, Mr. Isles. I wonder if you can answer it honestly."

"Do I believe in Lucy's research?" Graham said, stalling for time.

"No, Mr. Isles. Not, Do you believe in her research. Not, Do you believe in *her*. I want to know if you, having studied the evidence, agree with Miss Donne's conclusions."

"I've read her notes, but without having verified her facts—"

"They have been verified. You have my word on it. Factually, Miss Donne is in most respects entirely correct."

"Why would you verify that?" Graham said on a burst of skepticism. "Why aren't you bending over backwards to convince me the other way? Why the hell are you bothering to try and convince me of anything at all?"

"Because we need your help, Mr. Isles. We need your help very urgently—to head off unmitigated disaster—and to save Miss Lucy Donne."

But did Lucy want to be saved? She was aware of her perilous situation. The Marshal of Kallisfane had made it clear.

"You held your hand from me once," he said, "and if you failed that challenge, perhaps you won another, even so. I will grant you that. But it has only won you yet another challenge, and this one you may prefer to lose. For as you held your hand from me, so I will hold mine from you, to let you live and do as you will. Would you bring magic back into the world? Would you wake the old gods, the old dreamers and the ancient dreams? I will hold my hand in the hope that you might also summon the death that has long eluded me. And if you fail to open that door, no matter. You can serve me in other ways, in my house here. I have kept other scholars so. And so you might win your own life either way.

"But do you open the door on that other world, on that dead and deathless perfection that made me what I am, it will be otherwise. I will destroy you and all of your blood unto the ninth degree, until even the name of Donne will be erased from the world.

"I tell you plainly: this challenge, you might prefer to fail."

Yes. Indeed, yes. So a sensible woman might have hoped for rescue. An even more sensible woman might have given some thought to escape. But was Lucy a sensible woman? To live in his house, to plunder that library of stolen history, to plumb the depths of that ancient mind! The rewards of failure were rich, even if she would be a prisoner, dead to her family and her friends. Except perhaps for Graham Isles, who had inherited all the breadcrumbs that had marked her trail to this end. That was a thought to pull her up sharply. As far as Graham was concerned, she would not simply disappear.

Did that matter? By his own declaration he would not pursue a story no one wants to hear. He would only know.

And, a sinful inner voice added, he would never know that she had settled for failure. He would never know she had refused to try for the greater prize.

So it must have been that voice, rather than the thought of Graham's opinion, that roused in her a hot and prickly blush of shame.

———

As it happened, Graham was also none too sanguine about the thought of a rescue. Or rather, he thought rescuing Lucy from the Marshal of Kallisfane sounded like a fine idea; he just wasn't sure what role he was expected to play. Even after it was explained to him by Barrimond and the plowboy, it wasn't clear in his mind. "Persuade her," they said. "Make her listen to reason." But surely the telling point was whether or not she was in the Revenant's clutches? It seemed to him that the sensible order of proceeding was to extract her from her prison and *then* make her see reason. "We need to get her out quietly," said the plowboy, "and for that we need her cooperation. And for *that*, we need you. Right?"

Right, said Graham, though he said it with hidden irony, as if he could humor these men until they started to show some sense. Yet playing along had him riding in the back of the big black motorcar somewhere on the wrong side of midnight, dressed in imaginary armor and clutching a cardboard sword, on his way to rescue the princess before she could be sacrificed to the dragon. Though in fact, the idea seemed less absurd now, rushing through the cold, black night, than it had in the bureaucratic comfort of Barrimond's office.

"Sacrifice!" he had said. "Are you insane?"

"No," Barrimond had replied, "but the Marshal is."

"Well," the plowboy said, "say he has his moments. He's an old man, you know, and old men do have their moments. Most times he runs on the rails right enough."

"Yes," Barrimond said, "and the point is to get him back on the rails as soon as possible before any damage is done."

"Remove Miss Donne," said the plowboy, "and remove the temptation, like."

The temptation to do what? Suddenly there was no more time for explanations. It was down to the car and out in the night, and the sound of the engine droning back at them from the dark-windowed houses, and the quick sharp fire of the whiskey from the plowboy's flask. And then the city fell away into the dark.

Morning drew a mist out of the winter-wet ground. Lucy was out early enough to see the rising sun wrapped in a ball of foggy wool. She was weary, but a life-time habit of nervous energy won out over the condition of her heart—if its jackrabbit thumping was an injury and not just a symptom of her confusion. She walked out into the valley of Kallisfane without a thought for her health; but her walk was of necessity a thoughtful invalid's stroll.

Kallisfane Castle could be found on any map, though there were some odd discrepancies. Did the road cross the Fernsey River above Mimmenbrook or below? Was the castle on the southern spur of the Starsey Hills, or was it more southwesterly? But all the maps agreed there was no valley behind the castle, nothing but a blank space or a ripple as of hills. This morning the mist seemed to be conspiring with the mapmakers. A haze against the sky, a creeping whiteness against the ground, it erased colors, blurred edges, muted sound, as if this valley, the heart of the Marshal's demesne, might in the next moment efface itself entirely from the world. Or perhaps it had already done so. Perhaps where Lucy walked was no-place, no-time, nothing but a memory in the Marshal's skull. A fading memory, all that was left of the Empire-that-was.

And yet the black mud sucked at her shoes. Puddles bright as mirrors cupped in worn paving stones reflected her face, the edge of a wall. The thrushes singing in the woods that guarded the hilltops sang like the first springtime in the world.

In the valley lay a city. A city of white stone, all in ruins, though the mist filled in the gaps of fallen domes and tumbled walls, teasing the eye with long-lost grandeur. There had been a wide avenue here, palaces rising behind their colonnades, a statue, perhaps, on that great stone plinth that divided the way. Lucy sat there a moment to catch her breath and scrape the mud off her shoes. Her poor not-very-sensible shoes. They would never be the same again. Lucy sighed and pressed her hand over her heart, as if that could calm the queasy race and lag of her pulse. When she was walking the valley seemed perfectly quiet except for her own footsteps, the ring of distant birdsong chiming with the sunlight far above the fog, but now the silence was alive with hidden drips and scrapes and soft muddy sounds, as if the mist had grown feet to follow her with. But of course she likely was being followed by one of the Marshal's men. Walking away was not one of the options he had offered her.

Well, let them watch! she thought, a nice show of courage that did nothing to dispel the prickle creeping down her spine. She rose with a too-casual glance around and continued on. The ground mist was lifting above her head, hiding the sky and the tops of the surrounding hills, but here and there a shaft of milky sunlight broke through.

And where is she going, our Lucy, strolling on a misty dawn in early spring? At the end of this long avenue, where once the legions paraded and the wizard-philosophers strolled, lies the imperial palace. The Emperor Caedemus' palace, where one age was killed and another was erected on its grave. But she is only going there to appease her curiosity, to think . . . perhaps to decide . . .

———

The black motorcar stopped at an iron gate and the plowboy got out to talk to the guard. Graham lowered the window on his side, hoping the shock of fresh air would rouse him from the stupefaction of the drive. It was dawn, damp and cold, and Graham started to shiver without feeling any more awake. The real world was hot coffee, a razor, his own bed. He could not fathom what he was doing here.

The plowboy got back in and the motorcar pulled through the gate, wallowing in the ruts of the drive.

"Where are we?" Graham said.

"Kallisfane." The answer was curt. The man himself was pale with sleeplessness, stubbled and grim, and Graham had to admit that he looked more soldier than plowboy.

HOLLY PHILLIPS

"You're one of the Nameless Regiment, aren't you? One of the Marshal's own."

The big man grunted what was probably an affirmative.

"None too loyal, then, are you?" Graham's mild tone took the edge off the provocation.

"We're sworn to serve the Crown, same as any other regiment. And we serve the Marshal, too, believe me. He's his own worst enemy, when he gets to thinking on the past."

"How so?"

"Feels the weight of the years, like. The burden of his responsibilities. Well, you can imagine it, can't you, after all this time? Wanting to let it all go?"

"Yes. But I don't see what that has to do with Lucy Donne."

The plowboy-soldier kept his eyes on the road past the driver's shoulder, but Graham had the sense of an intelligence working behind that homely face.

"We reckon he thinks he can use Miss Donne to bring us all back to the way things used to be. Bring us all back to the days when he was an ordinary man, d'you see? Return the world to the way it was, and maybe return himself to the way *he* was . . . "

"But *how* will he use her? Use her how?"

"They was grim and bloody times—" He interrupted himself to say to the driver, "Take the east fork." The car turned. Graham caught a glimpse of the castle rearing up to their left, already falling behind. Where were they going? Graham started to ask, but the plowboy was talking again.

"People don't know what it was like in those days. They have these romantic notions that it was all storybook adventures and poetry and folksongs—people like Miss Donne, who think the

188

Marshal's a hard man doing a bloody job. Well so he is, and a good thing, too. Do you have the least notion of what this world would come to if he left his post? It'd be chaos. Your worst nightmares can't even touch what it would be to let the old gods walk again."

Graham was not immune to direful predictions, not when they echoed the fears that Lucy's work had raised, but still he persisted. "You haven't said what part Lucy has to play in all this."

"She's the sacrifice, man! Haven't you been listening? She's the life that opens the door the Marshal has been keeping shut all these years. She's the bloody key. Here," he said to the driver in the same rough tone, "park here, we'll have to go the rest of the way on foot."

"What—" Graham began.

"Right," the plowboy said, all soldier now. "We may just have a chance to take her away with no one the wiser until we're gone. The aim is to get her to come quietly back to the car, and that's your job. Say anything you need to—she's in danger, you're here to take her home—be a hero to her—"

"But—"

"Wake up, will you? We're saving the girl. We're saving the damn world!"

"But *why me*?"

The plowboy leaned to put his big face in Graham's. "You know the background, you know the girl, and I don't have time for arguments with men who don't know where their loyalties should lie. All right? There's men here who serve the Marshal before the Crown, and I can't take them all on, not if we're going to keep this quiet. You cooperate with me, you get the girl to cooperate with me, and we just drive away, no fuss, end of story. All right?"

The big man swung himself out of the car. After the briefest hesitation, Graham followed suit. But in that half-second pause, he had time to wonder what would happen to them after he had persuaded Lucy to cooperate. Were they going to be sent home and trusted to keep their mouths shut? Graham thought of Lucy's portfolio, all the stories no one wanted to hear. He climbed from the car into the misty morning. Birds were singing somewhere in the fog.

———————

The palace was roofed with mist, walled with air. Grand steps of once-white marble were broken and half buried by the fallen columns of the portico, but Lucy found she could pick her way between the disarticulated pillars, up the shattered stair. For the first time, as she scuffed her muddy shoes through the mold of windblown leaves, it struck her as odd, how lifeless the ancient Fane was. No moss to blur the carvings on the broken capitals, no grass to carpet the stairs, no bird-flitting or mouse-scurrying nearer than the treed battlements of the enclosing hills. *The end of everything*, he had said, *the end of life, an end without ending, an end with no hope of beginning, an end without even the hope of death* . . . As if everything could just stop, Lucy thought. Stop, freeze into crystal, her breath and blood, the air, the mist and the birds in the trees and the trees themselves. Like a book, she thought, a story captured between the covers, beginning and end all there, simultaneous, undifferentiated, a beginning never begun, an ending that never ended, the perfect story, unread, ideal. Yes. She did not at all understand what the Marshal had said about doing magic, or being magic, or the difference between them, but this she understood, the perfect, the completed world.

But the blood moved through her limping heart, the air moved into her lungs and out again, warm enough to make steam. She breathed out again, a deliberate puff, for the pleasure of seeing it hang for an instant in the milky brightness, and then went on into the palace. Her footsteps echoed around her, hinting, with the mist, of companionable ghosts.

Did he ever come here, the self-named Marshal of this place? *He* would have ghosts. In these rubble-mounds he would see the shape of rooms he had known, the fountained courts and lucent tiles and stone-filigree walls. Or would he? How long had he lived here as a mortal man, a soldier and then a captain of soldiers? Twenty years? Thirty? A scant handful of decades to set against the long centuries of ruin. Perhaps he wondered, as she did, which were the rooms of state, which the private apartments, which the emperor's own room where he had been stopped in the very act of summoning the end of time. Where he had been betrayed, killed by a trusted hand.

Here, where a pillared arch still stood, though the room beyond was adrift with shattered roof tiles and the pale stones of the further wall?

Here, where the broken roots of columns still marked out the line of a shady cloister?

Here, where a fountain's bowl fell into petal-shards like a teacup dropped just so in the center of the yard?

Here, where footsteps echoed, pat-patter-pattering even though Lucy was standing still.

Or maybe it was her heart, she thought, with the hum of invisible bees in her ears. She lowered herself to the flat top of a column's tumbled capital. Its leafy carvings sloughed away a skin of rotten stone under her fingers, crumbs of past beauty sifted into the dirt beneath her feet. The walls were mostly intact here, giving a shape and a sense of enclosure to the small courtyard, but the misty ceiling was lifting away, thinning against the blue sky. Sunlight, still diffused by damp, brightened the many shades of white of all the naked stone, walls, flagstones, fallen columns, broken bowl. There was even a ghost of color on the walls, rose and blue and ocher, scabrous as lichen if lichen could have grown in this place.

This dead place . . . save for the drift of the air, the far birdsong, the dripping of condensed mist from the many lips of stone. And the footsteps. Lucy was almost sure, despite a long silence that conjured up again the humming in her ears. The blood seemed to shrink away beneath her skin, leaving it tingling and cold. But of course, she knew she was being watched.

Yes, there, the unmistakable grit of shoe leather over dirty stone.

Sunlight found its way through clouds and mist to sparkle in the rainwater cupped by the shards of the fountain. Warmth pressed through the damp tweed of Lucy's jacket, and as though the sun confirmed something she already guessed, she was abruptly convinced that there was no magic here, neither in the place nor in her, and that all this morning held for her was an early walk and a mild sort of farce, grown men sneaking about in the wake of her curiosity. Rather like the new parlourmaid who hovers outside the drawing room door, holding her breath and fidgeting in her shoes, unsure whether she should go in to fetch the tea tray if there was still someone in the room. So Lucy thought, and she called out a cheerful, "Hullo!" which startled her in spite of herself, it had been so quiet before she spoke.

The silence itself seemed to be startled. Then an answering, "Lucy?" came cold and clear through the stony maze, and more footsteps, forthright ones, and then—she was dumbfounded, having refused to believe the familiarity of the voice—Graham Isles appeared in the archway on the sunny side of the court. He peered against the brightness, pale, stubbled, thoroughly disheveled, and said her name again, in as questioning a tone as before.

"Lucy?"

"Graham! But what—How on earth—" But then she remembered the portfolio, left for him a thousand years ago in the Left Luggage Office of Skillyham Station, and was silenced by a rush of guilt.

Graham glanced behind him before he crossed to where she sat. "I've lost him, I think. Or he's lost me. Listen—"

"Who?"

"Can you come? Right now? Right away? The driver's still with the car at the foot of the valley, but I think, if we climbed the hills, they don't seem very steep, we might manage to go very quietly all on our own."

He was looking around him as if he expected policemen with whistles, huntsmen with dogs. He was out of breath, and his shoes were even muddier than hers.

"Graham." She caught one of his hands, hot and damp with

193

sweat. "Stop a moment. Please explain. Where have you come from, who are you talking about, where to you want me to go?"

"There's no time," he said, but his hand closed around hers and he hunkered down beside her where she sat on her carved and crumbling stone. "Are you all right? I didn't expect to find you wandering about on your own. You look awfully pale."

So did Graham, but in the sunlight his eyes were the same dark amber as his favorite beer. A lovely color, in fact, which Lucy had never noticed before. He was otherwise entirely himself, and wonderfully alive and real in this—now that he was here she could think it—dreary graveyard of a place.

"Not exactly on my own," Lucy said, "but on a long leash, I think. Graham, I know why I'm here, but I haven't a clue where you come into it. Did they find out about the notes I left for you? Was it the Marshal's men who brought you here?"

"Yes, but not on his orders. Listen, they seem to think there's something dangerous about you being here. I mean, not just dangerous for you, but for everyone. Damn!" He looked around again, his hand tightening on hers. "There's really no time. I'm supposed to help get you away from him, but I'm not sure I like our chances much better once I have, so I thought, if we could slip away without them . . . We should just *go*, Lucy, and save the talk for later."

"But I don't—" —*want to*. She bit off the end, but her hand had gone limp in his grasp and the telepathy of touch must have told him. He stared up at her.

"They said he's going to sacrifice you. To raise the old gods. To bring the world back to the way it was."

"They're wrong!" she said fiercely, and twisted her hand out of his. "Whoever 'they' are. They're completely wrong. It's the other way round, it's exactly the other way . . . " She balked, catching a glimpse of something she hadn't quite seen before.

"Which other way?" Graham said, impatient.

"He . . . " Lucy balked again.

"Listen." Graham reclaimed her hand. "Lucy. I think we should just go. We should just get out of this, this whole thing, whatever it is, just get the hell out and—"

"And let everything go on as it has been."

"Yes! Holy fires and all, Lucy, do you hate this world so much you want to bring it crashing down around our ears?"

"No!" Lucy was shocked.

"Do you want to die for that?"

"But I'm not the one—And it's *change*, it's not—"

"Let's just go." Graham stood, pulling Lucy to her feet. "Lucy. Please. Let's just go."

She was caught, by the desperate pleading in his voice as much as by the hard grip of his hand, and it seemed as though that instant was the deciding one, as though, if she had not hesitated, if she had just moved, or spoken—but it was only a seeming. She could have changed nothing in that moment. It was only a pause before all the rest that was going to happen, happened. She looked up at him, at Graham, who was burning with impatience and determination, and then someone stepped into the archway on the sunny side of the courtyard. They looked. One of the Marshal's men, the big young man who had escorted Lucy off the train.

"Oh dear," Lucy said, feeling a guilty lick of humor at being caught.

"Oh damn," Graham said, in another tone entirely, and he pulled at Lucy's hand, turning, trying to move her, put her behind him, she wasn't sure. In any case, she stumbled against the fallen masonry she had been sitting on, and it broke, or something did, a crack that shook the air, and Graham was pulling her, very clumsily, so they both half-fell to the ground.

"Damn!" Graham said on a gasp. "Lucy. Go. If you can." But his hand was still holding hard to hers, and somehow, perhaps through that same telepathy, she realized he was shot, he had been shot by the large young man who carried not a book, but a gun.

Lucy looked up at him, but he was already dead. The Marshal of Kallisfane withdrew his sword with a meaty sound, and the large young man, looking stupid in his dead man's surprise, fell in a heap to the ground.

"Treachery," the Marshal said in his ordinary voice. "This is a good place for it."

Graham was falling, too, a slow continuation of the motion that had put them on their knees. His mouth was open as he fought for air. He still held Lucy's left hand very hard in his right. She used her free hand to grope under his jacket until she found the small hot hole in his side. His breath seemed to be stopped wetly in his throat, but still he managed to speak.

"I loved you," he said. "I never said. I never said."

His grasp weakened. Lucy clutched his hand hard, as hard as she could, pressing it with both her hands against her side, but still he let go, he let her go. She leaned over him to catch his gaze, but she could not, he was gone.

She was very conscious, in the silence, of the beating of her heart. If she had stopped the world, one minute ago, five minutes ago, an hour ago, he would be alive, forever and always. Graham. Who had loved her. If she had. If she had only known how.

"Perhaps now you are ready to try again," the Marshal said. His sword was smeared with blood—not dripping, only smeared, like her hand.

Would she say no because Graham who had died for her would want her to? No. She would say yes, yes, because only *yes* would end the deadlock of a thousand years, the deadlock that had killed him and all the untold others. Yes.

She was very slow, but he was patient. It was hard to let go of Graham, but it was really time she wanted to hold, and she could not, the moment was past. She stood, and looked at the Marshal, and wondered what he had really stopped, what impulse had died in the last emperor's brain. He tried to hand her his sword over Graham's body and she waved him brusquely away, back toward the broken fountain. But when she had followed him there she took the warm hilt again in her hand.

Her heart pounded out a fierce and primitive rhythm. If there had been words for it, they would have run something like, *you won't stop me, you won't bury me, I won't let you end me here.* The great weight of the Marshal's presence could not stifle it. She did not know what it was. Not magic. Perhaps only life in the face of death.

He knelt, as he had in the chapel, his eyes narrowed against the sun. Looking down, as she had looked down at Graham, Lucy saw his eyes were not black but brown, a dark tea-colored brown without red or gold to lighten them. He opened his shooting coat and shirt to bear his scarred breast. Lucy set the sword's point

197

there and stopped, seeing how her heartbeat trembled in her hands.

"Tell me your name," she said.

He told her. She drove the sword home.

He choked once, as Graham had, and died.

The world changed.

VIRGIN OF THE SANDS

Neil came out of the desert leaving most of his men dead behind him. He debriefed, he bathed, he dressed in a borrowed uniform, and without food, without rest, though he needed both, he went to see the girl.

The army had found her rooms in a shambling mud-brick compound shaded by palms. She was young, God knew, too young, but her rooms had a private entrance, and there was no guard to watch who came and went. Who would disturb Special Recon's witch? Neil left the motor pool driver at the east side of the market and walked through the labyrinth of goats, cotton, chickens, oranges, dates, to her door. The afternoon was amber with heat, the air a stinking resin caught with flies. Nothing like the dry furnace blast of the wadi where his squad had been ambushed and killed. He knocked, stupid with thirst, and wondered if she was home.

She was.

Tentative, always, their first touch: her fingertips on his bare arm, her mouth as heavy with grief as with desire. She knew, then. He bent his face to hers and felt the dampness of a recent bath. She smelled of well water and ancient spice. They hung a moment, barely touching, mingled breath and her fingers against his skin, and then he took her mouth, and drank.

"I'm sorry," she said, after.

He lay across her bed, bound to exhaustion, awaiting release. "We walked right into them," he said, eyes closed. "Walked right into their guns."

"I'm sorry."

She sounded so unhappy. He reached for her with a blind hand. "Not your fault. The dead can't tell you everything."

She laid her palm across his, her touch still cool despite the sweat that soaked her sheets. "I know."

"They expect too much of you." By *they* he meant the generals. When she said nothing he turned his head and looked at her. She knelt beside him on the bed, barred with light from the rattan blind. Her dark hair was loose around her face, her dark eyes shadowed with worry. So young she broke his heart. He said, "You expect too much of yourself."

She covered his eyes with her free hand. "Sleep."

"You can only work with what we bring you. If we don't bring you the men who know . . . who knew . . . " The darkness of her touch seeped through him.

"Sleep."

"Will you still be here?"

"Yes. Now sleep."

Three times told, he slept.

———————

She had to be pure to work her craft, a virgin in the heart of army intelligence. He never knew if this loving would compromise her with her superiors. She swore it would not touch her power, and he did not ask her more. He just took her with his hands, his tongue, his skin, and if sometimes the forbidden depths of her had him aching with need, that only made the moment when she slid her mouth around him more potent, explosive as a shell bursting in the bore of a gun. And he laughed sometimes when she twisted against him, growling, her teeth sharp on his neck: virgin. He laughed, and forgot for a time the smell of long-dead men.

"Finest military intelligence in the world," Colonel Tibbit-Noyse said, "and we can't find their blasted army from one day to the next." His black mustache was crisp in the wilting heat of the briefing room.

Neil sat with half a dozen officers scribbling in notebooks balanced on their knees. Like the others, he let his pencil rest when the colonel began his familiar tirade.

"We know the Fuhrer's entrail-readers are prone to inaccuracy and internal strife. We know who his spies are and have been feeding them tripe for months." (There was a dutiful chuckle.) "We know the desert tribesmen who have been guiding his armored divisions are weary almost to death with the Superior Man. For God's sake, our desert johnnies have been meeting them for tea among the dunes! So why the *hell*—" the colonel's hand slashed at a passing fly "—can't we find them before they drop their bloody shells into our bloody laps?"

Two captains and three lieutenants, all the company officers not in the field, tapped pencil ends on their notebooks and thumbed the sweat from their brows. Major Healy sitting behind the map table coughed into his hand. Neil, eyes fixed on the wall over the major's shoulder, heard again the rattle of gunfire, saw again the carnage shaded by vulture wings. His notebook slid through his fingers to the floor. The small sound in the colonel's silence made everyone jump. He bent to pick it up.

"Now, I have dared to suggest," Tibbit-Noyse continued, "that the fault may not lie with our intel at all, but rather with the use to which it has been put. This little notion of mine has not been greeted with enthusiasm." (Again, a dry chuckle from the men.) "In fact, I'm afraid the general got rather testy about the quantity and quality of fodder we've scavenged for his necromancer in recent weeks. Therefore." The colonel sighed. His voice was subdued when he continued. "Therefore, all squads will henceforth make it their sole mission to find and retrieve enemy dead, be they abandoned or buried, with an urgent priority on those of officer rank. I'm afraid this will entail a fair bit of dodging about on the wrong side of the battle line, but you'll be delighted to know that the general has agreed to an increase in leave time between missions from two days to four." He looked at Neil. "Beginning immediately, captain, so you have another three days' rest coming to you."

"I'm fit to go tomorrow, sir," Neil said.

Tibbit-Noyse gave him a bleak smile. "Take your time, captain. There's plenty of death to go 'round."

There was another moment of silence, this one long enough for the men to start to fidget. Healy coughed. Neil sketched the outlines of birds. Then the colonel went on with his briefing.

She had duties during the day, and in any event he could not spend all his leave in her company. He had learned from the nomads not to drink until he must. So he found a café not too near headquarters, one with an awning and a boy to whisk the flies, and drank small cups of syrupy coffee until his heart raced and sleep no longer tempted him.

A large body dropped into the seat opposite him. "Christ. How can you drink coffee in this heat?"

Neil blinked the other's face into focus: Montrose, a second-string journalist with a beefy face and a bloodhound's eyes. The boy brought the reporter a bottle of lemon squash, half of which he poured down his throat without seeming to swallow. "Whew!"

"We have orders," Neil said, his voice neutral, "not to speak with the press."

"Look at you, you bastard. Not even sweating." Montrose had a flat Australian accent and salt-rimmed patches of sweat underneath his arms. "Or have you just had the juice scared out of you?"

Neil gave a thin smile and brushed flies away from the rim of his cup.

"Listen." Montrose hunkered over the table. "There've been rumors of a major cock-up. Somebody let some secrets slip into the wrong ears. Somebody in intelligence. Somebody high up. Ring any bells?"

Neil covered a yawn. He didn't have to fake one. The coastal heat was a blanket that could smother even the caffeine. He drank the last swallow, leaving a sludge of sugar in the bottom of the cup, and flagged the boy.

"According to this rumor," Montrose said, undaunted, "at least one of the secrets had to do with the field maneuvers of the

Dead Squad—pardon me—the Special Desert Reconnaissance Group. Which, come to think of it, is your outfit, isn't it, Neil?" Montrose blinked with false concern. "Didn't have any trouble your last time out, did you, mate? No unpleasant surprises? No nasty Jerries hiding among the dunes?"

The boy came back, set a fresh coffee down by Neil's elbow, gave him a fleeting glance from thickly-lashed eyes. Neil dropped a couple of coins on the tray.

"How's your wife?" Neil said.

Montrose sighed and leaned back to finish his lemonade. "God knows. Jerries went and sank the mail ship, didn't they? She could be dead and I'd never even know."

"You could be dead," Neil said, "and she would never know. Isn't that a bit more likely given your relative circumstances?"

Montrose grunted in morose agreement, and whistled for the boy.

He stalled as long as he could, through the afternoon and into the cook-fire haze of dusk, and even so he waited nearly an hour outside her door. When she came home, limp and pale, she gave him a weary smile and unlocked her door. He knew better than to touch her before she'd had a chance to bathe. He followed her through the stuffy entrance hall to the airier gloom of her room. She stepped out of her shoes on her way into the bathroom. He heard water splat in the empty tub. Then she came back and began to take off her clothes.

He said, "I have three more days' leave."

She unbuttoned her blouse and peeled it off. "I heard." She

tossed the blouse into a hamper by the bathroom door. "I'm glad."

He sat in a creaking wicker chair, set his cap on the floor. "There's a rumor going around about some misplaced intel."

She frowned slightly as she unfastened her skirt. "I haven't heard about that."

"I had it from a reporter. Not the most reliable source."

The skirt followed the blouse, then her slip, her brassiere, her pants. Naked, she lifted her arms to take down her hair. Shadows defined her ribs, her taut belly, the divide of her loins. She walked over to drop hairpins into his hand.

"Who is supposed to have said what to whom?"

"There were no characters in the drama," he said. "But if it's true . . . "

"If it's true, then your men never had a chance."

This close she smelled of woman-sweat and death. His throat tightened. "They had no chance, regardless. Neither do the men in the field now. They've sent the whole damn company out chasing dead men." He dropped his head against the chair and closed his eyes. "This bloody war."

"It's probably just a rumor," she said, and he heard her move away. The rumble from the bathroom tap stopped. Water sloshed as she stepped into the tub. Neil rolled her hairpins against his palm.

Her scent faded with the last of the light.

———

He wished she had a name he could call her by. Like her intact hymen, her namelessness was meant to protect her from the forces she wrestled in her work, but it seemed a grievous thing.

She was so specific a woman, so unique, so much herself; he knew so intimately her looks, her textures, her voice; he could even guess, sometimes, at her thoughts; and yet she was anonymous. The general's necromancer. The witch. The girl. His endearments came unraveled in the empty space where her name should be, so he took refuge in silence, wishing, as much for his sake as for hers, that she had not been born and raised to her grisly vocation. From childhood she had known nothing other than death.

"How can you bear it?" he asked her once.

"How can you?" A glance of mockery. "But maybe no one told you. We all live with death. We all begin to die the instant we are born. Even you."

He had a vision of himself dead and in her hands, and understood it for a strange desire. He did not put it into words but he knew her intimacy with the dead, with death, went beyond this mere closeness of flesh. Skin slick with sweat-salt, speechless tongues and hands that sought the vulnerable center of being, touch dangerous and tender and never allowed inside the heart, the womb. He pressed her in the darkness, strove against her as if they fought, as if one or both might be consumed in this act without hope of consummation. She clung to him, spilled over with the liquor of desire and still he drank, his thirst for her unslaked, unslakable until she, wet and limber as an eel, turned in his arms, turned to him, turned against him, and swallowed him into sleep.

———

The battle washed across the desert as freely as water unbounded by shores, the war's tidal wrack of ruined bodies, tanks, and planes left like flotsam upon the dunes. The ancient, polluted city lay between the sea and that other, drier beach, and no one knew yet where the high tide line would be. Already the streets were full of the walking wounded.

Neil had errands to run. His desert boots needed mending, he had a new dress tunic to collect from the tailor—trivial chores that, performed against the backdrop of conflict, reminded him in their surreality of lying with two other men under an overhang that was too small to shelter one, seeing men torn apart by machine gun fire and feeling the sand grit between his molars, feeling the tickle of some insect across his hand, feeling his sergeant's boot heel drum against his kidney as the man shook, as they all shook, wanting to live, wanting not to die as the others died, wanting not to be eaten as the others were eaten by the vultures that wheeled down from an empty sky and that could not be trusted to report the enemy's absence, as they were brave enough to face the living when there was a meal at stake. In the tailor's shop he met a man he knew slightly, a major in another branch of Intelligence, and they went to a hotel bar for beer.

The place looked cool, with white tile, potted palms, lazy ceiling fans, but the look was a lie. Strips of flypaper that hung inconspicuously behind the bar twisted under the weight of captured flies. The major paid for two pints and led the way to an unoccupied table.

"Look at them all," he said between quick swallows.

Neil grunted acknowledgment, though he did not look around. He had already seen the scattered crowd of civilians, European refugees nervous as starlings under a hawk's wings.

"Terrified Jerry's going to come along and send them all back where they came from." The major sounded as if he rather liked the idea.

The beer felt good going down.

"As I see it," said the major, "this haphazard retreat of ours is actually going to work in our favor before the end. Think of it. The more scattered our forces are, the more thinly Jerry has to spread his own line. Right now they may look like a scythe sweeping up from the south and west," the major drew an arc in a puddle of spilled beer, "but they have to extend their line at every advance in order to keep any stragglers of ours from simply sitting tight until we're at their backs. Any day now they're going to find themselves overextended, and all we have to do is make a quick nip through a weak spot" he bisected the arc "and we'll have them in two pieces, both of them surrounded."

"And how do we find the weak spot?"

"Oh, well," the major said complacently, "that's a job for heroes like you, not desk wallahs like me."

Neil got up to buy the next round. When he came back to the table, the major had been joined by another man in uniform, a captain also wearing the "I" insignia. Neil set the glasses down and sat, and only then noticed the looks on their faces.

"I say, old man," the major said. "Rumor has it your section chief has just topped himself in his office."

"It's not a rumor," the captain said. "Colonel Tibbit-Noyse shot himself. I saw his desk. It was covered in his brains." He reached for Neil's beer and thirstily emptied the glass.

Major Healy, the colonel's aide, was impossible to find. Neil tracked him all over Headquarters, but although his progress allowed him to hear the evolving story of the colonel's death, he never managed to meet up with Healy. Eventually he came to his senses and let himself into Healy's cubbyhole of an office. The major kept a box of cigarettes on his desk. Neil seldom smoked, but, eaten by waiting, he lit one after another, the smoke dry and harsh as desert air flavored by gunpowder. When Healy came in, not long before sundown, he shouted "Bloody hell!" and slammed the door hard enough to rattle the window in its frame.

Neil put out his dog end in the overcrowded ashtray. Healy dropped into his desk chair and it tipped him back with a groan.

"Go away, captain. I can't tell you anything and if you stay I might shoot you and save Jerry the bother."

"Why did he do it?"

Healy jumped up and slammed his fist on his desk. "Out!" The chair rolled back to bump the wall.

"He sent the whole company to die on that slaughter ground and then he killed himself?" Neil shook his head.

The major wiped his face with his palms and went to stand at the window. "God knows what's in a man's mind at a time like that."

"Rumor has it he was the one who spilled our movements to the enemy." Neil was hoarse from cigarettes and thirst. "Rumor has him doing it for money, for sex, for loyalty to the other side. Because of blackmail, or stupidity, or threats."

"Rumor."

"I don't believe it."

Healy turned from the window. The last brass bars of light streaked the dusty glass. "Don't you?"

"Whatever he'd done, I don't believe he would have killed himself before he knew what had happened to the men."

"Don't you?"

"No, sir."

"If he was a spy, he wouldn't give a ha'penny damn about the men."

"Do you believe that, sir?"

Healy coughed and went to the box on his desk for a cigarette. When he saw how few were left he gave Neil a sour look. He chose one, lit it with a silver lighter from his pocket, blew out the smoke in a long thin stream.

"It doesn't matter what I believe," he said quietly. "Now give me some peace, will you? I have work to do."

The sun was almost gone. Neil got up and fumbled for the door.

———

Blackout enveloped the city. Even the stars were dim behind the scrim of cooking smoke that hazed the local sky. Though he might have wheedled a car and driver out of the motor pool, he decided to walk. Her compound was nearly a mile of crooked streets away, and it took all his concentration to recognize the turns in the darkness. Nearly all. He felt a kinship with the other men of his company, men who groped their way through the wind-built maze of dunes and sandstone desert bones, led by a chancy map into what could be, at every furtive step, a trap. He had seen how blood pooled on earth too dry to drink, how it dulled under a skiff of dust even before the flies came. Native eyes watched from dim doorways, and he touched the sidearm on his belt. With the war on the city's threshold, everyone was nervous.

Her doorway was as dim as all the rest. In the weak light that escaped her room her eyes were only a liquid gleam. She said his name uncertainly and only when he answered did she step back to let him in.

"I didn't think you'd come."

"I'm still on leave." A fatuous thing to say, but it was all he could think of.

She led him into her room where, hidden by blinds, oil lamps added to the heat. The bare space was stifling, as if crowded by the invisible. On her bed, the blue shawl she used as a coverlet showed the wrinkles where she had lain.

"It's past curfew," she said. "And . . . " She stood with her elbows cupped in her palms, barefoot, her yellow cotton dress catching the light behind it. Neil went to her, put his arms about her, leaned his face against her hair. She smelled of tea leaves and cloves.

"Of course you've heard," he said.

"Heard."

"About the colonel? Tibbit-Noyse's suicide?"

She drew in a staggered breath and pulled her arms from between them. "Yes." She returned his embrace, tipped her head to put her cheek against his.

He pulled her tighter, slight and strong with bone, and some pent emotion began to shake its way out of his body. As if to calm him, she kissed his neck, his mouth, her body alive against his. He could not discern if she also shook, or was only shaken by his tension. They stripped each other, clumsy, quick to reach the point of skin on skin. She began to kneel but he caught her arms and lifted her to the bed.

He came closer than he ever had to ending it. Weighing her down, hard against the welling heat between her thighs, he wanted, he ached, he raged with some fury that was not anger nor lust but some need, some absence without a name. Hard between her thighs. Hands tight against her face. Eyes on hers bright with oil flames. No, she said, and he was shaking again with the convulsive shudders of a fever, he'd seen malaria and thought this was some illness as well, some disease of heat and anguish and war, and she said No! and scratched his face.

He rolled onto his back and hardly had he moved but she was off the bed. Arms across his face, he heard her harsh breathing retreat across the room. The bathroom door slammed. Opened.

"Do you know about Tibbit-Noyse?"

Her voice shook. An answer to that uncertainty, at least.

"Know what?" he asked.

Her breathing was quieter, now.

"Know what?"

"That I have been ordered," she answered at last, "to resurrect him in the morning."

He did not move.

The bathroom door closed.

212

She had broken his skin. The small wound stung with sweat, or maybe it was tears, there beside his eye.

———•———

When she stayed in the bathroom, and stayed, and stayed, he finally understood. He rose and dressed, and walked out into the curfew darkness where, apparently, he belonged.

———•———

Next morning, Neil ran up the stairs to Healy's office and collided with the major outside his door.

"Neil!" Major Healy exclaimed. "What the devil are you doing here? Don't tell me. I'm already late." He pushed past and started down the hall.

Neil stretched to catch up. "I know. They're bringing the colonel back."

Healy strode another step, two, then stopped. Neil stopped as well, so the two of them stood eye to eye in the corridor. Men in uniform brushed by on their own affairs. Healy said in a furious undertone, "How the hell do you know about that?"

"I want to be there."

"Impossible." The major started to turn.

Neil grabbed his arm. "Morale's already dangerously low. How do you think the troops would react if they knew their superiors were bringing back their own dead?"

Healy's eyes widened. "Are you blackmailing your superior officer? You could be shot!"

"Sir. David. Please." Neil took his hand off the other's arm.

Healy seemed to wilt. "It's nothing you ever want to see, John. Will you believe me? It's nothing you ever want to see."

"Neither is all your men being shot dead and eaten by vultures while you lie there and do *nothing*."

Healy shut his eyes. "I don't know. You may be right." He coughed and started for the stairs. "You may be right."

Taking that for permission, Neil followed him down.

⊷•⊶

The company's staging area was a weird patch of quiet amidst the scramble of other units that had to equip and sustain their troops in the field. Trucks, jeeps, men raced over-laden on crumbling streets, spewing exhaust and profanity as they went. By the nature of their missions, reconnaissance squads were on their own once deployed, and this was never truer than for Special Recon. No one wanted to involve themselves with the Dead Squad in the field. The nickname, Neil thought, was an irony no one was likely to pronounce aloud today.

He and Major Healy had driven to the staging area alone, late, as Healy had mentioned, but when they arrived they found only one staff car parked outside the necromancer's workshop. The general in charge of Intel was inside with two men from his staff. When Healy parked his jeep next to the car, the three men got out, leaving the general's driver to slouch smoking behind the wheel. They formed a group in the square formed by rutted tarmac, prefabricated wooden walls, empty windows, blinding tin roofs. The compound stank of petrol fumes, hot tar, and an inadequate latrine.

The general, a short bulky man in a uniform limp with sweat, returned Neil's and Healy's salutes without enthusiasm. He didn't remark on Neil's presence. Neil supposed that Healy, as Special Recon's acting CO, was entitled to an aide.

The general checked his watch. "It's past time."

"Sorry, sir," Healy said. "We were detained at HQ."

The general grunted. He had cold pebble eyes in pouchy lids. "Any news of your men in the field?"

"No, sir. But I wouldn't expect to hear this early. None of the squads will have reached the line yet."

The general grunted again, and though his face bore no expression, Neil realized he was reluctant to go in. His aides had the stiff faces and wide eyes of men about to go into battle. Healy looked tired and somewhat sick. Neil felt a twinge of adrenaline in his gut, his breath came a little short. The general gave a curt nod and headed for the necromancer's door.

Inside her workshop, the walls and the underside of the tin roof were clothed in woven reed mats. Even the windows were covered: the room was brilliantly and hotly lit by a klieg lamp in one corner. An electric fan whirred in another, stirring up a breeze that played among the mats, so that the long room was restless with motion, as if the pale brown mats were tent walls. This, the heat, the unmasked stink of decay, all recalled a dozen missions to Neil's mind. His gut clenched again and sweat sprang cool upon his skin. There was no sign of her, or of Tibbit-Noyse. An inner door stood slightly ajar.

The general cleared his throat once, and then again, as if he meant to call out, but he held his silence. Eventually, the other door swung further open and the girl put her head through.

Neil felt the shock when her eyes touched him. But she was in some distant place, her eyelids heavy, her face open and serene.

215

He knew she knew him, but by her response his was only one face among five.

She said, "I'm ready to begin."

The General nodded. "Proceed."

"You know I have lodged a protest with the Sisterhood?"

The general's face clenched like a fist. "Proceed."

She stepped out of sight, leaving the door open, and in a moment she wheeled a hospital gurney into the room, handling the awkward thing with practiced ease. Tibbit-Noyse's corpse lay on its back, naked to the lamp's white glare. The heavy caliber bullet had made a ruin of the left side of his face and head. A ragged hole gaped from the outer corner of his eye to behind his temple. The cheekbone, cracked askew, whitely defined the lower margin of the wound. The whole of his face was distorted, the left eye open wide and strangely discolored, while the right eye showed only a white crescent. Shrinking lips parted to show teeth and a gray hint of tongue beneath the crisp mustache. The body was the color of paste and, bar an old appendectomy scar, otherwise intact.

The hole in Tibbit-Noyse's skull was open onto darkness. Neil remembered the Intel captain saying the man's brains had been scattered across his desk. But death was nothing new to him, and he realized he was examining the corpse so he did not have to look at the girl.

She wore a prosaic bathrobe of worn blue velvet, tightly belted at her waist. Her dark hair was pinned at the base of her neck. Her feet, on the stained cement floor, were bare. She set the brakes on the gurney's wheels with her toes, and then stood at the corpse's head, studying it, arms folded with her elbows cupped in her palms, mouth a little pursed.

An expression he knew, a face he knew so well. Another wave of sweat washed over him. He wished he had not come.

The fan stirred the walls. The lamp glared. Trucks on the street behind the compound roared intermittently by.

The girl—the witch—nodded to herself and went back into the other room, but reappeared almost at once, naked, bearing a tray heavy with the tools of her craft. She set this down on the floor at her feet, selected a small, hooked knife, and then glanced at the men by the door.

"You might pray," she said softly. "It sometimes helps."

Helps the watchers, Neil understood her to mean. He knew she needed none.

Her nakedness spurred a rush of heat in his body, helpless response to long conditioning, counter tide to the cold sweep of horror. Blood started to sing in his ears.

She took up her knife and began.

———

There is no kindness between the living and the dead.

Neil had sat through the orientation lecture, he knew the theory, at least the simplified version appropriate for the uninitiated. To lay the foundation for the false link between body and departed spirit the witch must claim the flesh. She must posses the dead clay, she must absorb it into her sphere of power, and so she must know it, know it utterly.

The ritual was autopsy. Was intercourse. Was feast.

Not literally, not quite. But her excavation of the corpse was intimate and brutal, a physical, a sensual, a savage act. As she explored Tibbit-Noyse's face, his hands, his genitals, his skin,

Neil followed her on a tour of the lust they had known together, he and she, the loving that they had enacted in the privacy of her room and that was now laid bare. As the dead man's secret tissues were stripped naked, so was Neil exposed. He rode waves of disgust, of desire, of sheer scorching humiliation, as if she fucked another man on the street, only this was worse, unimaginably worse, steeped as it was in the liquors of rot.

He also only stood, his shoulder by Healy's, his back to the rough matted wall, and said nothing, did nothing, showed, he thought, nothing . . . and watched.

When Tibbit-Noyse was open, when he was pierced and wired and riddled with her tools and charms, when there was no part of the man she had not seen and touched and claimed—when the fan stirred not air but a swampy vapor of shit and bile and decay—when she was slick with sweat and the clotting moistures of death—then she began the call.

She had a beautiful voice. Neil realized she had never sung for him, had not even hummed in the bath as she washed her hair. The men watching could see her throat swell as she drew in air, the muscles in her belly work as she sustained the long pure notes of the chant. The words were meaningless. The song was all.

When Tibbit-Noyse answered, it was with the voice of a child who weeps in the dark, alone.

The witch stepped back from the gurney, hands hanging at her sides, her face drawn with weariness but still serene.

"Ask," she said. "He will answer."

The general jerked his head, a marionette's parody of his usual brisk nod, and moved a step forward. He took a breath and then covered his mouth to catch a cough, the kind of cough that announces severe nausea. Carefully, he swallowed, and said, "Alfred Reginald Tibbit-Noyse. Do you hear me?"

A pause. "Y-ye-yes."

"Did you betray your country in a time of war?"

A pause. "Yes."

Neil could see the dead grayish lungs work inside the ribcage, the grayish tongue inside the mouth.

"How did you betray your country?"

A pause. "I sent my men." Pause. "To steal the dead." Pause. "Behind enemy lines."

The general sagged back on his heels. "That is a lie. Those men were sent out on my orders. How did you betray your country?"

A pause. "I sent my men." Pause. "To die." There was no emotion in the childish voice. It added calmly, "They were their mothers' sons."

"How did you know they were going to die?"

" . . . How could they." Pause. "Not be doomed."

"Did you send them into a trap?"

" . . . No."

"Did you betray their movements to the enemy?"

" . . . No."

"Then why did you kill yourself?" Against the dead man's calm, the general's frustration was strident.

" . . . I thought this war." Pause. "Would swallow us all." Pause. "I see now I was wrong."

Healy raised a hand to his eyes and whispered a curse. The general's shoulders bunched.

"Did you betray military secrets to the enemy?"

" . . . No."

"Who did you betray military secrets to?"

" . . . No one."

"Don't you lie to me!" the general bellowed at the riddled corpse.

"He cannot lie," the witch told him. Her voice was quietly reproachful. "He is dead."

" . . . I do not lie."

The general, heeding neither the live woman nor the dead man, continued to rap out questions. Neil could bear no more. He brushed past Healy to slip through the door. In the clean hot light of noon he vomited spit and bile, and sank down to sit with his back against the wall. After a minute, the general's driver climbed out of the staff car and offered him the last cigarette from a crumpled pack.

<hr />

The battle became a part of history. The tide of the enemy's forces was turned before it swamped the city; a new front line was drawn. The scattered squads of the Special Desert Reconnaissance Group returned in good time, missing no more men than most units who had fought in the desert sands, and carrying their bounty of enemy dead. Neil was given a medal for bravery on a recommendation by the late Colonel Tibbit-

Noyse, and a new command: twelve recruits from other units, men with stomachs already toughened by war. He led them out on a routine mission, by a stroke of luck found and recovered the withered husk of a major whose insignia promised useful intelligence, and on the morning of the scheduled resurrection, the second morning of his four-day leave, he went to the hotel bar where he had learned of Tibbit-Noyse's death and ordered a shot of whiskey and a beer.

He drank them, and several others like them, but the heat pressed the alcohol from his tissues before it could stupefy his mind. He gave up, paid his tab, and left. By this time the sunlight had thickened to the sticky amber of late afternoon. The ubiquitous flies made the only movement on the street. Neil settled his peaked cap on his head and blinked to accustom his eyes to the light, and when he looked again she was there.

She wore the yellow cotton dress. Her clean hair was soft about her face. Her eyes were wounded.

She said his name.

"Hello," he said after an awkward minute. "How are you?"

"My superiors have sent an official protest to the War Office."

"A protest?"

She looked down. "Because of the colonel's resurrection. It has made things . . . a little more difficult than usual."

"I'm sorry to hear that."

"You have not—" She broke off, then raised her eyes to his. "You have not come to see me."

"I'm sorry." The alcohol seemed to be having a delayed effect on him now. The street teetered sluggishly beneath his feet. His throat closed on a bubble of air.

"It was hard," she said. "It was the hardest I've ever had to do."

His voice came out a whisper: "I know."

Her dark eyes grew darker, and then there were tears on her face. "Please, John, I don't want to do this anymore. I don't think I can do this anymore. Please, help me, help me break free."

She reached for him, and he knew what she meant. He remembered their nights together, his body remembered to the roots of his hair the night he almost took her completely. He also remembered the scratch her nails left by his eye, and more than anything, he remembered her gruesome infidelity with Tibbit-Noyse—with all the other dead men—and he flinched away.

She froze, still reaching.

"I'm sorry," he said.

She drew her arms across her, clasped her elbows in her palms. "I understand."

He opened his mouth, then realized he had nothing more to say. He touched his cap and walked away. The street was uneasy beneath his feet, the sun a furnace burn against his face, and he was blind with the image he carried with him, the look of relief that had flickered in the virgin's eyes.

GIN

However much I might have hoped to forget it, the house is unmistakable. Mangy stucco and peeling green trim, waist-high wire fence that sags off its rusty poles, brown lawn so shorn it is more stubble than grass. The cab pulls up to the curb and when I pay the driver he looks philosophical about the size of the tip. He's probably known it was coming since he picked me up at the Greyhound station.

"Just here for a visit?" he'd asked with a glance at my knapsack. But I didn't encourage conversation and when I get out he doesn't say a word. He drives off as soon as the door is shut, leaving me to stand on the cracked cement and wait for anxiety to pounce. Fear, relief, guilt. I am sure I'm supposed to feel guilt, and the dread of returning to a place I never meant to see again. Waiting for it all beside the curb.

My mother's corpse was in the hospital morgue for more than a week before the lawyer's office tracked me down.

A dog barks out back, across the alley behind the house. It's such an ordinary neighborhood, neither middle class nor poor. Straight streets and short blocks of fifties bungalows with eighties sedans at the curbs. Roses across the street, dandelions next door, and green grass everywhere but here. Two summer weeks since my mother died, but I know the grass has been brown since the spring. Probably it has been brown since I

223

tossed my key on the kitchen table eight years ago. I bend and pick up my bag. The gate in the fence is gone. I take out the key the lawyer sent me and unlock the door.

They say smell is the surest trigger of memory. I am ready for tobacco smoke, old cooking and booze, the atmosphere my lungs had to readjust to every time I came home—*home*—The stench that greets me is so powerful, so heavy with decay, I stagger off the step. Cold saliva floods my mouth. I let the door hang open and run to the fence, where I lean on a post, wet with sweat and spitting.

My mother's corpse occupied the house for five days before the mailman reported a full mailbox and an unpleasant odor to the police.

The steel fence post is really a pipe, shaggy brown with rust inside, an unconvincing layer of silvery protection painted over blisters without. It is threaded at the upper end. I prop my forearm across the opening and think vaguely of spiders while I pick at flakes of silver and wonder about all the things a postman might discover on his rounds. A warm June breeze touches my face with the smells of cut grass and an early barbecue somewhere distant. I could just close the door and walk away. Why close the door, even? I could just walk away. Or take the bus to the hardware store at the strip mall on the highway, the new place that wasn't built back when I still lived here. I could buy a jug, take it to the gas station and fill it with gasoline, and come back here (walk, maybe, or hitch a ride saying my car was out of gas) and unscrew the cap and heave the whole thing in, light a match (I'd have to get matches at the hardware store, too, long wooden ones you could strike anywhere, the kind she used to light her cigarettes) and toss it in.

I could.

The windows are like blank screens inside the darkness of the house. The white blinds are drawn. I walk around, breathing through my nose because I don't want that stink inside my mouth, and open the blinds, the windows, the back door. The kitchen has dishes everywhere, tin cans black with mold, the living room the same only with dirty clothing. The bathroom is a nightmare of crusted hairs and vomit. The bedroom—I look at nothing, only stumble to the window and raise the blinds. Darkness persists: cardboard over the glass. I heave at the sash, which will not move. The smell is killing me. Flies bat against my face, my arms, my mouth. My ears sing and I think, quite clearly, *I'm going to faint.* I claw at the cardboard and old tape gives way, freeing a square of light and air.

Blankets twisted together on the floor. Clothing and shoes piled into chaos in the doorless closet. The mattress, bare, with a brackish coffin-shaped stain down the right-hand side.

Died in her sleep, the lawyer had said. Choked on her own vomit was more likely.

With the window clear, the room is cheerful with the glitter of glass. There must be a hundred bottles prisming rainbows against the yellowed paint of every wall, and even through the miasma of rot I can smell the juniper tang of gin.

———◦◦◦———

sunlight tears a web of woven silences and I
I
there was a dream of sleep
a terrible dream but all the dreams were terrible

djinns released from bottles hand-polished into lamps
heavy with light
cold though with heat hanging in the clarity
dreams
oh but once there was rest inside the perfect night
(there is no night more perfect than the darkness hidden
in the chambers of the heart)
peace before the light came storming in
before the flies
before I
died

I find a motel on the highway, a place where no one remarks on the absence of luggage or car. It is neither quiet nor clean, but there is a laundromat almost next door. After I shower and change into my one spare set of clothes I walk over and put my shirt and jeans into the wash. The place comforts me with its dryer heat and hot-cotton smells. Big and bright, a double line of washing machines set back to back down the middle, dryers on the walls, signs warning of laundry theft and the illegality of smoking. The rumble of trucks on the highway and six dryers running soothe me; the chirps of two brown babies in a double stroller sound like birds. Their mother sits dozing over a magazine, and though I can't stop the comparison (my mother sleeping off a hangover cure, cigarette a long tube of ash between yellow fingers, the old place a linoleum cave strewn with linty socks) it is a distant one. Everything is distant. Or I am distant from everything.

Yes. That seems true.

The mother gets up when a dryer dings and starts folding clothes. She's efficient: every time she finishes with one stack, another dryer is ready. So many clothes, and her breasts and arms are like pillows. The babies must be the youngest of a crowd. I learned from women like her, watching how they worked the machines (only three quarters then), how they folded, the giant bottles of Mr. Clean they thumped down on the conveyor belt at the grocery store. Learned what they bought, read the labels, figured it out. I did that with food, too, buying packages to cook and fruit I could eat raw. I even learned which store-bought treats to take to school, to trade for lunches made by other kids' moms. And on the days when I had nothing to trade, I sat at a library table and did my homework, or curled over a pinching stomach and slept with my head on my books.

My washing machine shimmies to a halt. I get up to toss sodden jeans into a dryer and then hold the door open for the mother with the two babies and six big trash bags of clean, folded laundry. She smiles without seeing me, her face shiny with sweat. When she is gone and I'm alone, I sit on the plastic bench with my back against the wall, watching the dryer turn over, turn over, turn over my clothes, and in my head I make a list: trash bags, Mr. Clean, rubber gloves. A cotton scarf to cover my hair.

In high school I called my hunger dieting, and though the councilors gave me lectures on self-esteem and videos on anorexia that I could not watch even if I wanted to on account of our television was pawned when I was ten, they never asked to speak to my mother. I've watched people for as long as I can remember, picking up the clues, and I was careful with my clothes, my hair, my anger. I never skipped school, except for the times when she destroyed my room and I had nothing to wear. And even then I could always get her to sign a note, once the check came and the first bottle was open, in the days before I learned how to sign her name myself.

---

night comes through spaces in every room
gaps in every wall permit a breeze
to stir the djinn
and the flies
a crooked bat cries hunger outside
as if dreams could so easily be swallowed
digested
gone
see?
I am still here
curled inside this bitter womb
where the djinn rested until released
by the polishing of hands
where there are no gaps
nightmares linger
and I

Flies spin about the house, excited by drafts, dizzy on the tides of rot. A night of open windows has reduced the smell. Though still powerful, it is not a presence that can crowd me out the door. A presence I can, just barely, live with. My scarved head bowed, I drop supermarket bags full of cleaning supplies by the kitchen door and without looking up, without taking stock, I begin to clear away the trash.

In the kitchen there is a deep drawer by the stove full to the brim with shards of china and glass. There are plastic plates, gas station cups, TV dinner trays, saucepans glazed with the remnants of overcooked macaroni, tin cans sprouting spoons, and in the dish drainer by the sink three scrubbed mugs of the kind shaped to fit inside a car's cup holders, but there are no china plates, there are no glass tumblers, there are no teacups painted with purple pansies. Confronted by the drawer of cutting edges, I realize I must cope with a problem she could not solve. The broken pieces are too sharp to be contained by plastic bags, too heavy for paper. I don't resist the temptation to shut the drawer again, I refuse it.

I avoid the room crowded with bottles (the wholeness of which is now utterly mysterious). In the room that I had once slept in I find a pile of boxes. The room is otherwise empty, its uncovered windows dusty and closed. I had not thought to try that door yesterday. The first breath of air inside smells of cardboard and the fruity perfume of the liquor store, but the stench crowds in behind me along with a trio of bluebottle flies. I edge along the stack of boxes and lift the sash. The flies hover at the threshold, but decline to fly through.

The first box I try is heavy with bottles. This stumps me. I had not thought about it—deliberately had not thought about it—and yet I must have done. Why else was I surprised? That she had not calculated her death, but let it come, or not come, as it chose. And it is still here, three bottles, exquisitely clear. Death. Or is it, in some hideous way, unrealized hope?

I cannot bear that she used my room to store her dissolution in. Yet I can. I will. I do. Where else, after all, should she have kept it? This has always been a small house. I leave the door open to the flies and carry an empty box with me to the kitchen where I pour in a burden of ruined shards. I am careful and cut myself only twice, though many slivers of glass and china wear the brown stains of her blood.

Nothing here is worth keeping. The trash bags bulge lumpy and black outside the door, waiting for the odd-job man who swore to have his pickup here by dark. Evening seems impossible. The buzz of flies and the hum of a lawn mower create a hollow place inside my skull where every sound I make, every creak of my joints and dry hiss of breathing, echoes. I fill more boxes.

I sort nothing, but I cannot keep myself from noticing what passes through my hands. When I was very small and she still shopped for us both, she would buy me cheap plastic toys, the ones from bins near the check-out line. I don't remember wheedling for them, as other children did. She bought them spontaneously, for generosity, or because she thought she should. And here they are, though I could have sworn they were all broken or lost by the time I walked away. Rubbery Santas with moveable limbs. Wind-up eggs with chicken feet. A blue monster with a goofy grin that cannot be more than a year or two old. This is a character in an animated movie I saw advertised, and I realize the obvious, that she has been buying these toys for herself. I find them under the coffee table, between the cushions of the orange couch, clotted with dust on the windowsills. Why? Why?

I leave her bedroom for last. I am down to my final package of trash bags and all the boxes are full, crowding the weed-cracked walk to the curb. I empty the closet with my eyes half closed, my mind a stupid tangle. I refuse to think, refuse to see, yet somehow I know when this dress in my gloved hands is torn all up one side, I know when the crotch of these trousers is stiff with urine and blood. Shaking, eyes swarming with black (flies, but I also have not eaten, nor drunk, I did not think to bring water or food, and would have swallowed none of it if I had) I fill the last of the bags and realize I have made a mistake.

The bright bottles still line the walls, and all the boxes are full.

When the odd-job man comes, I pay him in cash and he drops me at the motel on his way to the dump. He has promised to come tomorrow for the furniture.

Thank God. The laundromat is open all night.

———

light leaves but something lingers
vibration warmth sound something
something troubles the air
flies perhaps? searching for lost substance
(the djinn searching for hidden me)
where am I? here nowhere
else surrounded by nightmare
and some walls
lamps linger unlighted I reach
for brightness and find
only djinn
(dark beacon)

I want
I am wanting
where am I?

———•·◦·•———

I ride the bus in the morning, exhaustion riding me. I have not slept since I left home. (My home, that is, not hers.) It seems no matter how hard I scrub, no matter how hot the water is, I cannot rid myself of the stink of her death. The rented bed gives me no rest as I breathe, stifled, through motel sheets. There is a neon sign above my window. Light the color of beer bottles strobes in and out through the shut window with a rattle of papery wings. Last night I turned on the air conditioner for its noise and huddled under the thin blanket, shivering and wishing for day.

I unlock the door, but before I go in I take a tour of the outside. Sunlight illustrates the balding stucco and sagging eaves. Suddenly, I hear in my mind a realtor's phrase "project home" and recall the possibility of laughter. When I find the garden hose attachment and turn the tap to release a stream of first rusty, then clear water, I can believe I might drink from it later. It is going to be a hot day, and I have brought a box of crackers for my lunch.

The smell seems to have abated, but it rises when I begin to wrestle with the furniture, as if it has transmuted into dust. A haze forms as I lever the couch through the doorway, and it never quite abates. I go to the tap often, drink, douse my head. Water from my hair runs down my back beneath my shirt, mingling with sweat, then drying on the warm breeze. I remember this kind of interior weather, so different from the coast where I live now, June heat lifting off the earth to spin high moisture into clouds. White cumulus drift the arch of blue, but in a day or two there will be storms. I picture myself impossibly tall, lifting off the roof and letting the rain and lightning in.

Daylight is brutal to my mother's things. Cheap laminate and seventies upholstery are frayed by abuse, lacquered with stains. Couch and recliner, kitchen table and chairs, battered dresser wearing a thick layer of candle wax: they hunker on the brown grass like hobos waiting for a train. Weary and ready to collapse. By noon I have cleared out everything but my mother's bed.

I lie in the narrow shade at the back of the house where I cannot see the detritus of her days. The dead grass by the tap is damp from all the splashes I made getting clean. I cannot be clean, of course, my clothes are brown with filth, but I have rinsed hands, arms, face, neck. Lying down, my belly dips toward my spine, my shoulders quietly ache. I can feel the hairs stand up on my arms as they dry. I should be hungry but the water is cool in my stomach and requires no company.

A phrase my mother used when I tried to get her to eat: Thank you, love, but momma's tipple requires no company just now. She only called herself momma, I never did. When I spoke to her it was never as anything but mom.

She never hit me. She never failed to know when I came home, unless she was unconscious. She always asked how was I, how was school. I walked in one morning, having spent the night elsewhere (I knew a hundred places to sleep. Most of them would have surprised the people at school who only saw me in the library.) and found her sitting in the kitchen wrapped in the soft blue robe I had given her the Christmas before. Her glass was orange, so she was still working on her hangover, but she smiled at me, so the cure was nearly complete. There was a pack of cigarettes at her elbow, one lit in her hand, the box of matches by the bottle of gin with its cap screwed on tight. She always screwed on the cap between drinks.

She smiled, squinting through smoke to see my face, and said, quite sweetly, Hello, love. You're not home from school already, are you?

It's Saturday, mom.

Well, come give your old momma a kiss. She held open her arm, gesturing me in, and I stepped into her embrace.

Lord, aren't you a bony thing? she said. With a rusty chuckle she added, Better hope it lasts.

I gave her shoulders a squeeze and pulled away to go to my room. That was when I discovered her rages, the first time she had vented them on my things. Perhaps she had been looking for money, perhaps she had only noticed I wasn't there, I don't know. I was fourteen years old.

The flies have followed the furniture outside, or followed the flavor of water on the breeze. They light on my hands, my hair, the damp scarf I put to dry in the sun. The touch reminds me of the chore I have been avoiding. The bed with the coffin-shaped stain. I could put it off until the pickup man arrives, the double mattress is legitimately unwieldy, but I won't. The bottles still line the walls.

Even though they've been given the run of the house and the outer air, the flies still crowd together on the stain. I find myself easing my way around the bed, as if I won't disturb them when I shift the mattress. I know without looking that the blue-patterned fabric is crawling with maggots. I mean to avoid this horror by tipping the mattress from the far side, and carrying it with the underside next to my body. I must be calm and unhurried, strong and exact in my movements, for loathing writhes beneath my skin and panic rattles its hooves against my ribs.

But the mattress is too large. The steel bed frame takes up the center of the floor. And when I trip, and flail, and catch myself, I kick a bottle. A hundred gleaming cylinders roar beneath my feet, shattering the sunlight though every one of them is whole. Blind with light, bathed in sweat, battered by the hurtling wings and clinging, pattering, ubiquitous feet of flies, I

I can't tell the rest.

———

chaos fire the lamps are spilled the lamps
are spilled and the djinn
is free

———

The odd-job man has brought a friend, or perhaps it's his son, to help. When he sees all the furniture he says, "Sure you want me to take it all to the dump? Some of this is still good."

"No," I say. "The dump."

He looks at me, while the younger man scuffles his feet. "You should of told me you were shifting it all yourself. That's too much work for a girl, and in this heat."

"You'll need to do two trips," I say.

He looks at me, at the furniture, at his friend. "At least," he says.

I can see the messages they're passing one another. They mean to sell what they can. Double the wage they'll earn from me: a forty-pounder of rye to go with the case of beer.

I say, "That's everything," and go back inside. It's dusk, and I take the shades off the ceiling lights so I can see. Dry insect corpses spill out, covering my bare arms with the dust of their wings, but this scarcely troubles me. I am numb, now, like a soldier in combat. No, like a resident of hell. No. Like a daughter of this house. While the men curse their load into the truck and drive away, I sweep the living room floor. Dust rises, sepia as the walls. I sweep, cough, herd the dust bunnies into the center of the room. My mother called them ghost farts, something that never failed to make me laugh. I can remember sweeping when the broom was so tall I could barely control it. I rapped the handle twice against my forehead, but I kept on. The clean house was to be a surprise for my mother on her birthday. The only present I had to give her. When she came home.

When she came home I was asleep on the rough orange couch. I woke to hear her trying to tiptoe around the house. She was looking for me, in my room, in her room, not finding me. When she finally teetered into the living room I squeezed my eyes closed and pretended to sleep. She leaned over me, dark mother warm, and I could hardly breathe in her umbra of cigarettes and gin. Still, I did not stir. She stroked my hair off my forehead with the hand that held her cigarette. Ashes stung. She kissed me, and then groped her way to the recliner by the window. I heard her sit, and cough, and sigh. She fell asleep. When I got up in the morning I found the butt of her cigarette on the floor beneath her dangling hand. The coal had burned a black spot into the wood.

There is a galaxy of black spots on the floor revealed by my broom. Their constellations sketch out where the furniture used to be. This is the blue chair. This is the vinyl. This is the end of the couch. Stains make nebulae blurred by the atmosphere of dust. My head seems to drift high above me, orbiting the light bulb sun with the flies. The flies are only flies, restless in all this space. But their shadows dart near then far across the walls, waltzing to the music of the spheres. I myself, sweeping, can hear nothing but a distant ringing of bells.

—·—

presence, movement, life stirs up all the dreams
the djinn begins to stalk and I
crawling from my scattered womb
begin to stalk the djinn

—·—

Scrubbing out the bathroom I make a discovery: once I fail to distinguish my clean self from the rest of this place, it becomes less horrifying. It takes me in, and within it, I begin to transform. Washed by night breezes, rinsed by ammonia and sweat, the air slowly loses its heavy burden of rot. Moving the furniture probably also helped. The rooms echo like the inside of drums. I don't understand why, bright and empty, they seem smaller than they had dark and full.

The pickup man comes for the last load and I pay him for his time. He offers me a ride again, but there are two of them already in the cab and I know how filthy I am. Besides, what would I do but lie on the motel bed and think of cleaning? I might as well clean. I want this done. The pickup man shrugs and drives away, and I stand on the sidewalk for a moment. The sky deepens from blue to blue without ever quite becoming black. Neighbors' open windows reveal light, movement, talk. A television plays a happy gameshow tune. The streetlight at the end of the block wears a tall halo of moths. I turn and go back in.

I am lost
lost
where have all my landmarks gone?
only the walls remember me and I
cling to them
I would dream but the djinn is here too
lost and also clinging
we swallow each other
two snakes with a single tail
(but there is light
I am afraid the lamps are shining)

I have discovered fanaticism. As if burning eyes are watching me, I kneel, bow to the floor with my scrub brush in hand. My jeans are wet with brown sudsing water, the skin on my knees begins to chafe. My neck is stiff, my back aches, my arms and shoulders burn. I should rest. I should eat. I have an image in my mind, from some movie perhaps, of a woman in black scouring a vast stone floor. Penance, I think, but the word is not relevant. What is relevant is that the floors are coming clean.

GIN

I was sixteen when she finally learned to hate me. It was more than just the destruction of my things, my room, I learned not to take these things personally. But her rages were a mystery that struck when I wasn't there. So many times did I come home to be welcomed with a smile, a kiss in the heart of disorder, I began to wonder if it was really her doing. I invented a companion for her, someone she invited in and then sent away again before I came home. The thought of her befriending someone (a man, of course, in my mind) who could wreak such destruction in my home infuriated me far beyond the possibility of her guilt. I searched for clues to his presence amid the wreckage: cigarette butts of a different brand in the ashtrays, a ball cap left behind, a scribbled note, even, God help me, condoms in the bathroom trash. Even bruises on my mother's skin. Nothing. He was a phantom. A poltergeist. An absence.

And then one day I came home from school and she threw her glass at me. Get out, get out out *out!* It was a parrot's shriek, a trapped coyote's yell. Spittle wet her teeth, her chin. She pounded the kitchen table with her bottle, unable to stand. A knot of bruise on my forehead, my hair wet and stinging with gin, I left. Only for two days that time.

There is a thriving ant farm under the kitchen sink. I flood them with Mr. Clean and wash them all away.

———

if we had claws this djinn and I
would be piercing each other's skin
we share eyes with which to see
we mingle

this is not unfamiliar to me
this is not the first time
we have both been set free
together we watch the spaces
we wait for the living to come near
no need to wrestle

yet

———

Before I can clean the floor of her bedroom I have to carry out all the bottles. They are cool, smooth, heavy. They chime, two in each hand. Their juniper sting is stronger than decay even in the death room now; beyond the door it quarrels with the sweeter chemical scent of cleaning. I rank them in the center of the living room floor, two by two, four by four, gleaming rows. They are shockingly clean. Thick white glass, bright as ice, hoards the light. The labels are all gone, and I remember how she used to peel them away, incrementally, while she drank. She would run an absentminded fingernail underneath the edge, run it under, cutting not the paper but the glue, one stroke, then a drink, a pull on a cigarette, a strike of a match, then another stroke, another. She paced herself, matching the speed of her peeling to the frequency of her drinks. Only the last glass was poured from a pure bottle.

I have numbed myself to powerful smells. Though her room is heavy still with rot and gin, and soon lemon-fresh scent, it seems not much different to me than breathing a coastal fog, only warmer. A warm weight inside my lungs. It is late now, the neighborhood has gone quiet beyond the open windows, and even the flies seem slumberous, butting the nicotine walls. They are fewer than they were. Some have escaped, some, as I discover when I sweep, have died. Black freckles I took for burn scars scatter in the wavefront of my broom. Maggots, too, mark the edge of the mattress, writhing bits of rice. Some remnant of horror tugs the skin of my back. I bare my teeth, breathe across my cringing tongue as I harry them into the dust pan with the corpses of their forebears.

How many generations, it occurs to me to wonder, have bred in the two weeks since she died?

---

she is here she is here she is here
the djinn knows her almost
as well as I do
his dark excitement burrows
through me we are too close
even now two dragons
mating on the walls
I nestle I cling I
will not let him go
not now
that she is
finally here

She didn't entirely hate me. The mornings were still safe.

But instead of the sweetness of earlier greetings, she was often sad when I came in. Where you been, love? And I still could not find it in me to hate her, although I now kept all my books and clothes at school. She became, her house became, like the seething store of the subconscious, sheltered from my waking mind. I found an after-school job, I read in the library at lunch, I slept wherever I could, and only sometimes, only sometimes did I dream of going home. Where you been, love? Her voice drowning deep in sorrow and gin.

I have cleaned us into a corner, my bucket and me. Wet floorboards smell darkly of wet dog, patchily drying under the bare bulb. Cruising flies give the peripheral illusion that the light dangles from a swaying cord, but it is set into the ceiling socket, secure. To get the last crevices clean, I lean my forehead against the wall and, two-handed, scrub. I had been thinking accomplishment, completion, but the house conspires otherwise. So close, even the ammonia cannot disguise the odor arising from the plaster wall. Cigarettes and rot, rot, rot.

What a rotten mother you must have had, someone once said to me.

Not really, I said in reply.

But now I know the walls have to be cleaned as well.

———

now

now we fight
yes djinn is strong
desiring to be free but
I have death on my side
and I will not let him go
we tangle together our

242

GIN

skein of nightmares
and I no longer know where
he begins and I
end

———————

Seen close to, the yellowed plaster walls are not uniformly stained. There are gradations both gradual and stark, punctuated by dents as regular as hailstones. Working on my feet, scouring the walls, makes a change, but my shoulders burn with fiery wires along the bone. Wetness streaks the nicotine, paints vague shadows as wide as my brush. I cannot tell if I make anything cleaner, and the damp only seems to release the smell. The night meets a climax where time stills, stalls, stops. I move from kitchen to bathroom to living room to spare room, but time stays where it is, bound to midnight's back. Drowsy flies are caught in the bristles of my brush and drowned in my bucket of foam. Dark water slides down my arms to soak my shirt. It itches on my skin.

I never told her to stop drinking. I never asked her. I never begged. It would have been like asking the sun to stop setting. But no. Who ever asked the indifferent sun for anything? It would have been like asking the air not to fill my lungs. I had never known her sober. If she had quit she would have died.

———————

bound, struggling, we
follow her from room
to room we cling

243

as intimate as plaster
and paint

◦•◦

It occurs to me that I have never known pain before. Not like this, not really. The casual acquaintance of a lifetime has become an intimate friend, a lover, even, inhabiting my body, conquering muscle and bone. But still I work, at the edges of the army of bottles and then, last of all (to let the floor dry, of course) her room.

Nose to the plain of plaster, my head flirts with vertigo.

Flies caught in my bristles leave traces of themselves in my wake.

I did not mean to leave. I was anyway half gone, my best loved things in a locker at school. For many years that is how I have measured my life, by how much of it could fit in a high school locker. Green steel door with a ring for a padlock and tilted vents for air. It has made for a light, if somewhat cramped, existence. But I did not mean to leave.

◦•◦

intimate as tooth
and grin as blood
and skin as body
and breath as weeping
and death

◦•◦

Except that of course I lied when I said she never hit me.

My arms quiver in the air, rattle the brush against the wall.

The last wall in the last room and I am almost done. I let them hang for a moment at my side, enraptured by the shape and surge of fire along my limbs. I am heady with fatigue. The last wall in the last room. I lift my hands and begin again.

When I was seventeen, only three months from graduation, I spent a rare night at home. She was almost too far gone to say hello when I came in. I can't remember why I did, now. Did I, for once, have nowhere else to go? I don't know. I went into my room, that was almost empty but for the mattress on the floor, and lay down. I was tired. I must have been tired, because the known hated smog of tobacco smoke and booze and vomit and piss did not keep me awake, though I have always been sensitive to smells. I was asleep when she fumbled open the door, only slowly waking when she grabbed my hair, my arm, and dragged me up.

She was raving. Her split nails dug my scalp.

Get out get out now now *now*!

I remember how she hauled in her breath with a smoker's wheeze.

Out he's out he's out *he's out*!

I remembered the secret man I had searched for but never found.

OUT

she howled and spat and drove me, staggering, both of us, down the hall, her fist on my back, my sides, my head, pistons, hooves, pummeling through the kitchen, into the table, glass shattering, cut my foot, through the door

out.

I remember the blank, simple surprise I felt when she shut the door and locked it. I remember the damp cold of the spring night

on my bare legs and arms. I remember the gradual realization
of pain, and of the shirt that was my only covering, and of
the prickling damp of the bloody grass against my cut foot. I
remember how long the hour was that I stood there, how slow the
understanding that she was not going to let me back in.

I remember sitting on the front step with nowhere else to go.

I remember waiting for her to pass out so I could jimmy open
my bedroom window and collect my clothes.

I remember everything, but I still don't know why.

Why?

The wall is done.

---

when she begins to weep I
forget my strength I
forget death I
let him go oh yes
the djinn
is free

I stand in the middle of the floor and through my tears I see the
shapes my wet brush has made. Made, discovered, disinterred.
There is a creature, a fly/dragon/genie who pours upward from
an open bottle, no feet, many grasping claws

and a woman

a tiny tiny ragdoll woman

caught between his jaws.

when she begins to weep I
forget my fear I
forget pain I
let him go oh yes
the djinn
is free
and so
am I

I have not been back to the house since that night. In the meantime, my mother's corpse, what the heat and flies had left of it, was cremated, her ashes enclosed inside a brown cardboard box and given to me. I paid fees I couldn't really afford and signed papers at the lawyer's office. The house was everything, and the lawyer explained about probate, about how, with certain restrictions, certain clauses, I could put it on the market even before the courts had proved my mother's estate. She had, astonishingly, left almost no debts at all. An unpaid electricity bill, property taxes for the year before. Once my checks were cashed, I would be broke, but I would be free of obligation, and whatever the house realized was mine.

I called the real estate agent, and she asked me to meet her there with the key. Easier, she said, to give me her opinion on the spot, and she would have more documents for me to sign. So here I am, earlier than I meant to be. At first I think I will meet the agent outside, but though I wait on the crumbling sidewalk for pain, for grief, nothing comes. There is just this house, this yard, this street. There was rain two nights ago, but now the sky is bright. Across the street a robin flirts with a sprinkler, chasing a bath and a meal. For no reason (of course I have a reason) I take out the key and go in.

The place is empty and, though somewhat battered, clean. It will only take some paint to make it new, and maybe some rugs. My footsteps echo off the walls as I walk from room to room. Even to my sensitive nose there is no trace of smell. The bottles are all gone, hauled away by the odd-job man for the cost of the deposit, and the three that were still full of gin.

And on the bedroom wall, there is nothing. Nothing. Except, perhaps, hidden in the traces of my cleaning, the delicate remnants of wings.

QUEEN OF THE
BUTTERFLY KINGDOM

The woman from the embassy called again this morning, as she does every morning. The negotiations are continuing, she said. They had not been apprised of any changes.

Changes, I said. I was deeply impressed by her choice of word; but then, I am always intrigued by people's private lexicons. Of course I knew she meant "changes in the situation," but that only meant there were no fresh rumors of torture, no dead men displayed for the evening news. Change. Well, yes, injury is change. Death is certainly change.

We'll let you know as soon as we hear anything new, she said.

Don't let your life stop, was my distant mother's advice. Another phone call, messages from another world, the real world of home. Carry on, my mother said. Carry on as best you can.

I stood in this borrowed kitchen, the glazed tiles cold beneath my feet, Ryan's blue terrycloth robe cinched around my waist, my teacup cooling in my hand. I wanted to think about the word "changes." I wanted to let it carve new pathways through the erosion patterns in my brain, and why not? I'm a writer. I would never say, Words are my life, because that is too extravagant, too grandiose, but it is secretly true. My vocation is to turn the nothing of dreams into books on the shelves. Magic! See me build my castles in the air! My bare feet were cold, and I decided my mother was right. I made a fresh cup of tea and carried it up the many stairs of this narrow city house to the attic that the absent owners converted to a children's playroom, and that I have in my turn made into a kind of office. My desk is an old door propped across two piles of bankers boxes full of the manuscripts and contracts I couldn't bear to leave behind. I turned on the laptop and without checking my email (there is no cable connection up here) I opened a new document in Word.

The white screen, the blank page. This is the novel I came here to write. No, no. I came here because I am in love, but this is the novel I could not write at home.

I had to get up again and go down three flights to the living room where a pile of Ryan's mail waits for him to come back—come home, I almost said. I always compose in manuscript format, it's so much easier than reformatting later, but I find the intricacies of this foreign address impossible to remember. I went back upstairs and typed it in at the top left-hand corner of the screen, then keyed down a few spaces and typed the title.

Queen of the Butterfly Kingdom

Then I looked at it again, and tried it with a "The" at the beginning, but no. Too definite. There's something dreamy about it the other way.

Queen of the Butterfly Kingdom

A few more spaces down, and I typed Chapter One.

And then, after a while, I got up and went down two flights to shower and put on some clothes.

Like other cities, this one is composed of hidden neighbor-hoods—neighborhoods, that is, that look like undifferentiated city to the unaccustomed small-town eye. I have been exploring since we first arrived, although Ryan teased me, calling me a scaredy-cat and a hick Canuck. I didn't mind. On the one hand, I was feeling cat-like then, slinking close to the walls with my sides sucked in, somewhat inclined to growl; and on the other hand I loved the sound of those words snapped together like a couple of birch twigs brittle with ice. Hick Canuck. At an embassy dinner he whispered it in my ear to make me laugh, his voice two soft puffs of air against my neck, like kernels of corn exploding. Hick Canuck. Especially delicious since, by the standards of this ancient country, so was everybody at the table, from the Ambassador on down.

But what Ryan didn't see, being busy with briefings even before the team left with the special envoy, was how, like a cat, I expanded my territory in cautious circles. I hate to hurry these things. It seemed rash to venture out into the streets and the stores—the buses! My God!—before I even knew how the light switches worked, the telephone, the stove. I mean "know" in the intimate sense, the habitual sense that does not even register the smells and sounds of home. When I am a foreigner, I am an explorer, continually amazed at tourists who can simply visit a place like this. Eventually, though, I discovered the side streets and main streets, the children's parks and the botanical parks and the jogging trails, the street with the bakeries, the street with the hardware stores, the street with the whores. Neighborhoods are such subtle things here I had to watch which way the neighbors turned when they left their doors, which way they came from with their string bags full of food. I thought that if I bought a string bag and filled it at the right butcher's shop and wine store

I would cease to be a stranger, or at least a foreigner, but it hasn't worked out that way. At home the bus drivers wave even when I'm not catching the bus, the café owner teases me if I don't get my usual decaf latté with no foam. Here I don't know how to ask for no foam, and though I go to the neighborhood café they have yet to notice that I always scrape it off with my spoon.

At least when I go at the quiet time after lunch I can sit at my regular table. Not the one in the window, it's too big for one person, but the one against the wall just down from the window corner. Today I came too early, however, and had to sit at a table in back. As I struggled through my order (I have memorized the words, but they still come out of my mouth as sounds) I consoled myself with the thought that really, there is no café in the world where a writer can't open her notebook and sit, pen in hand, entirely at home.

I opened my notebook, and sat, pen in hand.

A drop of rain fell on the page, blurring the forgotten words of last week. *Keep it fresh and strange*, the notebook said. I couldn't remember what "it" was. Something from the novel. Magic? Love? More raindrops fell, spattering on the tabletop, pinging off the saucer beneath my glass.

"Lady, you are so far out of your place I could not find you."

I looked up to see the rainbird perched like a crow on the back of an empty chair.

"You found me," I pointed out. "Here you are."

"And here *you* are." The rainbird spread his arms in a gesture at the café, the waiters, the hissing espresso machine. Crystal droplets scattered from his feathers like shining beads from a broken necklace. "I wonder why, when you have all the worlds and time."

I ducked my head and smoothed the damp-rippled page. His black glass eyes were hard to meet. "Where would you have me go?"

" 'Go', lady? You are the center. To you the worlds bend like grass in the rain."

As he spoke more rain fell, a pattering that mingled with the roar and sigh of steam, like liquid consonants in a whispered hiss. What language did they speak? I did not know, and then I did: it was the poetry of the grass that bowed towards my chair, an invisible meadow sketched out in the gleam of spiderwebs and dew. The waiter walked by, oblivious, and the grass laughed and danced aside.

"Come, lady. We are here." The rainbird leaned forward on his perch, his hands between his knees, avid as a boy. "Give us your tale."

"I have no stories in me," I said sadly. "The only one I know these days is out there in the real world somewhere, unfinished, out of reach."

He tossed his head and snapped his beak in annoyance. I thought I saw a bright fragment of a severed wing fall to the floor, but when I looked the floor was carpeted in a moss of jewels, beads of dew catching the light and colors of the busy street outside.

"Lady," the rainbird said, "that story is not worthy of you. Are you not the hero, the villain, the mystery, the queen? In *that* story you barely figure. You have made yourself an afterthought, a figment, a shadow by the fireless hearth. As far as you are concerned, *that* story is no story at all."

I sat in sullen silence. He was talking about Ryan's story,

Ryan's captivity, Ryan's peril. What he was talking about was no story at all. It was my life. Mine, and Ryan's, for as long as Ryan lived.

"Listen, lady." The rainbird was coaxing now. "Spin your own tale. Spin *our* tale, yours and mine. Come away with me, come back to your true place. Come home."

While he spoke the elegant grasses moved around me, draping me in shining cobwebs, winding me a cloak of rain-gemmed strands. In every droplet there shone a story, as round and complete as a world, and in every story shone my face crowned in flames or petals or thorns.

My face, but not Ryan's. However hard I looked, the only story he figured in was his own.

"Come home," the rainbird said, and when I echoed him, "home," I felt the shining strands drawn across my mouth and nose, not a cloak but a muffling shroud. "Am I supposed to bury myself in my dreams?"

"Not bury," said the rainbird. "Live!"

But as I sat there, pen in hand, life was wearing chains many miles to the east.

"Even an empty hearth can make a story," I said. I closed my notebook, paid my tab, and left without another word.

<hr />

Morning again, still no news, and I climbed up to the attic to make another attempt at work. Once there, however, I discovered I had failed to save yesterday's aborted beginning, and I had to open a new document. And then, of course, I had to go back downstairs to the living room for an envelope with this address

254

on it, and then it occurred to me to wonder if I should be using this address on my manuscripts at all. Even if Ryan—

Even if Ryan comes back, this posting was only supposed to be for two years. Where will I be when it comes time to discuss the book with an editor? I needed to call my agent, there were so many things I should have discussed with her before I left. It all happened so quickly, and now here I am where morning is the middle of the night back home. Email, I thought, but the only connection is in Ryan's office, and I just— How can I explain myself to you? It wasn't the pain of missing him while sitting in his space, the space he hasn't even had a chance to make his own. It was the outrageousness, the sheer humiliating cliché of being the woman who felt the pain, the woman who had been left behind. I can't escape the pain, but surely I can escape the cliché? Suddenly my mother was the wisest person I knew. Waiting, after all, is still a kind of life.

So I went out for food. Shopping is surprisingly painless, even for someone who is effectively a deaf-mute. Everything has a price on it, or on its shelf, and for all the weirdnesses and seemingly perverse and willful oddities of this foreign land, the cash registers still show an electronic total and the bills are all numbered in their corners just as you would expect. I do prefer fresh food, however; not only for the usual reasons, but because this alien packaging can be deceptive. Ryan and I had been eating breakfast cereal for a week when he came home laughing from a reception to say he had been served our cereal with bits of sausage and mustard perched on the little squares. I had the dreadful sense that he had told our mistake to his fellow guests, who would have laughed and offered up dumb foreigner stories of their own. I should have laughed, too, but I was overcome by that wretched playground feeling of having innocently worn the wrong tights, the wrong backpack, the wrong brand of shoes to school. What's got into you? Ryan asked me, but his voice was tender, tinged with a kind of wonder. To myself, having published a scant handful of books, I am barely a writer, but to Ryan I am an artist and therefore mysterious, even a little exalted. Where do you go? he asks me when he catches me dreaming. Where were you just now? I am too shy to answer honestly. My books are public, my airy castles open for daily tours, but my imagination is still as secret as a locked bedroom door. Read my next book, I say, and he promises me he will.

I walked back from the shops with the handle of my string bag cutting into my fingers, and looked up outside the house to notice, almost simultaneously, the fresh post-rain light slipping under the hem of the clouds and the officious Mercedes parked illegally at the curb. The driver's door was swinging open (perhaps the movement that had caught my eye) and Alain Bernard climbed out into the narrow street. Alain is fairly young and fairly important, and he had something to do with Ryan's appointment to the envoy's staff. I don't know the details. They might be friends, but then again, they might not.

This, of course, was not what I thought when Alain climbed out of the car. You can guess what I did think. Or can you? I'm not sure you can call it thinking, it's more like the floor of your mind giving way, like a sudden shove out of a mental window, so your heart takes flight and your stomach plummets. Alain took an urgent step toward me and I dropped my bag, loosing a single orange into the street. I wanted to fend him off, to go away, to pretend I hadn't seen him, but even in that dreadful moment the writer in me was thinking how inadequate that single orange was. In the movie version of my life it would have been a dozen oranges cascading over the blackened bricks, leaping and rolling, caroming off the curb in an extravagant emotional collapse. But what does a woman living alone, a woman who can barely force herself to swallow past the loneliness and fear, want with a dozen oranges? I bought exactly two, and one was still peering out at me through the string bars of its cage.

Oh, God! No, don't think it, it's nothing like that, there's no bad news! Alain, who read everything in that single wobbling orange, snatched up the fruit and then snatched up me, holding me tight against his double-breasted diplomatic wool while he cursed himself in both official languages, his feet awkwardly straddled across the fallen bag. This was very dramatic but I'm not really fond of drama outside of books. I stiffened like an offended cat and after a moment Alain let me go.

Jesus, he said, I'm such an asshole. I just came to see how you are.

I'm fine, I told him. I should have also told him he wasn't an asshole, which he isn't, but I did not. I bent and gathered my suddenly pitiful bag from between his polished black toes and held it mutely open like a beggar's cup to receive the escaped orange. He dropped it in with a precise movement of finger and thumb, and that picture—his hand with its watch and starched cuff, my white, nail-bitten fingers, the orange—looked like another frame from the same movie, the kind of image that makes the instructor hit pause and say to her class, Now what is the director trying to say with this shot? To which I say, God knows. Me, I've always written for my characters and let theme take care of itself.

Alain followed me down the area stairs and in by the basement door. Thanks to my mother's advice I wasn't embarrassed by a dirty kitchen: no depressed sink full of dishes, no distractedly unswept floor. I put the groceries away and filled the kettle, but Alain said I looked like I needed a drink. Taking this to mean he wanted one, I led him upstairs to the living room where Ryan keeps a supply. I will drink for pleasure but not for comfort, and the afternoon whiskey tasted like medicine.

You haven't called me, Alain said. Tell me how you've been.

I've been waiting, I said.

I look at this and think how cold I must have sounded to poor Alain, who after all has better things to do in this crisis than hold a hostage's girlfriend's hand—at least, I hope to God he has better things to do. Are we all just waiting, waiting, waiting? This is my faith: that somewhere, men and women who have known Ryan far longer than I, who have worked with him in situations exactly as crucial and frightening as this one, are talking, pleading, promising, blustering, threatening, using every psychological trick and political strategy to bring him and the others home. And yet here is Alain, drinking Ryan's whiskey and looking at me with an intense, intimate, questioning pain in his eyes. Shall I tell you my secret thought? I am not vain. I swear I am not, I may never recover from the astonishment of Ryan's declaration of love—for me! of all people!—and yet, fairly or not, I can't help but question the source of Alain's concern. He has always watched me too closely, with too much tension around his eyes. But how would I know? Maybe what I see there isn't wanting but guilt. He was still calling himself names when he left. I locked the door behind him, went up all those stairs, and turned the computer on. To hell with the address. I typed the title, spaced down, and once again tapped out Chapter One.

Morning. The same phone call, the same woman, the same lack of news. No news is good news, the koan of cynical times. For an instant after I hung up the telephone I wanted, I desired, I longed to be with Ryan, wherever he is. Let me wear the blindfold and the chains, let me sit in the dark, in the icy water of the flooded cell. Only let me be there instead of here, like this, thinking this, alone. But then I had to laugh, for Ryan was probably longing just as powerfully, and infinitely more sensibly, to be here with me. I toasted a piece of bread I knew I wouldn't eat and sat with the plate between my elbows and my teacup pressed against my chin. Ryan and I usually share a pot of coffee in the morning, but these days the caffeine sends unbearable twitches down my nerves. I can't tell you now all the things I thought sitting at the table this morning, but I know my mind circled a long, long way before it looped back to the city, the house, the novel waiting unwritten upstairs.

The kitchen only has windows looking out on the skinny garden in back. Gardens are important here. This one is very tasteful, with clean, patterned bricks and shade-loving plants, and right now all the beds are full of narcissus and crocus, their watercolor hues freshly painted by the rain. At home there is snow on the ground, but here we have flowers and new leaves on the trees. After a while I pulled my notebook out of the bag that had been sitting on the counter since yesterday, and just then I saw the first flicker of movement at the top of the garden wall. Just a pale flash at first, as if someone in the lane had tossed a bit of burning trash into the yard. But no: the paleness clung, and doubled itself, and became two paws. The rest of the intruder followed in swift installments, an elbow, a head and foreleg, a torso and a tail, until a cat entire dropped down into the bushes at the foot of the wall.

Tiger, tiger, burning bright. The rain striped his orange sides with sullen smoke. He shook himself, irritable with damp, and stood upright, a cat-man with flowing robes and a turban that was all fringe and flame. He fussed with the set of his coat as he stalked fastidiously through the shaggy grass of the lawn toward my door. His knock was an impatient tattoo. I opened cautiously, thinking of the varnished doorframe and the dark timbers of the ceiling.

"Madame." He bowed himself inside, his clothes rustling like starched silk. He wore a scent like sandalwood and burning cedar. I don't know what he smelled when he sniffed the air. "You have had a visitor."

He spoke as if he had a right to be offended, which put my hackles up. "Alain. A friend."

"If he were a friend he would know better than to interrupt you at your work."

"I was not working."

"Why not?"

I made an exasperated gesture, already fed up with his peremptory air. He changed his manner, bowed and rubbed his furry cheek against my hand.

"Madame. Don't scold me, I beg you. I think only of you."

Threads of smoke and steam rose about him, heady with the

scent of dreams. The mutter of the rain outside blurred into the drowsy murmur of flames.

"I won't scold," I said, seduced by his warmth. "But—"

"Say me no buts. Only hear me out, I pray." The firecat sat opposite me in Ryan's chair, and smoke wove itself into braids and wreaths about the table and the room. "I ask for nothing, I have no needs and no desires. I do not ask for comfort, and I do not hunger for the food laid out for another man's return. But lady, others do. Let me protect you. Let me hide you away—"

"From what?" I said. I made my tone sharp enough to cut through the insinuating strands of smoke that stroked my face.

The firecat smiled. "Why, lady, from these interruptions and intrusions, these visitors and telephone calls, these newspapers and—"

"And this real world?"

"Real? Is your absent lover more real than I?"

"Ryan is real." If I had not been surprised I would not have felt such dismay. My voice was hoarse, my hands curled into fists. "Ryan is real."

"More real than I? What is he but a memory, an invention, a dream? What do you have of him but an echo in your skull—and what, then, am I? Do you call me less than that?"

"He is real," I said again, and as if I could make it true by saying it: "He is alive. He is more alive than you ever were."

The firecat stood and loomed over me, his paws on the table, flames flickering up from the wood like tiny, incandescent wings. "I will show you what is real," he purred. "I will show you what is real and what is not. I will show you just how real, and how unreal, *you* are, for a start."

But before he could the silence of that tall, narrow, empty house was shattered by the telephone.

Don't drop anything, Alain said, it's only me.

He wanted to take me out to dinner. You need to get out, he said, as if he had found me huddled in a broom closet, soft as a mushroom, pale as a fish in a cave. The trouble is that as wrong as Alain was, he was also right. I am tender and sad. But he was winkling me out of my shell like a raccoon with a snail, and I could not summon the strength of will to say no, even though I knew how it would be. Alain trying to alleviate my loneliness, and me knowing it is impossible. My loneliness has too specific a cause, it requires too specific a cure.

This evening, not knowing where Alain was taking me, I dressed in what I persist in thinking of as my grown-up clothes—clothes in silk and wool, clothes I bought new. To be honest with you, though I look good in them, I don't like them much. When I wear them I feel as though they are also wearing me. As Ryan says, I prefer clothes that have been beaten into submission before I put them on.

Oh, let me laugh, let me laugh. If black humor isn't funny at midnight, when should it be? But having thought that phrase, having permitted entry to those words, beaten and submission, they became a hammer and chisel carving a bloody path of empathy across the inside of my skin. I wanted to tell Ryan, Hold fast to your integrity; if you have to, you can afford to let your dignity go. But is that true? Or is that just the writer in me wanting to be wise?

If Ryan were a character in a book I was writing, I would peel him like an onion. I would strip away a layer of him for every succeeding stage of his capture and confinement, make him denser, simpler, truer—smaller—for every door he is dragged through, every narrower, darker, harder cell he inhabits, until he is so small and pure he can slip through the bars of his cage, the keyhole of his door. I would leave his captors bewildered, humbled by their own powerlessness and by the weakness of their fortress keep that keeps nothing of worth, all the treasure flown, thin and light and free as a butterfly on the warming breeze.

And as a writer, I would not do it gently. If Ryan were an invention of mine I would be cruel to him, even savage. His layers of humor, temper, affection, fear would be stripped away—I would strip them away—like layers of skin. I would pare him down to the delicate framework of bone, all the vulnerable leverage points of his being exposed. God, it's too easy to think of ways to torture a human being. I can come up with dozens without effort, it's as if they wait, a noisome crowd of tallow-sweated men, leaning against some unmarked door in the mind. Why is it so easy? Is it only my own fear, the inevitable recognition of my own body's mortal tenderness? Or do we all have a storeroom of horrors in our minds? Perhaps it is only a part of our human legacy, a psychic equivalent to the rusted iron maidens they display in the museums here. Ryan and I saw several of these displays when he played the tourist with me before he was called away. He, too, will have a store of horrors pressing against the doors of his mind. If he were a character of mine, we would share those horrors, neither of us truly alone in the dark as I wrote the story of his ideal. At least he would have me, even if I were the author of his pain.

At least I would have my victim, him.

Alain arrived with a smile hung across the face of his worry and took me to a restaurant so quiet and civilized it was like a Victorian library. The waiters whispered in French and Alain answered in his earthy Gaspesian drawl, which made me smile. We really are all hicks beneath the wool. We are the children of loggers and trappers and cowboys, the grandchildren of the intrepid or disgraceful younger sons, and we are sometimes childlike, I think, in this subtle and sinister ancient world. We are all explorers here. We are voyageurs, and we are Iroquois in the royal court, where the racks are kept well-oiled and ready for use. We'll get them back, Alain said, but I can't help but wonder if this is another case of arrows vs. guns.

This morning the telephone did not ring.

I feel as though I have become a character in a novel—or less even than that: a painted icon traced out in tarnished gold. I am Woman Who Waits By Phone. Did I sleep through the ring? I wasn't asleep, I could chart for you the course of my night hour by hour, tell you to the minute the time the garbage truck rumbled by, to the minute when the natural light first overtook the light from the streetlamp outside. I did not sleep—yet, did I dream I was awake? I know I did not, but somehow the knowledge cannot touch my doubt. And then getting up—did the jangling springs of this antique bed drown the electronic burble of the modern phone? did the water thundering into the sink? the growl of the kettle working itself up to a boil? On every other day since Ryan left, the telephone's ring has burst into the house and rummaged through the air of every room, invasive as a policeman or a thief, yet this morning it might have been drowned by the windy rush of air into my lungs.

I did all the predictable things: checked the dial tone twice, checked that the handset was in its cradle three times, started to call the embassy and stopped. How many times? I don't remember. *Don't tie up the line* joined forces with *Don't ask for news if you are afraid of what you might hear* to weigh me down with chains. I wanted to call. I wanted to shower and dress and go out for coffee as if this were just another day of waiting. How is this different? Because I have not been told that I am still in suspense. I am in suspension about my own suspense. I might be falling and not even know. I find that this is perhaps not unendurable—and is this the real human tragedy, that so little is unendurable? Or is it that we so often have no choice but to endure?—nevertheless, I also find I cannot do anything *but* endure. It is I who have been stripped to the bone. Without skin I am cold, without muscles I am immobile, without nerves I am numb. I sit in this last, smallest, darkest cell, this cell without a window or a door, this cell without even cracks in its walls, and I am at the end of my inventions. They sit outside the door, powerless and mute. I have carried myself into the dead heart of the maze, and here I sit still alone, waiting to become so small, so light, so close to nothing that I can evaporate into the air. Waiting. The only sound is the sound my blood makes as it marches past my ears. Waiting.

When the telephone finally rings, it clamors like a bugle, loud enough to shake down the walls. This house is two hundred and eighty years old, and bricks and timbers, floorboards and chimneypots that have stood for longer than my country has had a name are crumbling around my ears. Dust stops up my throat and burns my eyes so that I am blind with tears. There is light, but I cannot see; air, but I cannot breathe. I grope through the crumbs of brick and splinters of oak until I touch the smooth anachronistic plastic of the phone.

It rings again and lightning flashes through the bones of my hand. Dust glows blue and an ominous ruddy smoke-shadow hovers over the jackdaw piles of shattered beams. I lift the receiver to my ear.

"Hello," I say, my voice harsh with dust. "Hello?"

An unfamiliar voice with a familiar accent says my name.

"Yes," I say, a husk of a word.

"Please hold."

Hold? There is nothing beneath my feet, I am dangling over a void at the end of this telephone cord, of course I hold! The receiver clicks and hums, and then static bursts over me like a storm of bees.

"Go ahead," says a voice as distant as the moon.

Thinking the voice is speaking to me, I say, "Hello?" and so I miss a word or two, perhaps my name.

"Is this thing working? Hello? Are you there?"

Ryan, rescued, is shouting at me from God knows where, a helicopter, a submarine, the far side of the moon.

"I'm here," I say. "I'm here. When are you coming home?"

And suddenly the air is full, not of dust, but of wings.

THE LONG, COLD GOODBYE

Berd was late and she knew Sele would not wait for her, not even if it weren't cold enough to freeze a standing man's feet in his shoes. She hurried anyway, head down, as if she hauled a sled heavy with anxiety. She did not look up from the icy pavement until she arrived at the esplanade, and was just in time to see the diver balanced atop the railing. Sele! she thought, her voice frozen in her throat. The diver was no more than a silhouette, faceless, anonymous in winter clothes. Stop, she thought. Don't, she thought, still unable to speak. He spread his arms. He was an ink sketch, an albatross, a flying cross. Below him, the ice on the bay shone with the apricot-gold of the sunset, a gorgeous summer nectar of a color that lied in the face of the ferocious cold. The light erased the boundary between frozen sea and icy sky; from where Berd stood across the boulevard, there was no horizon but the black line of the railing, sky above and below, the cliff an edge on eternity. And the absence the diver made when he had flown was as bright as all the rest within the blazing death of the sun.

Berd crossed the boulevard, huddled deep within the man's overcoat she wore over all her winter clothes. Brightness brought tears to her eyes and the tears froze on her lashes. She was alone on the esplanade now. It was so quiet she could hear the groan of tide-locked ice floes, the tick and ping of the iron railing threatening to shatter in the cold. She looked over, careful not to touch the metal even with her sleeve, and saw the shape the suicide made against the ice. No longer a cross: an asterisk bent to angles on the frozen waves and ice-sheeted rocks. He was not alone there. There was a whole uneven line of corpses lying along the foot of the cliff, like a line of unreadable type, the final sentence in a historical tome, unburied until the next storm swept in with its erasure of snow. Berd's diver steamed, giving up the last ghost of warmth to the blue shadow of the land. He was still faceless. He might have been anyone, dead. The shadow grew. The sun spread itself into a spindle, a line; dwindled to a green spark and was gone. It was all shadow now, luminous dusk the color of longing, a blue to break your heart, ice's consolation for the blazing death of the sky. Berd's breath steamed like the broken man, dusting her scarf with frost. She turned and picked her way across the boulevard, its pavement broken by frost heaves, her eyes still dazzled by the last of the day. It was spring, the 30th of April, May Day Eve. The end.

Sele. That was not, could never have been him, Berd decided. Suicide had become a commonplace this spring, this non-spring, but Sele would never think of it. He was too curious, perhaps too fatalistic, certainly too engaged in the new scramble for survival and bliss. (But if he did, *if* he did, he would call on Berd to witness it. There was no one left but her.) No. She shook her head to herself in the collar of her coat. Not Sele. She was late. He had come and gone. The diver had come and gone. Finally she felt the shock of it, witness to a man's sudden death, and flinched to a stop in the empty street. Gaslights stood unlit in the blue dusk, and the windows of the buildings flanking the street were mostly dark, so that the few cracks of light struck a note of loneliness. Lonely Berd, witness to too much, standing with her feet freezing inside her shoes. She leaned forward, her sled of woe a little heavier now, and started walking. *She* would not go that way, not *that* way, she would *not*. She would find Sele, who had simply declined to wait for her in the cold, and get what he had promised her, and then she would be free.

But where, in all the dying city, would he be?

Sele had never held one address for long. Even when they were children Berd could never be sure of finding him in the same park or alley or briefly favored dock for more than a week or two. Then she would have to hunt him down, her search spirals widening as he grew older and dared to roam further afield. Sometimes she grew disheartened or angry that he never sought her out, that she was always the one who had to look for him, and then she refused. Abstained, as she came to think of it in more recent years. She had her own friends, her own curiosities, her own pursuits. But she found that even when she was pursuing them she would run across Sele following the same trail. Were they so much alike? It came of growing up together, she supposed. Each had come too much under the other's influence. She had not seen him for more than a year when they found each other again at the lecture on ancient ways.

"Oh, hello," he said, as if it had been a week.

"Hello." She bumped shoulders with him, standing at the back of the crowded room—crowded, it must be said, only because the room was so small. And she had felt the currents of amusement, impatience, offense, disdain, running through him, as if together they had closed a circuit, because she felt the same things herself, listening to the distinguished professor talk about the "first inhabitants," the "lost people," as if there were not two of them standing in the very room.

"We lost all right," Sele had said, more rueful than bitter, and Berd had laughed. So that was where it had begun, with a shrug and a laugh—if it had not begun in their childhood, growing up poor and invisible in the city built on their native ground—if it had not begun long before they were born.

Berd trudged on, worried now about the impending darkness. The spring dusk would linger for a long while, but there were no lamplighters out to spark the lamps. In this cold, if men didn't lose fingers to the iron posts, the brass fittings shattered like rotten ice. So there would be no light but the stars already piercing the blue. *Find Sele, find Sele.* It was like spiraling back into childhood, spiraling through the city in search of him. Every spiral had a beginning point. Hers would be his apartment, a long way from the old neighborhood, not so far from the esplanade. *He won't be there*, she warned herself, and as if she were tending a child, she turned her mind from the sight of the dead man lying with the others on the ice.

Dear Berd,

I cannot tell you how happy your news has made me. You are coming! You are coming at last! It seems as though I have been waiting for a lifetime, and now that I know I'll only have to wait a few short weeks more they stretch out before me like an eternity. Your letters are all my consolation, and the memory I hold so vividly in my mind is better than any photograph: your sweet face and your eyes that smile when you look sad and yet hold such a melancholy when you smile. My heart knows you so well, and you are still mysterious to me, as if every thought, every emotion you share (and you are so open you shame me for my reserve) casts a shadow that keeps the inner Berd safely hidden from prying eyes. Oh, I won't pry! But come soon, as soon as you can, because one lifetime of waiting is long enough for any man . . .

———•◦•◦•———

Sele's apartment was in a tall old wooden house that creaked and groaned even in lesser colds than this. Wooden houses had once been grand, back when the lumber was brought north in wooden ships and the natives lived in squat stone huts like ice-bound caves, and Sele's building still showed a ghost of its old beauty in its ornate gables and window frames. But it had been a long time since it had seen paint, and the weathered siding looked like driftwood in the dying light. The porch steps groaned under Berd's feet as she climbed to the door. An old bell pull hung there. She pulled it and heard the bell ring as if it were a ship's bell a hundred miles out to sea. The house was empty, she needed no other sign. All the same she tried the handle, fingers wincing from the cold brass even inside her mitten. The handle fell away from its broken mechanism with a clunk on the stoop and the door sighed open a crack, as if the house inhaled. It was dark inside; there was no breath of warmth. All the same, thought Berd, all the same. She stepped, anxious and hopeful, inside.

Dark, and cold, and for an instant Berd had the illusion that she was stepping into one of the stone barrow-houses of her ancestors, windowless and buried deep under the winter's snow. She wanted immediately to be out in the blue dusk again, out of this tomb-like confinement. Sele wasn't here. And beyond that, with the suicide fresh in her mind and the line of death scribbled across her inner vision, Berd had the sense of dreadful discoveries waiting for her, as if the house really were a tomb. *Go. Go before you see . . .* But suppose she didn't find Sele elsewhere and hadn't checked here? Intuition was not infallible—her many searches for Sele had not always borne fruit—she had to be sure. Her eyes were adjusting to the darkness. She found the stairs and began to climb.

There was more light upstairs, filtering down like a fine gray-blue dust from unshuttered windows. Ghost light. The stairs, the whole building, creaked and ticked and groaned like every ghost story every told. Yet she was not precisely afraid. Desolate, yes, and abandoned, as if she were haunted by the empty house itself; as if, having entered here, she would never regain the realm of the living; as if the entire world had become a tomb. *As if.*

It was the enthusiasm she remembered, when memory took her like a sudden faint, a shaft of pain. They had been playing a game of make-believe, and the game had been all the more fun for being secreted within the sophisticated city. Like children constructing the elaborate edifice of Let's Pretend in the interstices of the adult world, they had played under the noses of the conquerors who had long since forgotten they had ever conquered, the foreigners who considered themselves native born. Berd and Sele, and later Berd's cousins and Sele's half-sister, Isse. They had had everything to hide and had hidden nothing. The forgotten, the ignored, the perpetually overlooked. Like children, playing. And for a time Sele had been easy to find, always here, welcoming them in with their bits of research, their inventions, their portentous dreams. His apartment warm with lamplight, no modern gaslights for them, and voices weaving a spell in point and counterpoint. *Why don't we . . . ? Is there any way . . . ? What if . . . ?*

What if we could change the world?

The upper landing was empty in the gloom that filtered through the icy window at the end of the hall. Berd's boots thumped on the bare boards, her layered clothes rustled together, the wooden building went on complaining in the cold, and mysteriously, the tangible emptiness of the house was transmuted into an ominous kind of inhabitation. It was as if she had let the cold dusk in behind her, as if she had been followed by the wisp of steam rising from the suicide's broken head. She moved in a final rush down the hall to Sele's door, knocked inaudibly with her mittened fist, tried the handle. Unlocked. She pushed open the door.

"Sele?" She might have been asking him to comfort her for some recent hurt. Her voice broke, her chest ached, hot tears welled into her eyes. "Sele?"

But he wasn't there, dead or alive.

Well, at least she was freed from this gruesome place. She made a fast tour of the three rooms, feeling neurotic for her diligence (but she did have to make sure all the same), and opened the hall door with all her momentum carrying her forward to a fast departure.

And cried aloud with the shock of discovering herself no longer alone.

They were oddly placed down the length of the hall, and oddly immobile, as if she had just yelled *Freeze!* in a game of statues. Yes, they stood like a frieze of statues: Three People Walking. Yet they must have been moving seconds before; she had not spent a full minute in Sele's empty rooms. Berd stood in the doorway with her heart knocking against her breastbone, her eyes watering as she stared without blinking in the dead light. Soon they would laugh at the joke they had played on her. Soon they would move.

Berd was all heartbeat and hollow fear as she crept down the hallway, hugging the wall for fear of brushing a sleeve. Her cousin Wael was first, one shoulder dropped lower than the other as if he was on the verge of turning to look back. His head was lowered, his uncut hair fell ragged across his face, his clothes were far too thin for the cold. The cold. Even through all her winter layers, Berd could feel the impossible chill emanating from her cousin's still form. Cold, so cold. But as she passed she would have sworn he swayed, ever so slightly, keeping his balance, keeping still while she passed. Keeping still until her back was turned. Wael. Wael! It was wrong to be so afraid of him. She breathed his name as she crept by, and saw her breath as a cloud.

If any of them breathed, their breath was as cold as the outer air.

Behind Wael was Isse, Sele's beautiful half-sister. Her head was raised and her white face—was it only the dusk that dusted her skin with blue?—looked ahead, eyes dark as shadows. She might have been seeing another place entirely, walking through another landscape, as if this statue of a woman in a summer dress had been stolen from a garden and put down all out of its place

274

and time. Where did she walk to so intently? What landscape did she see with those lightless eyes?

And Baer was behind her, Berd's other cousin. He had been her childhood enemy, a plague on her friendship with Sele, and somehow because of it her most intimate friend, the one who knew her too well. His name jumped in Berd's throat. He stood too close to the wall for Berd to sidle by. She had to cross in front of him to the other wall and he *had* to see her, though his head, like Wael's, was lowered. He might have been walking alone, brooding a little, perhaps following Isse's footsteps or looking for something he had lost. Berd stopped in front of him, trembling, caught between his cold and Isse's as if she stood between two impossible fires.

"Baer?" She hugged herself, maybe because that was as close as she dared come to sharing her warmth with him. "Oh, Baer."

But grief did not lessen her fear. It only made her fear—made *them*—more terrible. She had come too close. Baer could reach out, he only had to reach out . . . She fled, her sleeve scraping the wall, her boots battering the stairs. Down, down, moving too fast to be stopped by the terror of what else, what worse, the dark lobby might hold. Berd's breath gasped out, white even in the darkest spot by the door. It was very dark, and the dark was full of reaching hands. The door had no handle. It had swung closed. She was trapped. No. No. But all she could whisper, propitiation or farewell, was her cousin's name. "Baer . . . " *please don't forget you loved me.* "Baer . . . " *please don't do me harm.* Until in an access of terror she somehow wrenched open the door and sobbed out, feeling the cold of them at her back, "I'm sorry!" But even then she could not get away.

There was no street, no building across the way. There was no way, only a vast field of blue . . . blue . . . Berd might have been stricken blind for that long moment it took her mind to make sense of what her eyes saw. It was ice, the great ocean of ice that encircled the pole, as great an ocean as any in the world. Ice bluer than any water, as blue as the depthless sky. If death were a color it might be this blue, oh! exquisite and full of dread. Berd hung there, hands braced on the doorframe, as though to keep her from being forced off the step. She forgot the cold ones upstairs; remembered them with a new jolt of fear; forgot them again as the bears came into view. The great white bears, denizens of the frozen sea, exiles on land when the spring drove the ice away. Exiles no more. They walked, slow and patient and seeming sad with their long heads nodding above the surface of the snow; and it seemed to Berd, standing in her impossible doorway—if she turned would she find the house gone and nothing left but this lintel, this doorstep, and these two jambs beneath her hands?—it seemed to her, watching the slow bears walk from horizon to blue horizon, that other figures walked with them, as white-furred as the bears, but two-legged and slight. She peered. She leaned out, her arms stretched behind her as she kept tight hold of her wooden anchors, not knowing anymore if it was fear that ached within her.

And then she felt on her shoulder the touch of a hand.

She fell back against the left-hand doorjamb, hung there, her feet clumsy as they found their new position. It was Baer, with Wael and Isse and others—yes, others!—crowding behind him in the lobby. The house was not empty and never had been, no more than a tomb is empty after the mourners have gone.

"Baer . . . "

Did he see her? He stood as if he would never move again, his hand outstretched as though to hail the bears, stop them, call them to come. He did not move, but in the moment that Berd stared at him, her heart failing and breath gone, the others had come closer. Or were they moved, like chess pieces by a player's hand? They were only *there*, close, close, so close the cold of them ate into Berd's flesh, threatening her bones with ice. Her throat clenched. A breath would have frozen her lungs. A tear would have frozen her eyes. At least the bears were warm inside their fur. She fell outside, onto the ice—

—onto the stoop, the first stair, her feet carrying her in an upright fall to the street. Yes: street, stairs, house. The door was swinging closed on the dark lobby, and there was nothing to see but the tall, shabby driftwood house and the brass doorknob rolling slowly, slowly to the edge of the stair. It did not fall. Shuddering with cold, Berd scoured her mittens across her ice-streaked face and fled, feeling the weight of the coming dark closing in behind her.

———

Dear Berd,

I am lonely here. Recent years have robbed me of too many friends. Do I seem older to you? I feel old sometimes, watching so many slip away from me, some through travel, some through death, some through simple, inevitable change. I feel that I have not changed, myself, yet that does not make me feel young. Older, if anything, as if I have stopped growing and have nothing left to me but to begin to die. I'm sorry. I am not morbid, only sad. But your coming is a great consolation to me. At last! Someone dear to me—someone dearer to me than anyone in the world—is coming towards me instead of leaving me behind. You are my cure for sorrow. Come soon . . .

Berd was too cold, she could not bear the prospect of canvassing the rest of Sele's old haunts. Old haunts! Her being rebelled. She ran until the air was like knives in her lungs, walked until the sweat threatened to freeze against her skin. She looked back as she turned corner after corner—no one, no one—but the fear and the grief never left her. Oh, Baer! Oh, Wael, and beautiful Isse! It was worse than being dead. Was it? Was it worse than being left behind? But Berd had not earned the grief of abandonment, no matter how close she was to stopping in the street and sobbing, bird-like, open-mouthed. She had no right. She was the one who was leaving.

At least, she was if she could find Sele. If she could only find him this once. This one last time.

She had known early on that it was love, on her part at least, but had been frequently bewildered as to what kind of love it was. Friendship, yes, but there was that lightness of heart at the first sight of him, the deep physical contentment in his rare embrace. She had envied his lovers, but had not been jealous of them. Had never minded sharing him with others, but had always been hurt when he vanished and would not be found. Love. She knew his lovers were often jealous of her. And Baer had often been jealous of Sele.

That had been love as well, Berd supposed. It was not

indifference that made Berd look up in the midst of their scheming to see Baer watching her from across the room; but perhaps that was Baer's love, not hers. Baer's jealousy, that was not hers, and that frightened her, and bored her, and nagged at her until she felt sometimes he could pull her away from Sele, and from the warm candlelit conspiracy the five of them made, with a single skeptical glance. He had done it in their childhood, voicing the doubting realism that spoiled the game of make-believe. "You can't ride an ice bear," he had said—not even crushingly, but as flat and off-hand as a government form. "It would eat you," he said, and one of Berd and Isse's favorite games died bloody and broken-backed, leaving Baer to wonder in scowling misery why they never invited him to play.

Yet there he was, curled, it seemed deliberately, in Sele's most uncomfortable chair, watching, watching, as Sele, bright and quick by the fire, said, "Stories never die. You can't forget a story, not a real story, a living story. People forget, they die, but stories are always reborn. They're real. They're more real than we are."

"You can't live in a story," Baer said, and it seemed he was talking to Berd rather than Sele.

Berd said, "You can if you make the story real."

"That's right," Baer said, but as though he disagreed. "The story is ours. It only becomes real when we make it happen, and there has to be a way, a practical way—"

"We live in the story," Sele said. "Don't you see? *This* is a story. The story *is*."

"This is real life!" Baer mimed exasperation, but his voice was strained. "This story of yours is a *story*, you're just making it up. It's pure invention!"

279

"So is life," Sele said patiently. "That doesn't mean it isn't real."

Which was true; was, in fact, something Berd and Sele had argued into truth together, the two of them, alone. But Berd was dragged aside as she always was by Baer's resentful skepticism—resentful because of how badly he wanted to be convinced—but Berd could never find the words to include them in their private, perfect world, the world that would be perfect without him—and so somehow she could not perfectly immerse herself and was left on the margins, angry and unwilling in her sympathy for Baer. How many times had Berd lost Sele's attention, how many times had she lost her place in their schemes, because Baer was too afraid to commit himself and too afraid to abstain alone? Poor Baer! Unwilling, grudging, angry, but there it was: poor Baer.

And there he was, poor Baer, inside a cold, strange story, leaving Berd, for once, alone on the outside with Sele. With Sele. If only she were. *Oh Sele, where are you now?*

It seemed that the whole city, what was left of it, had moved into the outskirts where the aerodrome sprawled near the snow-blanked hills. There had been a few weeks last summer when the harbor was clear of ice and a great convoy of ships had docked all at once, creating a black cloud of smoke and a frantic holiday as supplies were unloaded and passengers loaded into the holds where the grain had been—loaded, it must be said, after the furs and ores that paid for their passage. Since then there had been nothing but the great silver airships drifting in on the southern wind, and now, as the cold only deepened with the passage of equinoctial spring, they would come no more. *Until,* it was said, *the present emergency has passed.* Why are some lies even told?

Everyone knew this was the end of the city, the end of the north, perhaps the beginning of the end of the world. The last airships were sailing soon, too few to evacuate the city, too beautiful not to be given a gorgeous goodbye. So the city swelled against the landlocked shore of the aeroport like the Arctic's last living tide.

The first Berd knew of it—it had been an endless walk through the empty streets, the blue dusk hardly seeming to change, as if the whole city were locked in ice—was the glint and firefly glimmer of yellow light at the end of the wide suburban street. She had complained, they all had, about the brilliance of modern times, the constant blaze of gaslight that was challenged, these last few years, not by darkness but by the soulless glare of electricity. But now, tonight, Berd might have been an explorer lost for long months, drawing an empty sled and an empty belly into civilization with the very last of her strength. How beautiful it was, this yellow light. Alive with movement and color, it was an anodyne to grief, an antidote to blue. Her legs aching with her haste, Berd fled toward, yearning, rather than away, guilty and afraid. And then the light, and the noise, and the quicksilver movement of the crowd pulled her under.

It was a rare kind of carnival. More than a farewell, it was a hunt, every citizen a quarry that had turned on its hunter, Death, determined to take Him down with the hot blood bursting across its tongue. Strange how living and dying could be so hard to tell apart in the end. Berd entered into it at first like a swimmer resting on the swells. Her relief at the lights that made the blue sky black, and at the warm-blooded people all around her steaming in the cold, made her buoyant, as light as an airship with a near approximation of joy. *This* was escape, oh yes it was.

The big houses on their acre gardens spilled out into the open, as if the carpets and chandeliers of the rich had spawned tents and booths and roofless rooms. Lamps burned everywhere, and so did bonfires in which the shapes of furniture and books could still be discerned as they were consumed. The smells wafting in great clouds of steam from food carts and al fresco bistros made the sweet fluid burst into Berd's mouth, just as the music beating from all sides made her feet move to an easier rhythm than fear. They were alive here; she took warmth from them all. But what storerooms were emptied for this feast? Whose hands would survive playing an instrument in this cold?

The aerodrome's lights blazed up into the sky. Entranced, enchanted, Berd drifted through the crowds, stumbling over the broken walls that had once divided one mansion from the next. (The native-born foreigners had made gardens, as if tundra could be forced to become a lawn. No more. No more.) That glow was always before her, but never within reach. She stumbled again, and when she had stopped to be sure of her balance, she felt the weight of her exhaustion dragging her down.

"Don't stop." A hand grasped her arm above the elbow. "It's best to keep moving here."

Here? She looked to see what the voice meant before she looked to see to whom the voice belonged. "Here" was the empty stretch between the suburb and the aerodrome, still empty even now. Or perhaps even emptier, for there were men and dogs patrolling, and great lamps magnified by the lenses that had once equipped the lighthouses guarding the ice-locked coast. This was the glow of freedom. Berd stared, even as the hand drew her back into the celebrating, grieving, furious, abandoned, raucous crowd. She looked around at last, when the perimeter was out of view.

"Randolph!" she said, astonished at being able to put a name to the face. She was afraid—for one stopped breath she was helpless with fear—but he was alive and steaming with warmth, his pale eyes bright and his long nose scarlet with drink and cold. The combination was deadly, but Berd could believe he would not care.

"Little Berd," he said, and tucked her close against his side. With all their layers of clothing between them it was hardly presumptuous, though she did not know him well. He was, however, a crony of Sele's.

"You look like you've been through the wars," he said. "You need a drink and a bite of food."

And he needed a companion in his fin de siècle farewell, she supposed.

"The city's so empty," she said, and shuddered. "I'm looking for Sele. Randolph, do you know where he might be?"

"Not there," he said with a nod toward the aerodrome lights. "Not our Sele."

"No," Berd said, her eyes downcast. "But he'll be nearby. Won't he? Do you know?"

"Oh, he's around." Randolph laughed. "Looking for Sele! If only you knew how many women have come to me, wondering where he was! But maybe it's better you don't know, eh, little Berd?"

"I know," said little Berd. "I've known him longer that you."

"That's true!" Randolph said with huge surprise. He was drunker than she had realized. "You were pups together, weren't you, not so long ago. Funny to think . . . . Funny to think, no more children, and the docks all empty where they used to play."

A maudlin drunk. Berd laughed, to think of the difference between what she had fled from and what had rescued her. All the differences. Yet Randolph had been born here, just the same as Wael and Isse and Baer.

"Do you know where I can find him, Randolph?"

"Sele?" He pondered, his narrow face drunken-sad. "Old Sele . . . "

"Only I need to find him tonight, Randolph. He has something for me, something I need. So if you can tell me . . . or you can help me look . . . "

"I know he's around. I know!" This with the tone of a great idea. "I know! We'll ask the Painter. Good ol' Painter! He knows where everyone is. Anyone who owes him money! And Sele's on that list, when was he ever not? We'll go find Painter, he'll set us right. Painter'll set us right."

So she followed the drunk who seemed to be getting drunker on the deepening darkness and the sharpening cold. The sky was indigo now, alight with stars above the field of lamps and fires and human lives. Fear receded. Anxiety came back all the sharper. Her last search, and she had only this one night, this one night, even if it had barely begun. And the thought came to her with a shock as physical as Baer's touch: it was spring: the nights were short, regardless of the cold.

She searched faces as they passed through fields of light. Strange how happy they were. Music everywhere, bottles warming near the fires, a burst of fireworks like a fiery garden above the tents and shacks and mansions abandoned to the poor. Carnival time.

Berd had never known this neighborhood, it was too far afield even for the wandering Sele and her sometimes-faithful self. All she knew of it was this night, with the gardens invaded and the tents thrown open and spilling light and music and steam onto the trampled weeds and frozen mud of the new alleyways. They made small stages, their lamplit interiors as vivid as scenes from a play. Act IV, scene i: the Carouse. They were all of a piece, the Flirtation, the Argument, the Philosophical Debate. And yet, every face was peculiarly distinct; no one could be mistaken for another. Berd ached for them, these strangers camped at the end of the world. For that moment she was one of them, belonged to them and with them—belonged to everything that was not the cold ones left behind in the empty city beside the frozen sea. Or so she felt, before she saw Isse's face, round and cold and beautiful as the moon.

No. Berd's breath fled, but . . . no. There was only the firelit crowd outside, the lamplit crowd within the tent Randolph led her to, oblivious to her sudden stillness, the drag she made at the end of his arm. No cold Isse, no Wael or Baer. No. But the warmth of the tent was stifling, and the noise of music and voices and the clatter of bottle against glass shivered the bones of her skull.

The Painter held court, one of a hundred festival kings, in a tent that sagged like a circus elephant that has gone too long without food. He had been an artist once, and had earned the irony of his sobriquet by turning critic and making a fortune writing for twenty journals under six different names. He had traveled widely, of course, there wasn't enough art in the north to keep a man with half his appetites, but Berd didn't find it strange that he stayed when all his readers escaped on the last ships that fled before the ice. He had been a prince here, and some princes did prefer to die than become paupers in exile. Randolph was hard-pressed to force himself close enough to bellow in King Painter's ear, and before he made it—he was delayed more than once by an offered glass—Berd had freed her arm and drifted back to the wide-open door.

It seemed very dark outside. Faces passed on another stage, a promenade of drunks and madmen. A man dressed in the old fashioned furs of an explorer passed by, his beard and the fur lining of his hood matted with vomit. A woman followed him wearing a gorgeous rug like a poncho, a hole cut in the middle of its flower-garden pattern, and another followed her with her party clothes torn all down her front, too drunk or mad to fold the cloth together, so that her breasts flashed in the lamplight from the tent. She would be dead before morning. So many would be, Berd thought, and her weariness came down on her with redoubled weight. A stage before her, a stage behind her, and she—less audience than stagehand, since these performers in no wise performed for her—stood in a thin margin of nowhere, a threshold between two dreams. She let her arms dangle and her head fall back, as if she could give up, not completely, but just for a heartbeat or two, enough to snatch one moment of rest. The stars glittered like chips of ice, blue-white, colder than the air. There was some comfort in the thought that they would still shine long after the human world was done. There would still be sun and moon, snow and ice, and perhaps the seals and the whales and the bears. Berd sighed and shifted her numb feet, thinking she should find something hot to drink, talk to the Painter herself.

She looked down, and yes, there was Isse standing like a rock in the stream of the passing crowd.

She might have been a statue for all the notice anyone took of her. Passersby passed by without a glance or a flinch from Isse's radiating cold. It made Berd question herself, doubt everything she had seen and felt back at the house. She lifted her hand in a half-finished wave and felt an ache in her shoulder where Baer had touched her, the frightening pain of cold that has penetrated to the bone. Isse did not respond to Berd's gesture. She was turned a little from where Berd stood, her feet frozen at the end of a stride, her body leaning toward the next step that never came. Still walking in that summer garden, her arms bare and as blue-white as the stars. Berd rubbed her shoulder, less afraid in the midst of carnival, though the ache of cold touched her heart. Dear Isse, where do you walk to? Is it beautiful there?

Something cold touched Berd's eye. Weeping ice? She blinked, and discovered a snow flake caught in her eyelashes. She looked up again. Stars, stars, more stars than she had seen moments ago, more stars than she thought she would see even if every gaslight and oil lamp and bonfire in the north were extinguished. Stars so thick there was hardly any black left in the sky, no matter how many fell. Falling stars, snow from a cloudless sky. Small flakes prickled against Berd's face, so much colder than her cold skin they felt hot. She looked down and saw that Baer and Wael had joined Isse, motionless, three statues walking down the impromptu street. How lonely they looked! Berd had been terrified in the house with them. Now she hurt for their loneliness, and felt an instant's powerful impulse to go to them, join them in their pilgrimage in whatever time and place they were. The impulse frightened her more than their presence did, and yet . . . She didn't move from the threshold of the tent, but the impulse still lived in her body, making her lean even as Isse leaned, on the verge of another step.

Snow fell more thickly, glittering in the firelight. It was strange that no one seemed to notice it, even as it dusted their heads and shoulders and whitened the ground. It fell more thickly, a windless blizzard that drew a curtain between Berd and the stage of the promenade, and more thickly still, until it was impossible that so much snow could fall—and from a starlit sky!—and yet she was still able to see Wael and Baer and Isse. It was as though they stood not in the street but in her mind. She was shivering, her mouth was dry. Snow fell and fell, an entire winter of snow pouring into the street, the soft hiss of the snowflakes deafening Berd to the voices, music, clatter and bustle of the tent behind her. It was the hiss of silence, no louder than the sigh of blood in her ears. And Isse, Wael, and Baer walked and walked, unmoving while the snow piled up in great drifts, filling the street, burying it, disappearing it from view. There were only the three cold ones and the snow.

And then the snow began to generate ghosts. Berd knew this trick from her childhood, when the autumn winds would drive fogbanks and snowstorms onto the northern shore. The hiss and the monotonous whiteness gave birth to muttered voices and distant calls, and to the shapes of things barely visible behind the veil of mist or snow. People, yes, and animals like white bears and caribou and the musk oxen Berd only knew from the books they read in school; and sometimes stranger things, ice gnomes like white foxes walking on hind legs and carrying spears, and wolves drawing sleds ridden by naked giants, and witches perched backwards on white caribou made of old bones and snow. Those ghosts teased Berd's vision as they passed down the street of snow, a promenade of the north that came clearer and clearer as she watched, until the diamond points of the gnomes' spears glittered in the lamplight pouring out of the tent and the giants with their eyes as black as the sky stared down at her as they passed. Cold filled her, the chill of wonder, making her shudder. And now she saw there were others walking with the snow ghosts, people as real as the woman who wore the beautiful carpet, as solid as the woman who bared her breasts to the cold. They walked in their carnival madness, as if they had blundered through the curtain that had hidden them from view. Still they paid no notice to the three cold ones, the statues of Baer and Isse and Wael, but they walked there, fearless, oblivious, keeping pace with the witches, the oxen, the bears.

And then Randolph grasped Berd's sore shoulder with his warm hand and said, "Painter says Sele's been sleeping with some woman in one of the empty houses . . . Hey, where'd everybody go?"

For at his touch the snow had been wiped away like steam from a window, and all the ghosts, all the cold ones, and all the passersby were gone, leaving Berd standing at the edge of an empty stage.

"Hey," Randolph said softly. "Hey."

It was perfectly silent for a moment, but only for a moment. A fire burning up the street sent up a rush of sparks as a new log went on. A woman in the tent behind them screamed with laughter. A gang of children ran past, intent in their pursuit of some game. And then the promenade was full again, as varied and lively as a parade.

Berd could feel Randolph's shrug and his forgetting through the hand resting on her shoulder. She could feel his warmth, his gin-soaked breath past her cheek, his constant swaying as he sought an elusive equilibrium. She should not feel so alone, so perfectly, utterly, dreadfully alone. They had gone, leaving her behind.

"No." No. *She* was the one who was leaving.

"Eh?" Randolph said.

"Which house?" Berd said, turning at last from the door.

"Eh?" He swayed more violently, his eyes dead, lost in some alcoholic fugue.

"Sele." She shook him, and was surprised by the stridency in her voice. "Sele! You said he was in a house with some woman. Which house?" Randolph focused with a tangible effort. "That's right. Some rich woman who didn't want to go with her husband. Took Sele up. Lives somewhere near here. One of the big houses. Some rich woman. Bitch. If I'd been her I'd've gone. I'd've been dead by now. Gone. I'd've been gone by now . . . "

Berd forced her icy hands to close around both his arms, holding him against his swaying. "Which house? Randolph! *Which house?*"

———

My dearest Berd,

I'm embarrassed by the last letter I wrote. It must have given you a vision of me all alone in a dusty room, growing old before my time. Not true! Or, if it is, it isn't the only

truth. I should warn you that I have been extolling your
virtues to everyone I know, until all of my acquaintance
is agog to meet the woman, the mysterious northerner, the
angel whose coming has turned me into a boy again. You
are my birthday and my school holiday and my summer all
rolled into one, and I cannot wait to parade you on my arm.
Will it embarrass you if I buy you beautiful things to wear? I
hope it won't. I want shamelessly to show you off. I want you
to become the new star of my almost-respectable circle as
you are the star that lights the dark night of my heart . . .

4198 Goldport Avenue.

There *were* no avenues, just the haphazard lanes of the
carnival town, but the Painter (Berd had given up on Randolph
in the end) had added directions that took into account new
landmarks and gave Berd some hope of finding her way. Please,
oh please, let Sele be there.

"It's a monstrous place," the Painter had said. His eyes were
greedy, unsated by the city's desperation, hungry for hers. "A
bloody great Romantic pile with gargoyles like puking birds and
pillars carved like tree nymphs. You can't miss it. Last time I was
there it was lit up like an opera house with a red carpet spilling
down the stairs. Vulgar! My god, the woman has no taste at all
except for whiskey and men. Your Sele will be lucky if she's held
onto him this long."

His eyes had roved all over Berd, but there was nothing to see
except her weary face and frightened eyes. He dismissed her, too
lazy to follow her if she wouldn't oblige by bringing her drama

to him, and Randolph was so drunk by then that he stared with sober dread into the far distance, watching the approach of death. Berd went alone into the carnival, feeling the cold all the more bitterly for the brief warmth of the Painter's tent. Her hands and feet felt as if they were being bitten by invisible dogs, her ears burned with wasp-fire, her shoulder ached with a chill that grew roots down her arm and into the hollow of her ribs. Cold, cold. Oh, how she longed for warmth! Warmth and sunshine and smooth pavement that didn't trip her hurting feet, and the proper sounds of spring, waves and laughter and shouting gulls, rather than the shouting crowd, yelping as though laughter were only a poor disguise for a howl of despair. She stumbled, buffeted by strangers, and wished she could only *see*, if she could only *see*. But Wael and Isse and Baer were near. She knew that, even in the darkness; heard their silence in the gaps and blank spaces of the noisy crowd, felt their cold. And oh, she was frightened. She missed them terribly, grieved for them, longed for them, and was terrified that longing would bring them back to her, as cold and strange and wrong as the walking dead.

But she would not go that way, not that way, she would not.

Berd stumbled again. Under her feet, barely visible in the light of a bonfire ringed by dancers there lay a street sign that said in ornate script Goldport Ave. She looked up, past the dancers and their fire—and what was that in the flames? A chair stood upright in the coals and on the chair an effigy, please let it be an effigy, burning down to a charcoal grin—she dragged her gaze up above the fire where the hot air shivered like a watery veil, and saw the pillared house with all its curtains open to expose the shapes dancing beneath the blazing chandeliers. Bears and giants and witches, and air pilots and buccaneers and queens. Fancy dress, as if the dancers had already died and moved on to a different form. Berd climbed the stairs, the vulgar carpet more black than red after the passage of many feet, and passed through the wide-open door.

She gave up on the reception rooms very soon. They were so hot, and crowded by so many reckless dancing drunks, and the music was a noisy shambles played by more drunks who seemed to have only a nodding acquaintance with their instruments. Perhaps the dancers and the musicians had traded places for a lark. Berd thought that even were she drunk and in the company of friends it would still seem like a foretaste of hell, and she could feel a panic coming on before she had forced a way through a single room. Sele. Sele! Why wouldn't he come and rescue her? She fought her way back into the grand foyer and climbed the wide marble stairs until she was above the heads of the crowd. Hot air mingled with cold. Lamps dimmed as the oil in the reservoirs ran low, candles guttered in ornate pools of wax; no one seemed to care. They would all die here, a mad party frozen in place like a story between the pages of a book. Berd sat on a step halfway above the first landing and put her head in her hands.

"There you are. Do you know, I thought I'd missed you for good."

Berd burst into tears. Sele sat down beside her and rocked her, greatcoat and all, in his arms.

He told her he had waited on the esplanade until his feet went numb. She told him about the suicide. She wanted to tell him about his sister, Isse, and her cousins, but could not find the words to begin.

"I saw," she said, "I saw," and spilled more tears.

"It isn't a tragedy," Sele said, meaning the suicide. "We all die, soon or late. It's just an anticipation, that's all."

"I know."

"There are worse things."

"I know."

He drew back to look at her. She looked at him and saw that he knew, and that he saw that she knew, too.

"Oh, Sele . . . "

His round brown face was solemn, but also serene. "Are you still going?"

"Yes!" She shifted so she could grasp him too. "Sele, you have to come with me. You must, now, you have no choice."

He laughed at her with surprise. "What do you mean? Why don't I have a choice?"

"They—" She stammered, not wanting to know what she was trying to say. "Th-they have been following me, Wael and Baer and Isse. They've been following. They want— They'll come for you, too."

"I know. I've seen them. I expect they'll come soon."

"I'm sorry. I know it's wrong, but they frighten me so much. How can you be so calm?"

"We did this," he said. "We wanted change, didn't we? We asked for it. We should take what we get."

"Oh, Sele." Berd hid her face against his shoulder. He was only wearing a shirt, she realized. She could feel this chill of his flesh against her cheek. She whispered, "I can't. It's too dreadful. I can't bear to always be so cold."

"Oh, little Berd." He stroked her hair. "You don't have to. I've made my choice, that's all, and you've made yours. I don't think, by now, there's any right or wrong either way. We've gone too far for that."

She shook her head against him. She wanted very much to plead with him, to make her case, to spin for him all her dreams of the south, but she was too ashamed, and knew that it would do no good. They had already spun their dreams into nothing, into cold and ice, into the land beyond death. Anyway, Sele had never, ever, in all their lives, followed her lead. And at the last, she could not follow his.

They pulled apart.

"Come on," Sele said. "I have your things in my room."

The gas jet would not light, so Berd stood by the door while Sele fumbled for candle and match. Two candles burning on a branch meant for four barely carved the shape of the room out of the darkness. It seemed very grand to Berd, with heavy curtains round the bed and thick carpets on the floor.

"A strange place to end up," she said.

Sele glanced at her, his dark eyes big and bright with candlelight. "It's warm," he said, and then added ruefully, "It was warm. Anyway, I needed to be around to meet some of the right people. It's such a good address, don't you know."

"Better than your old one." Berd couldn't smile, remembering his old house, remembering the street sign under her feet and the shape in the bonfire outside.

"Anyway." Sele knelt and turned up a corner of the carpet. "My hostess is nosy but not good at finding things. And she's been good to me. I owe her a lot. She helped me get you what you'll need."

"The ticket?" Berd did not have enough room for air in her chest.

"Ticket." Sele handed her the items one at a time. "Travel papers. Letters."

"Letters?" She was slow to take the last packet. Whose letters? Letters from whom?

"From your sponsor. There's a rumor that even with a ticket and papers they won't let you on board unless you can prove you aren't going south only to end up a beggar. Your sponsor is supposed to give you a place to stay, help you find work. He's my own invention, but he's a good one. No," he said as she turned the packet over in her hands, "don't read them now. You'll have time on the ship."

It was strange to see her name on the top envelope in Sele's familiar hand. He had never written her a letter in her life. She stowed them away in her pocket with the other papers and then checked, once, twice, that she had everything secure. *I can't go.* The words lodged in her throat. She looked at Sele, all her despair—at going? at staying?—in her eyes.

"You're right to go," Sele said. "Little Berd, flying south away from the cold."

"I don't want to leave you." Not *I can't,* just *I don't want to.*

"But you will."

She shivered, doubting, torn, and yet knowing as well as he that he was right. She would go, and he would go too, on a different journey with Isse and Wael and Baer. So cold. She hugged him fiercely, trying to give him her heat, wanting to borrow his. He kissed her, and then she was going, going, her hand in her pocket, keeping her ticket safe. Running down the stairs. Finding the beacon of the aerodrome even before she was out the door.

On the very threshold she looked out and saw what she had not thought to look for from the window of Sele's room. Inside, the masquerade party was in full swing, hot and bright and loud with voices and music and smashing glass. Outside . . .

Outside the ice had come.

It was as clear as it can be only at the bottom of a glacier, where the weight of a mile of ice has pressed out all the impurities of water and air. It was as clear as glass, as clear as the sky, so that the stars shone through hardly dimmed, though their glittering was stilled. Berd could see everything, the carnival town frozen with every detail preserved: the tents still upright, though their canvas sagged; the shanties with the soot still crusted around their makeshift chimneys. Even the bonfires, with their half-burnt logs intact, their charcoal facsimiles of chairs and books and mannequins burned almost to the bone. In the glassy star-light Berd could even see all the little things strewn across the ground, all the ugly detritus of the end of the world, the bottles and discarded shoes, the dead cats and dead dogs and turds. And she could see the people, all the people abandoned at the last, caught in their celebratory despair. The whole crowd of them, men and women and children, young and old and ugly and fair, frozen as they danced, stumbled, fucked, puked, and died. And, yes, there were her own three, her own dears, the brothers and sister of her heart, standing at the foot of the steps as if they had been caught, too, captured by the ice just as they began to climb. Isse, and Wael, and Baer.

The warmth of the house behind Berd could not combat the

dreadful cold of the ice. The music faltered as the cold bit the musicians hands. Laughter died. And yet, and yet, and yet in the distance, beyond the frozen tents and the frozen people, a light still bloomed. Cold electricity, as cold as the unrisen moon and as bright, so that it cast the shadows of Baer and Wael and Isse before them up the stairs. The aerodrome, yes, the aerodrome, where the silver airships still hung from their tethers like great whales hanging in the depths of the clear ocean blue. Yes, and there was room at the right-hand edge of the stairs where Berd could slip between the balustrade and the still summer statue of Wael, her cousin Wael, with his hair shaken back and his dark eyes raised to where Berd stood with her hand in her pocket, her ticket and travel pass and letters clutched in her cold but not yet frozen fist. The party was dying. There was a quiet weeping. The lights were growing dim. *Now or never*, Berd thought, and she took all her courage in her hands and stepped through the door.

My darling, my beloved Berd,

I wish I had the words to tell you how much I love you. It's no good to say "like a sister" or "like a lover" or "like myself." It's closer to say like the sun that warms me, like the earth that supports me, like the air I breathe. And I have been suffering these past few days with the regret (I know I swore long ago to regret nothing, even to remember nothing I might regret, but it finds me all the same) that I have never come to be with you, your lover or your husband, in your beloved north. It's as though I have consigned myself to some sunless, airless world. How have

I let all this time pass without ever coming to you? And now it is too late, far too late for me. But I am paid with this interminable waiting. Come to me soon, I beg you. Save me from my folly. Forgive me. Tell me you love me as much as I love you . . .

CASTLE ROCK

Claude propped the flashlight on a rock and put a match to the fire, urging the damp tinder to catch. Flames nibbled at the edges of the kindling, reluctant, then hungry, then bright and dancing. The night eddied around him, smelling of frost beyond the smoke. The tarp overhead rustled with rain and falling needles from the autumn larches. Claude hovered over the fire, nudging the sticks into a better arrangement.

Making his way through the orchard and into the woods had only been ordinarily spooky, no worse than being sent out to the woodshed after dark, but now that he was here, in this place with the night's work ahead of him, the fire was essential, a defense against the night. More than that, a companion to someone who had never been alone.

Provisionally satisfied with the fire, he turned to the bag he had stashed here after school. Having a secret was as strange as being alone, but here it was, his bag full of stolen things, elements for the final spell. They didn't look like much tumbled out onto the ground. A jumble of clothes; a tangle of leaves and moss; a book; a mask. Only the mask looked magical, better even than it had in the art room at school. Claude held it up against the fire so the new coals gleamed through the eye holes, and shivered. He had been doubting the magic; now he doubted any of this was a good idea. But no. That thrill of danger was vindication, proof he was right and Paul was wrong. His brother had always had the power to ruin a story, to spoil the game. Well, tomorrow the game would be finished, but at least Paul would know what it was he had betrayed and killed. That was Claude's promise to himself: for the rest of their lives, Paul would have to know.

Claude laid the mask aside and began stuffing the stolen clothes, to make them look like a body.

———

Paul dreamed of a fire burning in a stone hearth, people coming and going at his back, a subterranean mutter of a voice. He woke so gradually he was still halfway in the dream place even as he stirred, rediscovering his limbs under the weight of the blankets. It was early—he could tell by the cold on his face that his mother had not yet got up to turn on the furnace—and he might have slipped back into the dream-muttering darkness of sleep, except . . . Except the house shifted, or the air did, or Paul's own bones did, whispering to him that his twin was awake. Or maybe he just heard the subliminal squeak of a floorboard. His door opened. He let his mouth go slack and pretended he was still asleep.

If Claude had said his name he might have gone on pretending, but instead of trying to wake him, Claude was moving around the room, rifling through Paul's dresser drawers. Quietly. As though he was trying *not* to wake Paul.

"The hell do you think you're doing?" Paul said, keeping his eyes closed for effect.

Claude's reply was a flop of clothes across the bed. Startled, Paul jerked up onto one elbow and glared. But Claude only gave him a cool, remote glance and said in his game voice, "Get up. It's nearly dawn. There's no time to be lost."

"It's *dawn*?" Paul's voice cracked, violently enough to give him pause. *Changing at last?* Then he took another look at his brother's face and his heart sank. Claude was pale, his eyes dark with fever and his lips bitten and chapped. You couldn't argue with Claude when he was like this, you could only fight, and Paul was starting to dread their fights. So although he couldn't dredge up any enthusiasm, he did at least wrestle his clothes under the covers where he could dress in the warmth of his bed.

He let Claude haul him downstairs, pretending he was still half asleep, hoping his inertia would slow Claude down enough that he'd get fed up and quit. But Claude shoved an egg-and-ham sandwich into Paul's hand, and he had to juggle it while he worked his feet into his shoes. The cat got in the way, scavenging for dropped bits of scrambled egg. He wolfed down what he could and was still licking ketchup off his palm as his brother dragged him out the door.

The stupid thing was, Paul was actually enjoying himself. It felt good to throw water on his brother's fire, to be the brake on his brother's runaway train. And the thing that let him enjoy it was the fact that Claude's fire was proof against anything Paul could throw at it. Claude was like a force of nature, and even if Paul was sick of their games, even if he was growing up and moving on, there was something reassuring about Claude's refusal to leave it all behind. Really fucking annoying, but also reassuring, as if Claude were holding their boyhood treasures safe, refusing to change even in this season of changes. Fighting to keep just one important thing between them from changing.

So he let Claude drag him past the frost-burned garden and through the orchard where the late apples hung like pale winter suns among the dying leaves.

———

But then the Tyrant made his fatal mistake, Claude said, building the story the way he built the spell. The story was the spell. They stopped in the orchard to pick apples mealy with frost, because the orchard and garden were the domain of the Cooks, and the Cooks' support was food. *Sustenance,* Claude said, *for the final battle,* but Paul was checking the frosted grass for bear shit: the bears always got over the orchard fence in the fall. But there are no bears in the castle kitchens. Claude wanted to give his brother a shove, a kick in the ass, but that would end everything, making them nothing more than quarreling boys. He was sweating with the effort of building the castle around them, the castle-keep they had lived in most of their lives. Here, hidden in the apple trees, were the kitchens with the vast smoke-blackened beams overhead all hung with hams and sausage links and herbs. It was perpetually firelit and smelled like the farmhouse kitchen when their mother used the big wood-fired range for cooking Christmas dinner, roast turkey and fried onions and smoke. The vast structures of the keep had once been so real they had almost blinded him—them—to the outer world, so they could creep down corridors and scale towers and serve, disguised, in banqueting halls without having to acknowledge the trees and fields hidden in the stony walls. Now, without Paul to help him summon it, the keep eluded him, thin as a ghost in sunlight, and the apples were only apples, the floor frosted grass, the ceiling the brightening sky.

But the magic was there. It had to be there. Claude reached for it with everything he had.

Even after their long resistance, the story went, *the good people of the keep were unprepared. It was the best fortune they could have asked for, the Tyrant's arrogance that let him risk this momentary weakness for the sake of greater power, but their subtle, resisting magics were still piecemeal, scattered in their hidden places. They needed to be gathered, quietly, secretly, into the weapon that would bring the Tyrant down before he could attain his greatest power and hold the keep forever in his iron fist.*

The end, Claude thought. One way or another, the end.

"C'mon, Paul," he said, risking the entire spell. "Give me some help here."

Paul sighed, his breath making a cloud in the air. But then he said, offhand, as if it didn't matter, "We have to see the Cellarer."

That was all Claude needed, the open door to the keep. He took a deep breath and felt the morning come alive with the rising sun.

"The Cellarer, yes. His magics are the deepest and darkest. The Cellarer, and then the Lady of Fountains for her blessing and her shield."

———————

"Come on!" Claude said, like a much younger boy, and he took off running.

For a split second Paul thought about just standing there and letting Claude run alone. But it couldn't be done. When his twin ran, he felt it in his bones. They *couldn't* run alone; he *couldn't* trail behind. Your twin ran, and you ran, and the running was like a twin-engine boat carrying you both along. You had to win, but the need was inseparable from the knowledge that so did he, and that if you ran like hell and won this time, next time it would be him. Which was frustrating—knowing you could never, ever really win, for good and all? Infuriating!—but also essential. They were two horses in harness, a matched pair, running.

They reached the orchard fence at the same time, but Paul made a cleaner vault, putting him a stride ahead. He slanted across the lower field where the mown grass hid treacherous hollows. He ran with his arms out for balance, the air sharp and cold in his lungs, and scarcely noticed when the sleepy magpies started up from the fence at the edge of the woods and flew up toward the head of the valley.

Claude, close behind him and breathless, said, "The Tyrant's spies. They won't be able to tell him exactly what we're doing, but we'll have to be fast."

Paul, spurred by annoyance, ran harder, but he couldn't widen the distance between them. And then there was the fence, barbed wire rusted and broken with age, and the trees where you couldn't run. Well, you could, the undergrowth wasn't heavy, but the forest was for silence. Woodcraft. Ghosting through the trees. Paul negotiated the aged wire and slipped through the bushes with the barest rustle of cloth. Hoping to spot some wildlife, he told himself, but with Claude's breath panting in his ear and his own heart pounding, it really was like old times.

And the Cellarer, great, brooding, temperous man, was not to be approached lightly.

He was dark as old tree roots, narrow-faced and tough with blazing black eyes. As with all the keep's people, Claude could see him only from the corner of his inner eye. It was a face he'd only ever known from the inside. (He thought of the mask he'd made, the Tyrant's face modeled in plaster of Paris on his own, and felt a sharp heart-thump of . . . something. Fear? What comes before fear, when it might turn out to be excitement after all.) But the cellar door was one of the realest things about the keep, based on an old miner's test shaft carved out of the valley wall.

The steep rock face rose out of the trees, gray granite under a collage of lichen, ferns, miniature trees. It smelled different from the woods, a cold mineral scent, and it seemed always to cast a heavy shade whatever the time of day. This early in the day, the mine opening was black, so dark he could barely make out the rough stones choking the sloping shaft a few meters in.

"The door's open," he whispered. He did not have to say that was a good sign. Paul knew the Cellarer's ways as well as he did.

They crept inside, something they had done so often it could have been an everyday sort of thing, but it never was. Some places have a soul, and the Cellarer's door was one. There was always an awareness here, a listening silence, and all the years of the game—the time they'd built a snow rampart across the cave mouth to defend the Cellarer's realm against the Tyrant's arrogant new captain of guards; the time they had spent the night watching their too-small fire die and knowing the coming darkness would herald the Cellarer's most potent initiation—had only deepened the life of the place, focusing that awareness until it was intense enough to burn the heart or the mind. Claude slipped into the darkness with all his skin tingling with life, and when he felt Paul moving at his side, he knew that the magic would speak.

The choked shaft was not deep, but it was deep enough for echoes.

We know your need, and will meet it, but there is a price to be paid.

Paul knew it was Claude's voice, but the echoes took the words and gave them back changed, alive. It was the darkness speaking rather than the boy, or the boy speaking for the dark. Paul felt his own throat resonate to the echo, a shaft no different from the mine's.

The price of freedom, the Cellarer said, and both boys listened, shivering, to hear what the price of freedom was. Then Paul realized, and whispered with something like real awe, "Freedom is the price."

Claude caught his breath, and for a moment past and future balanced like a pair of scales. For a moment, Paul could sense the honorable end to the game, the farewell, the free passage through the open door. That was what the story meant—what Claude meant—of course it was. *The Tyrant's final mistake.* Paul got it. The game worked; their life worked; what had been out of gear was meshing smoothly again. He could play the game, yes, and love it the way he used to do, and then—not quit—but lay it down like a book they had read to the satisfying conclusion. The End.

The release from guilt, from resentment, was like a benediction. Like (not that he would never think this in words) love.

"Come," said the Cellarer/Claude. "Take what you need. You

307

may only use it this once, but if you strike hard and true, that once will do for all."

So they moved forward to gather up the talismans, the weapons, the rocks glinting like the Cellarer's eyes with pyrite and quartz.

———•∗•———

The keep was all around them then, a shadow so vivid in Claude's mind it turned the trees to ghosts of themselves, cobwebs and tapestries on the ancient walls. Sunlight was striking the ramparts on the far side of the outer bailey and the lesser denizens of the keep were beginning to stir. Yes, they cast shadows like birds and deer, but the keep was half wild and all magic, and what would you expect? Claude had lost track of how many innocent forest creatures had been turned into voiceless slaves, how many treacherous servants had been transformed into mule deer, coyotes, grouse. If trees and bushes clung to the cracks in the old walls, what did that say but that the Tyrant had stolen even the gentle power of the woods to build his stronghold, or that the woods were slowly wearing away at the Tyrant's cruel power, or both. So it was right, it was fitting, that the outer bailey *had the appearance of* a hay meadow ringed by trees and hills, and it was right that the great gate leading into the inner bailey *seemed like* a rocky ridge cutting the valley farm almost in two. And it was obvious, if you know how to look, that the magpies chuckling in the shorn grass had human shadows, and that the shadows hid whispered comments behind their hands. The Tyrant's spies. They would steal even your thoughts if you had not learned how to hide them behind a screen of words.

"If anyone asks," Paul said as they jogged across the field, "we're just taking the banqueting cloths to the laundry."

So they became pageboys with license to go anywhere, easy even for the magpie-spies to overlook. The Laundress was one of the Lady of Fountain's guises, her humblest, as the pageboys were *their* humblest, and Claude was a little disappointed—a little irritated, in fact, that Paul's contribution to the story had them taking the path of least grandeur. Didn't he understand this was the great climax of all their stories? Didn't he get that this was the end?

But maybe—Claude's heart gave another of those out-of-rhythm bumps—maybe Paul *didn't* get it. Maybe he thought he was coming back to the game. *Maybe it didn't have to end.*

Instantly Claude's mind was racing through the possibilities, trying to find the path that would let the story continue past this day's assault. But for the story to go on the Tyrant would have to survive. He was the reason for all the quests, the secret tasks, the battles. He was the force that drove the entire game. And in his potency he *could* survive, Claude knew. This was a desperate chance, the Cellarer's magic weapons cobbled together in a hurry to take advantage of this one instant's vulnerability. So it *could* fail. Looked at logically, it probably *would* fail, and the Tyrant would keep his power and his throne.

But if he did, what would the consequences be?

The Lady, the Cooks, all the lesser denizens who came and went according to the story's demands. Even the Cellarer. None of them was powerful enough to best the Tyrant or even defend against his full wrath—if they had been, there never would have been a story or a game. So to attack the Tyrant openly, and fail . . .

Even if they survived, what kind of story would remain to be acted out? The Tyrant's evil had always been mostly potential, the threat they dodged or foiled in a thousand subtle ways. To unleash it in all its power, to expose themselves to the full force of the Tyrant's hatred and rage, the hatred and rage they had been provoking and evading all these years . . .

Claude felt queasy threads of panic squirming beneath his skin. Because he had made the elementary mistake of all young wizards: he had thought he was in control of the magic, but he was himself entrained in the spell he had set in motion. They both were, the story and all its characters were. The Tyrant was already waiting for them in his place of power, and as terrible as the consequences would be if they attacked him and failed, Claude literally could not imagine the consequences of not attacking him at all. Because he, Claude, had made the Tyrant real. The Tyrant was real, and awake, and waiting.

So the story had to end. It *had* to end. And yet . . .

The panic did not diminish, but it began to wind itself through other strands, a briar patch of anger.

Because if the story *didn't* end, and the Tyrant survived in all his fury, then maybe that would serve Paul right. Even if Claude had to share in the consequences. Maybe that was no more than Paul the traitor deserved.

At least, that was one way the story might go.

The Lady of Fountains had her place in the valley, as the Cellarer had his. The spring that provided drinking water to the farmhouse was one of the imaginary keep's anchor-points, one of the places where the game had something tangible to latch on to. Like the mine shaft, it was a forbidden place, but unlike the mine it was not forbidden because it was dangerous. No, it was forbidden because the water must not be sullied; the spring must be kept pure. And so, as the Cellarer was a dangerous man full of dark secrets, the Lady was vulnerable and aloof. She was one of the wild powers that needed protecting from the Tyrant's wicked greed as much as she was one of the powers that did the protecting. And so even her Laundress guise was delicate and wary.

In fact, the Laundress was one of the elements of the story Paul was most fond of, not least because he had made her up himself. She was a girl, half human, half wild, who let her magic mingle with the wash-water so that it could protect the dreams of those who slept between her sheets. When Paul was visited by nightmares or couldn't sleep for thoughts of his fights with Claude, he took clean sheets from the linen closet and pretended they came from the Laundress's cauldrons, and such was the magic of the game that it always worked. The Laundress was imaginary, yet somehow her spells were real.

Would it still work, Paul wondered, when the game was done?

The Lady's pool coiled like a sleeping cat in the elbow of the western hill. The water was shallow and very clear, shaded by rocks and trees and the gently thumping pump house that squatted on the bank. On that cold autumn morning the pool was fringed with ice, crystals more delicate than communion wafers. Paul knelt on the flat Summoning Stone and broke off a piece of ice to slip onto his tongue. It gave a taste much wilder than the water that came from the tap at home, the essence of ice formed in a hollow of stone and flavored by the weeping of trees, and he realized it was too late in the year to summon the Laundress from her clouds of steam. This cold, clear silence was the Lady's signature and her rightful realm.

"Lady," he whispered, his breath a cloud, and although he did not really listen for her answer, he felt a strangely adult pang of longing for the days, the very recent days, when he would listen with all his soul. What would become of the Lady without the game? Would she . . . die? A crazy thought, but it went with that moment of sadness. *Goodbye,* Paul thought. *Goodbye.*

"Lady," said Claude, kneeling beside him, "we beseech your blessing. Please. Give us a sign. Is this the right thing to do?"

Paul gave him a sidelong look. Was *what* the right thing to do? Ending the game? The run through the cold morning had stung color into Claude's cheeks, but it looked like rouge painted over his pallor. His face was tight with strain; sweat dewed his temples and his downy lip. For the first time it occurred to Paul that his brother was actually sick, fighting a fever of the body as well as the mind. God knew, he probably hadn't slept all night, gearing himself up for the final play. Compassion twinged in Paul's chest. *Let's get this done,* he thought, for both their sakes.

"The Cellarer has given us our task," he said in the best game voice he could summon. "We do not seek to be released from our duty, only to be confirmed in it. Lady, give us your blessing."

"Lady," Claude whispered, the words barely more than breath smoking on the air, "give us a sign."

—◦⊷∗⊶◦—

"Lady, give me a sign."

Claude knelt in the chill purity of the Wellhouse, watching the reflection of the sky upheld by pillars that were immense even in their ruination. They had fulfilled their task in the laundry, hiding in the steam from the Tyrant's spies, and the Laundress had beckoned them inwards, through all the concealing bustle to the hidden door to the ancient holy place, the door she in her Laundress guise was there to protect. Now they were within (and he blessed Paul for finding the way through) and his heart ached for the Lady's recognition of his dilemma, for a touch of the Lady's gentle grace. *A sign.* He held the fate of the Tyrant, the fate of the keep, in his hands. What should he do?

"The price," he whispered, though there was no echo to pick up the words and speak them anew. "The price of freedom."

He could hear Paul breathing beside him, and in the far distance, no louder than his heartbeat, the rhythmic thumping of the laundry's mangles. Even here they were within the keep. Here, they were within the keep as it should have been if the Tyrant had never come—as it might be again once the Tyrant was gone. Was that Claude's sign? Was that the only answer he was going to get?

No. The sun was still rising above the eastern ramparts, and now a long shaft of autumnal sunlight slipped through the pillars to brush the Lady's pool with gold. Her benison. And then, with a whisper of wings, a black bird followed the sunlight down to the water's edge. It was a crow, one of the birds of war, drinking from the Lady's own water. There was Claude's answer, as clear as if she had spoken in words, and he was glad—oh, most bitterly glad!—or perhaps he was only bitter. But there was no arguing, the Lady was an oracle in this place. There would be war. They would take the Cellarer's martial spells to the Tyrant's stronghold, they would strike, and they would bear the consequences together, win or lose.

They bowed to the Lady's invisible presence and rose. The crow started up and flew ahead of them through the trees.

Paul was itching to run again. It was obvious Claude was leading him to the Tyrant's tower, what they had called the castle rock in the days before the game had expanded to fill the whole valley with the keep. Back then, when the farm had encompassed their world, the farmhouse had been the witch's forest cottage and the castle rock the place where they had been sent on their fairytale quests. Sometimes their mother had played the role of the witch, sending them off to gather ingredients for her magical spells— getting the boys out of the house and out of her hair, Paul had come to realize. But it was those games that had given rise to *the* game, and it was the castle rock, a steep-sided lump of granite like an island in the upper field, that had formed the nucleus of the keep.

I'm the king of the castle, and you're the dirty rascal!

He remembered that from when they were so small the castle rock was a mountain they could not explore in a day. He could remember shouting until the noise shook the birds from the trees, and he felt some of the same rambunctious energy bubbling up from inside. He would have laughed if Claude had not been so intent; would have run if Claude had not been holding them to a cautious jog. The valley's magpies had gathered at the

314

sunlit margin of the field, flashing peacock-green from their tails even through the mist rising off the frosty grass. And Paul had to admit to himself, the mist drifting about the foot of the rock was a beautiful touch. Like the Cellarer's echo, like the Lady's still pool. Like a goodbye. It drew a bittersweet thread through his ebullience, a lick of nostalgia for something that was almost, but not quite, gone.

So he tried hard, and he could almost see the Tyrant's tower rearing up in its ruinous magnificence; he could almost see the Tyrant's guards gathering up their weapons, preparing to question what business they had with the Master of the Keep. And when Claude yelled at him to run, he ran with all his heart.

———————

The tower was as overgrown as the outer walls and they had to fight their way through more than the baffled guard. Hawthorn and ash were still bright with berries, as was the prickly oregon grape clinging in the cracks of the stone. Claude hauled himself up by the thin, tough trunks of the stunted trees, his hands growing sticky with sap, his heart pounding madly with exertion and fierceness and fear. He could hear the cries of the Tyrant's spies alerting their master to the assault, but there was no help for it, it was impossible to take the Tyrant unawares. Claude could only put his faith in the Cellarer's magic and the Lady's blessing, in the weight of stones in his pockets and the whisper of crow wings in his ears. *You are not alone,* he told himself, *you are the champion of the keep, you have allies and protections the Tyrant knows nothing of.* So he told himself, though fear crowded the air from his straining lungs. And then he remembered that

315

this was his spell, that even the Tyrant himself was bound up in his, Claude's, spell, and he grew confused.

The castle rock did not have a proper peak, rather, a saucer-like declivity ringed in a low, rough battlement very like a lookout tower's roof. The hollow had accumulated a mulch of drifted leaves and a clump of shallow-rooted birches had grown and died there, leaving black-and-white trunks to stand like so many gravestones. It had always felt like a *place* to Paul, not just a part of the sprawling landscape like the woods or the wider hills, but a *place*, singular and alive. It had its own silence, its own moods, its own relationship with the sun and rain and moon. It was a place to claim and be claimed by, and it was a shock, a real fist-in-the-guts shock to see that it had been claimed by someone other than the twins. It was a trespass that trembled on the verge of sacrilege.

The figure stood among the grave-trees, sneering down at the valley, too arrogant even to turn and acknowledge the twins' approach. It should not have been impressive, slouching and dressed like a tramp as it was, but therein lay the proof of its power. Arrogant, yes, and mad, outside the rules even of the story that had created it, a story that would have dressed it in robes of velvet and chains of gold. But it scorned the story, you could see that in its white and misshapen face. It scorned everything, all the rules, and in contempt imposed its own rules on whatever part of the world that did not fight back. *That* was the Tyrant.

That was the *Tyrant*, Paul thought, and he shook with the urgency to get his fist out of his crowded pocket.

"In the Lady's name," he bellowed, and threw the first stone.

Claude threw a stone; he had to, with Paul firing one missile after another. Paul was finally consumed by the game, screaming war cries and taunts as he threw stone after stone, and it was as if the game had suddenly chosen him over Claude. There was a sickening disjuncture in Claude's head. He threw stones with all the strength in his arm—and how had he carried so many in his pockets? There seemed no end to them—he pelted that arrogant figure with its coarse and sneering face—that white plaster face that was his face inside—and some part of the world came adrift. If the castle rock had come unmoored and scudded off above the hills he would not have been surprised; if it had revealed itself to be the tower he called it, tall as a skyscraper and black as hell, he would not have been surprised. The surprise, the horror, was that it did neither. It was just a battered island of granite left behind by a glacier some thousands of years ago, its feet in the hay meadow and its head not even as high as the tops of the cedars that grew at the edge of the field. It was just the castle rock where they had used to play when they were little boys.

But if that was true, then what was that thing?

Who was that thing?

That man?

Staggering under the blows of the ensorcelled—no, the mine-rubble stones. Flinching under the diving attacks of the excited crows. Throwing up an arm to shield his head, falling back against the dead trees, bleeding horribly from his head, his face, his mouth a gaping shattered ruin.

Paul was a machine, throwing stone after stone. Claude was

a machine too, a puppet played upon by his terrible spell. He threw another stone, feeling his own face stretched into a mask of horror, and another stone that fell short, and the next one he managed somehow to throw far out over the field, and then, with the last stone still in his hand, he had torn himself free.

"Stop it! You're killing him! You're killing him! STOP!"

Paul couldn't stop. He saw the blood, but knew it was impossible—some trick of Claude's, red paint, his own fevered imagination—and the air was in constant motion, confusing him, as if the wheeling of the crows had got inside his head, filling his skull with random motion, shuffled fragments of darkness and light. His own movements, the wind-up and the throw, joggled his eyes. It was a weird, claustrophobic kind of blindness, and he was deafened by his own panting breaths, the shouts in his throat that had no more meaning to him than the barks of a dog. And he couldn't stop. He was weeping and he couldn't stop. And then Claude screamed.

The birds flew up into the sunlight.
The crows. A woodpecker in the trees. The magpies in the grass.
They flew up high.
You could see their shadows moving across the ground.

Paul, wiping the sweat and tears from his face, was the first to move forward. He was shaking, but the world had expanded

318

again beyond the reaches of his skull. It was so quiet suddenly, just the birds calling from high above the hills. He felt that something horrible had stopped, like a car crash, a car crash that was him. He stepped toward the figure, Claude's scarecrow, that was hung up among the trunks of the dead birch trees.

That was blood, there.

That was an eye exposed by a torn lid, as if the lid had opened from the top down.

That was a tooth emerging like a giant maggot from the torn cheek and shattered jaw.

That was a bubble of blood swelling from the nostril of the broken nose. That was a bubble of air, that swelled, slowly, like a bubble-gum bubble carefully blown, until it popped and there was no more. No more air, no more blood.

That was a man, and they had killed him.

"I did this." It was a whisper. Claude didn't even know that he was speaking out loud. "*I* did this. I *did* this."

He kept saying it, over and over, like a chant. I *did this. I* did *this.* I *did this. I* did *this.* Paul heard him at the far distant edges of his mind, and then suddenly there was nothing but Claude's voice drilling a hole in his skull. Paul spun around and yelled, "*What* did you do? Shut up! *What did you do?*"

Claude was as white as a cold marble statue of himself, and his eyes showed white all around the rims of the iris. He did not look away from the dead man when he spoke.

"He wasn't real. He was just a mask. Some clothes, a book. I made him real." Claude started to tremble, and then he was crying. "He was the Tyrant, and I made him real."

And then we killed him.

But that thought was intolerable. Paul had never had an intolerable thought before and he did not know what to do with this one. He had to get rid of it. Get rid of it. His hands made an involuntary gesture, as if he could throw it away, but his arms ached from throwing all those stones, throwing them so hard, killing the Tyrant, killing the game.

"I made him real."

"Shut up," Paul said—he had no room to shout with that thought inside him. He staggered away, thinking he could throw it up if he couldn't throw it away. He had stones in his guts. He was going to shit himself, wet his pants. He was going to come apart at the seams, there was going to be nothing left of him, nothing left but a book, some clothes, a mask. The birds were circling down, the crows and the magpies, curious and drawn to blood. Paul staggered to the rough edge of the castle rock's top, sure he was going to puke, but when he got to the edge he just . . . went down. He ran right into the flocking magpies, put up his arms against the accidental scratches of their claws and went on running. He hurtled down the steep side of the rock, skidded on his heels, fell flat on his back and leapt up, not even caring if he could breathe. He heard the birds calling. Over the noise of his running, the uneven whimper of his breath, he could hear his brother calling for him to wait.

"Come on, Claude," Paul said, but it was only a whimper, and he did not dare to stop, to turn back and call and wave until Claude caught up with him. "Come on, Claude, come *on*," he said, and he thought Claude must be coming down behind him, he *had* to be coming down behind him, because Paul knew there were only two choices: run, or come apart like an exploding grenade.

He jumped the last meter down to the level field, stretched out his stride, and with his brother close behind him ran for home.

———•••———

"Paul, wait." Claude had no breath to shout and his cry was lost in the muttering of the troubled birds.

The birds, he thought. The war birds, the Tyrant's orphaned spies. The gore crows that grew fat on the battlefield's dead.

"We can't just leave him here. Paul, wait."

But Paul ran, a small figure and strangely slow—strangely, because he was so quickly gone.

Claude turned back to face his dead.

The mask was ruined, the face shattered to show the flesh beneath. Had they really thrown that hard? How could they have thrown that hard? They were just boys.

You are in the service of the keep, said the Cellarer, *do you think you would have been chosen if you were not man enough?*

Alexander the Great was leading armies when he was your age, the Cooks said in their gossipy way.

And the Lady's gentle voice murmured, *You have done nothing but what we laid upon you to do.*

But that wasn't true. It had been Claude's spell. It was all right that Paul had run—no it wasn't! Fucking Paul, *how could you?*—but it was just that Claude should deal with the consequences alone. It had been his spell. His was the responsibility, and—

He drew a deep breath.

—his was the power.

He had made the Tyrant real. They had both killed him, but *he* had made the Tyrant *real*.

He had no fire, no ingredients with which to build a new spell. But this was the place of power, the Tyrant's tower, the hinge-point of the keep, and it was now also a place of sacrifice.

Let the sacrifice be not in vain, said the Lady of Fountains.

Use it, said the Cellarer. *It's there, for good or ill. Use it to do what needs to be done.*

Claude, bowed beneath the weight of his responsibilities, knelt at the corpse's side and began to summon the keep.

———

"Did you guys manage to get yourselves some lunch? I'm sorry I was so late with the groceries. Annie asked for a lift to town and we ended up having lunch together after her appointment. Did you get some of the zucchini loaf out of the freezer? I hope? Please eat the zucchini loaf. If it's not gone by next June I may actually have to kill myself. You can build my tomb out of zucchini-loaf bricks. Sorry, morbid humor. Are you okay, Paul? You're looking kind of rough. What were you guys up to today? Out before breakfast. Did you even eat before you . . . Paul, are you crying? What's wrong? Did you have a fight? Is that why Claude's in hiding? Paul. Stop crying. Tell me what happened. Paul, talk to me. Where's your brother? *Where's Claude?*"

———

He built the keep stone by stone.

He began with the places he knew well: the Cellarer's door,

the laundry and the Wellhouse, the kitchen with its massive hearths. He built the walls along the line of the surrounding hills, and he built the single gate with its gatehouse that rested where the farmhouse stood in his mother's world. He built the stables, the armory, the many shrines. He built the clerics' studies and the chatelaine's offices and the ladies' solar, but there were no clerics scratching with their pens, no chatelaine jingling her keys, no ladies toying with their jewels and their little dogs. There were no little dogs and no hounds in the kennels; no horses in the stables; no hawks in the mews. No cats in the sunlight; no rats in the cellars; no mice in the walls. No soldiers, no servants; no ambassadors or slaves. But the baileys stood cobbled and sodded within the massive bulk of the keep. The keep stood, thick-walled and many-roofed, riddled with secret passages and cellars tunneling away into an abyss even the Cellarer could not plumb. And at last, but also first and always, the tower stood, the castle rock that was the foundation for all the rest. A great, massy tower, though not so tall as it seemed with the Tyrant's arrogance stealing the light from the sky. This was the tower as it should have been, as it was once and as it will be now the Tyrant is dead, and at its base, deep in the earth, lies the keep's crypt. Claude built the long winding stairway, stone by stone, and when it was done, every step solid in his mind, he began to drag the Tyrant's corpse down from the tower's peak.

Step by step. Stone by stone.

It was dark as night inside, but that didn't matter. He had it all in his mind.

They were out until long after dark, Paul and his mother, calling
Claude's name and shining their flashlights into the trees. The
woods weren't so thick in the daytime, but everywhere you shone
your light there was a tree, and where there was a tree you couldn't
see beyond. *Claude!* A frightened grouse exploded like a bomb in the
bushes, sounding like an entire flock as it made its escape. *Claude!*

They found the camp he'd made, with the tarp and the
blackened fire pit. *That would be reassuring,* their mother said,
if he were actually here. But he wasn't, just the tarp and a few
unburned sticks. This was where he had made it, Paul knew. This
was where he had made the Tyrant—*I made him real*—no. No.
This was where he plotted the last play in the game.

Were you fighting?

No.

Oh, come on, Paul, look at you. Look at your hands.

We weren't.

What?

We weren't fighting. We were just . . . playing.

Playing. Playing with what?

He always wanted to play the same stupid game.

What game?

You know. He felt like he was lying. He had never known the
truth could be a lie. *The game we used to play as kids.*

*But what happened? Christ, Paul, what do you think I'm going
to do to you? I just want to know where my son is!*

As if, at that moment, she had only one. As if she had only the
one who was not there.

I don't know where he is. I went one way and he went the other. That's all I know!

In the morning she called the Search and Rescue team.

He dug the grave with a shard of rock and his hands.

There was nothing else, and that was right. It was real magic he was doing here—not evil magic, though it was bloody and dark. This burial at the tower's heart was the true end, the only proper kind of end, which is also a beginning. He was setting a foundation stone; he was planting a seed. He dug the grave with his hands in the hard, stony earth, shedding blood into the dirt where it would mingle with the Tyrant's, and that, too, was right. It was his own power he was burying here; his spell. He shed sweat into the tower's foundations, and tears. He vomited a thin acrid bile of remorse and fear. And it was all right, it was *right*, this is what magic *is*.

The Cellarer told him so, and the Lady did not disagree.

They searched all the next day, all the day after that. Paul clung to his mother's side until she chased him away like a stray dog; then he walked in the line where the experienced searchers told him to walk. They had a helicopter out, flying over the sparsely wooded hills. They had dogs, trained animals and neighbor's pets who counted the twins as friends. Paul walked along the bank of the stream that ran down the west side of the valley, knowing with a knot of guilt in his gut that as soon as the searchers climbed the castle rock they would find—

325

But he wasn't there. Claude. He wasn't where Paul had left him. The searchers said so, and they had climbed to the top, looked all around.

Paul couldn't believe it. He *didn't* believe it, and on the third evening he went up the valley himself, exhausted and sick with shame. He had fought with his mother. She wasn't speaking to him. She wasn't speaking to anyone, just looking, looking, looking, and calling Claude's name until she was as hoarse as a crow. So when the rest of the searchers were giving up for the day—night was falling and a wintry cold seemed to be pouring down from the deep blue spaces between the stars—he went back up the valley and climbed castle rock in the dark. Claude was there, as Paul had known he would be, sitting in a litter of dead leaves and smashed plaster and pages torn from a book. When Paul reached the top of the rock Claude looked up, and for a long time they just stared at each other in the last of the daylight. Claude was filthy, bloody, smelling of piss. He looked strangely old, as if the three days had been three years in a fairy hill. He did not speak. They had once been able to read each other's minds, but Paul could not guess what Claude saw when he looked at him. Paul found it harder and harder to meet his eyes and finally he had to look away.

But he was still strong enough to pull his brother up and help him down to level ground.

STORY NOTES

THREE DAYS OF RAIN

I wrote "Three Days" as a tribute to one of the greatest American short story writers, Ray Bradbury. His stories are so often about people trembling on the edge of some great beginning or ending in their lives, and are so full of the power of nostalgia, of the human need to cling to the idea of Home even in the strangest lands, even at the end of the world. Also, and not coincidentally, it typically takes me three days to write the first draft of a short story.

Of course, there is also a certain amount of ecological despair at the story's heart. If you've ever flown into Phoenix, Arizona, and seen all the lawns and golf courses and swimming pools shining under the desert sun . . .

COLD WATER SURVIVAL

For the longest time "Cold Water Survival" was a title in search of a story. Then the fabulous Ellen Datlow asked me to write something for her Lovecraft tribute anthology. My favorite Lovecraft story is probably "Shadow over Innsmouth," but I had recently seen Werner Herzog's great Antarctic documentary, *Encounters at the End of the World*, and the breaking up of the massive southern ice sheets was very much on my mind. So "At the Mountains of Madness" became my inspiration, and the story was born.

By the way, I went in with the firm intention to disallow all tentacular activity, but by the end the sneaky little bastards had crept in, in spite of everything I could do.

BROTHER OF THE MOON

Yet another story that arises from my fascination with 20th-century history. This one comes from the collapse of the USSR and its satellites. Originally I meant to write about a mercenary company that takes over a country with the attitude that they cannot possibly do a worse job than any of their employers, but then I caught sight of the relationship between our hero and his sister, and the plangent tone of love and loss took hold. Weirdly, considering the undercurrents of war, incest, and suicide, I think it's one of my sweeter stories, with a rare happy ending.

THE RESCUE

In the USSR and elsewhere, political dissidents, and especially the rebellious children of the powerful, were sometimes sent to mental hospitals to be tortured in the name of re-education. The people who did this were morally insane. Hence the story.

I have to say, I think it's one of the tightest, creepiest, most psychologically subtle pieces I've ever done, and I love the way the haunting keeps almost to the background until the end. I take no credit for any of that, by the way. This is one of those stories that just used me as an intermediary to get itself down on the page.

COUNTRY MOTHERS' SONS

I was offered a commission to write a werewolf story, and I was so happy to be asked that I accepted without much thought. *Sure, I'd love to!* was swiftly followed, however, by, *Oh crap, now what do I do?* As far as I can remember, my original idea was to write about the crazy guy who lived in the woods outside a neighboring town. How I got from there to a widow in post-WWII Europe I'm not entirely sure, but I like the way her narrative slowly fills in what she doesn't want to say out loud, even to herself. It's a fairly self-conscious literary story, and I'm not sure how well it fitted into the anthology it was commissioned for. I'm very fond of it, though. I love the image of the pigeons on the rooftops worshipping the moon.

PROVING THE RULE

This novella was one of my very first commissions, for an anthology about wizards, and as with "Country Mothers" I had blithely accepted before it occurred to me how seldom I write about conventional magic-user types. In my stories, magic tends to be what happens to my characters, not what they do. So I had to think for a while before I came up with an angle on the idea that I liked, and then it took me a few false starts before I hit upon the early Electric Era setting. That was what really brought the story to life—that, and the image of Graham waiting for Lucy in the pub, so grudgingly in love.

VIRGIN OF THE SANDS

"Virgin" was more consciously inspired by other people's fiction than most of my stuff. Olivia Manning's *Levant Trilogy* and Michael Ondaatje's *The English Patient* both lent me images and ideas; and the latter, particularly, suggested a sensuality, and a sexuality, that is rather unusual in my writing. I was surprised, though, when the story was picked by two different erotica anthologies. To me it's a horror story—very much a horror story—about the dehumanizing aspects of war.

GIN

For my excellent mother's sake I should say that "Gin" does not arise from my personal experience. I think the story really came from the sense I had as a child, of glimpsing the strange inner lives of other children's families. Certainly the setting is drawn from the neighborhoods I lived in back then: the closed-in house with the dried-out lawn, silence on the outside hinting at the desperation within. The drawer full of broken dishes came from a dream. The mattress full of maggots was a waking inspiration. It still makes me shudder.

QUEEN OF THE BUTTERFLY KINGDOM

This must be the single most intimate story I've ever written. At its heart lies a deep conflict I carry within me, between my very pragmatic and skeptical self who keeps the difference between fantasy and reality extremely clear, and the self who lives in and by my imagination. But what really inspired me—or at least, what energized me—to write "Queen" was the purchase of a very expensive bodhran that I could not afford. I keenly remember walking down an icy street in Ottawa in January, the sun blazing out after an ice storm, the wind blowing skaters down the Rideau Canal, and the whole story, beginning to end, hitting me with such force that I skidded into the nearest café, drum and all, and wrote down the first couple of scenes.

THE LONG, COLD GOODBYE

This is one of my very favorite stories. I loved writing about all that cold. I wrote the story in June, and I can remember looking up from the computer and being thoroughly disoriented by the green grass and flowers outside my window. But it is the tenderness at the heart of the story, and the bittersweet sense of the friendship that should have been a love affair, that makes it live for me.

Mind you, if it unsettles anyone who lives, as I do, on land stolen from indigenous peoples by false or broken treaties, then that's definitely a bonus.

CASTLE ROCK

I went to high school with two sets of twins. One pair, identical boys, seemed entirely happy with their lot, but the other pair, a brother and sister, were cruelly divided by her congenital bone ailment. The brother-twin seemed to live under a perpetual shadow of guilt. I think those two pairs became a kind of template for me: the doubled self, and the doubled self divided. Add a wary fascination with the cloudy boundary between imagination and delusion, and voila: Castle Rock.

PUBLICATION HISTORY

"Three Days of Rain" © 2007 by Holly Phillips. Originally appeared in *Asimov's*.

"Cold Water Survival" © 2009 by Holly Phillips. Originally appeared in *Asimov's*.

"Brother of the Moon" © 2007 by Holly Phillips. Originally appeared in *Fantasy*.

"The Rescue" © 2010 by Holly Phillips. Originally appeared in *Postscripts*.

"Country Mothers' Sons" © 2010 by Holly Phillips. Originally appeared in *Full Moon City*.

"Proving the Rule" © 2008 by Holly Phillips. Originally appeared in *Book of Wizards*.

"Virgin of the Sands" © 2006 by Holly Phillips. Originally appeared in *Lust for Life*.

"Gin" © 2006 by Holly Phillips. Originally appeared in *Eidolon*.

"Queen of the Butterfly Kingdom" © 2007 by Holly Phillips. Originally appeared in *Interfictions*.

"The Long, Cold Goodbye" © 2009 by Holly Phillips. Originally appeared in *Asimov's*.

"Castle Rock" is original to this collection.

ABOUT THE AUTHOR

Holly Phillips is the author of the novels *The Burning Girl* and *The Engine's Child*. She is also the author of many short stories, many of which have been collected in her World Fantasy Award-nominated collection, *In the Palace of Repose*, and have appeared in such magazines as *Asimov's, Fantasy, Clarkesworld, Weird Tales, Beneath Ceaseless Skies, On Spec*, and anthologies such as *Full Moon City, Interfictions, Shine*, and *Lovecraft Unbound*.